BROKENHEARTED

Just as the Fort Smith Kid's thumbs went over each set of gun hammers respectively, the Ranger raised the big Colt he'd carried cocked and hanging down his thigh beside his empty holster.

Without a word to the Kid, Sam had taken quick but careful aim, making sure his shot had his full concentration. Then he'd squeezed the Colt's trigger with finality.

"Holy God—!" the Kid started to shout, trying to swing the shotguns down at the Ranger in time. But he didn't get the words out of his mouth. Nor did he get both shotguns cocked before the Ranger's bullet sliced through his heart, blowing part of it out his back. It thumped onto the stone steps behind him. A smear of blood and fragments of dark muscle matter streaked upward, as if pointing toward the ornate bordello doors.

As the Kid fell, the single shotgun he'd managed to cock flew backward, hit the stones and exploded in a blue-orange streak. . . .

LAWMAN FROM NOGALES

Ralph Cotton

A SIGNET BOOK

SIGNET
Published by New American Library, a division of
Penguin Group (USA) Inc., 375 Hudson Street,
New York, New York 10014, USA
Penguin Group (Canada), 90 Eglinton Avenue East, Suite 700, Toronto,
Ontario M4P 2Y3, Canada (a division of Pearson Penguin Canada Inc.)
Penguin Books Ltd., 80 Strand, London WC2R 0RL, England
Penguin Ireland, 25 St. Stephen's Green, Dublin 2,
Ireland (a division of Penguin Books Ltd.)
Penguin Group (Australia), 250 Camberwell Road, Camberwell, Victoria 3124,
Australia (a division of Pearson Australia Group Pty. Ltd.)
Penguin Books India Pvt. Ltd., 11 Community Centre, Panchsheel Park,
New Delhi - 110 017, India
Penguin Group (NZ), 67 Apollo Drive, Rosedale, Auckland 0632,
New Zealand (a division of Pearson New Zealand Ltd.)
Penguin Books (South Africa) (Pty.) Ltd., 24 Sturdee Avenue,
Rosebank, Johannesburg 2196, South Africa

Penguin Books Ltd., Registered Offices:
80 Strand, London WC2R 0RL, England

First published by Signet, an imprint of New American Library,
a division of Penguin Group (USA) Inc.

First Printing, October 2011
10 9 8 7 6 5 4 3 2 1

For Mary Lynn . . . *of course*

PART 1

Chapter 1

———◆———

Sierra Madre Occidental, Mexico

Arizona Ranger Samuel Burrack rode toward Rosas Salvajes on a copper-colored black-point dun. He'd left Black Pot, his Appaloosa stallion, boarded at the Ranger badlands outpost near Nogales. Though he didn't like leaving Black Pot behind, there was no denying that the stallion needed a rest. Besides, he reminded himself, the black-point dun had proven itself with distinction time and again in this dry desert furnace.

How long had he been down here? Two months . . . ? Longer . . . ?

He'd lost track of time since he'd crossed the border at Nogales to begin his search for Luis and Teto Torres and their *Asesinos de Arma*, or Gun Killers Gang. But it didn't matter. It wouldn't matter until the job was done.

He knew that time was the first civil element a lawman needed to shed once the Arizona Territory border fell out of sight. This was not his first trip into the wilds of Mexico in search of bad men, and he didn't want it to be his last.

The dun turned quarterwise on the loose sandy hillside and shuffled down it in a stream of spilling gravel and a rise of dust. At the bottom of the hill, Sam patted the horse's withers for a job well done and rode on toward Rosas Salvajes, or Wild Roses. In the near distance, adobe, plank and stone buildings rose out of the wavering sand flats stretching out before him.

The weathered buildings stared out at him from behind the half-circling remnants of an ancient fortress wall, which was left over from the Spanish, who had built and ruled the village with iron fists. Roofs of clay tile, tin and wood shingles stood glaring from within a bed of white sand and blinding sunlight. He looked away to protect his eyes.

Three of the Torres gang lay dead in his wake over the five-hundred-mile stretch from Sonora to Durango.

The first to fall had been an Arizona outlaw named Jake Furrows. Sam had left him dead on a side street out in front of a cantina on the outskirts of Sonora, a single bullet through his heart. The second Gun Killer member was a Mexican gunman known as El Lagarto.

The Lizard . . . , Sam thought, touching the heels of his boots to the dun's sides.

He had killed the Lizard in the fishing village of Punta de Pescado on the sandy coast of the Gulf of California, lingering long enough to watch as a gathering crowd of fishermen's wives picked through the dead man's saddlebags and clothing before dragging him away beneath a flock of jabbering seagulls.

The third Gun Killer he'd crossed off his list had been an Arkansan named Lloyd Grelow, also known as the Fort Smith Kid. Sam had found the Kid waiting for him halfway up the long set of stone steps leading to the ancient and majestic Sueños Hermosos—Beautiful Dreams—Bordello in Durango. The Kid had stood above him on the stone steps, holding a pair of twin sawed-off shotguns in his hands. The young Ranger couldn't imagine why the Kid had done that, chosen shotguns, when a perfectly good ivory-handled Colt stood in a holster on his hip. But that had been his call.

Sam shook his head thinking about it.

He also had no idea why Grelow chose such a place as the Beautiful Dreams Bordello for such a reckoning, though he supposed that didn't matter either. Lit up high on ground cocaine and peyote, the Kid had not been in his right mind. Sam remembered the Kid's wide eyes shining down at him like black, wet glass.

"Ever think you'd die on your way up to a whorehouse, Ranger?" he'd called down to Sam. White cottony spittle clung to either corner of his lips.

Sam hadn't answered. How could he have replied to such a question as that? He'd been more concerned with those two double barrels on the steps above him than he was in making conversation. The Kid held the shotguns propped upward on either hip, poised and ready. Well . . . almost ready, Sam reflected.

The first thing Sam had noticed was that the big shotgun hammers weren't cocked, and that was all he needed to see. Just as the Fort Smith Kid's thumbs went over each set of gun hammers respectively, the Ranger raised the big Colt he'd carried cocked and hanging down his thigh beside his empty holster.

Without a word to the Kid, Sam had taken quick but careful aim, making sure his shot had his full concentration. Then he'd squeezed the Colt's trigger with finality.

"Holy God—!" the Kid started to shout, trying to swing the shotguns down at the Ranger in time. But he didn't get the words out of his mouth. Nor did he get both shotguns cocked before the Ranger's bullet sliced through his heart, blowing part of it out his back. It thumped onto the stone steps behind him. A smear of blood and fragments of dark muscle matter streaked upward, as if pointing toward the ornate bordello doors.

As the Kid fell, the single shotgun he'd managed to cock flew backward, hit the stones and exploded in a blue-orange streak, peppering two iron-trimmed oak doors that marked the entrance of Beautiful Dreams. Splinters flew from the doors.

Atop the steps, a young prostitute who had been watching felt the sting of splinters nip at her bare shoulder. She had screamed, dropped the black cigar she'd been smoking and vanished inside behind one of the partially open doors.

From that day to this, Sam had followed the gang's tracks along stretches of sandy beach, through forests of cedar and pine, across wavering desert flats and down rocky hillsides.

And now to Wild Roses . . . , he told himself. Beneath him, the copper dun kept a brisk pace in spite of the fiery heat rising with the beat of its hooves on the burning sand.

From the hayloft above a plank-and-adobe livery barn, a young, red-haired Scots-Irish woman named Erin Donovan gazed out at the approaching Ranger atop the copper-colored dun. The dun's black stockings and matching mane and tail took on a sheen of silvery sand as dust rose and drifted behind it.

"It is him," she murmured quietly, knowing that her brother, Bram, lay unconscious on a blanketed pallet of straw in a corner behind her. Her brother had spent another bad night shivering and rambling out of his head. Throughout the heat of the day, he had remained unconscious, sweating heavily, which the doctor had said was the best thing for him. *That, and plenty of clean, cool water*, she reminded herself, to help wash the venom from his system.

She continued to gaze out at the lone rider on the coppery, black-point dun, watching him stop more than a hundred yards from town, draw a rifle from his saddle boot, check it and lay it across his lap. All the while he stared toward Wild Roses as if he could see her—as if he was looking into her eyes deep enough to see the edges of her soul.

Nonsense. Stop it, she scolded herself. Her life had neither the time nor the space for such farm girl romanticism. Still, her gaze lingered on the Ranger, staring as she might under different circumstances, as if he were some dusty cavalier, some king's knight in armor come to save her.

Yet these were not different circumstances, she

thought, taking a quick glance over her shoulder as her brother moaned under his shallow breath and lay drenched in sweat. There was no changing her situation, and there were no knights, no dashing horsemen riding in her direction. There was only her and her brother, Bram. Both were wanted by the law in Texas—and here came a lawman. One who would do them dirt? she wondered.

Had Bram not stumbled upon a large desert rattlesnake a week ago, they would have vanished with the Torres brothers and lived under the protection of the Gun Killers' fierce reputation until Texas had forgotten them both.

Unfortunately, that was not to be the case. The snakebite in Bram's ankle had changed everything. Instead of taking shelter with the Gun Killers, poor Bram lay locked in a life-and-death struggle, snake venom coursing through his veins, and after only one robbery.

The Torres brothers had left them here—all of them apart from the wild-eyed gunman Matten Page. Page had stayed behind to kill the Ranger when he arrived. At least that was what the Torres brothers had ordered him to do. It appeared to Erin that his greatest interest was trying to catch her alone with no way out of a room except past him.

She looked back out at the rider and the drift of dust he and his black-point dun had left trailing them. Speaking of Page, it was time for her to go to the cantina and tell him the Ranger was here. After all, that was her job—that was what she'd promised to do.

She stood up to leave the loft, but instead of turning away and climbing down the ladder, she lingered at the open door, staring out at the Ranger as he and the dun drew closer to the edge of Wild Roses.

"What do you see out there, little darling?" the voice of Matten Page said behind her.

She spun around with a start and saw him step up off the ladder and walk toward her.

"Oh!" she said, collecting herself quickly. "I was just on my way to find you!"

"It didn't look that way to me," Page said, a harsh expression on his bearded face. He stopped close to her, stooped a little and gazed out toward the lone rider nearing the edge of town.

"I—I think this might be him," she said quietly.

"I think you just might be right, little darling," Page replied, studying the rider closely.

Erin stared in silence.

Page straightened, turned to her and looked her up and down, as he did at every opportunity. He always stood too close to her, and his eyes always watched her in a manner that made her feel uncomfortable.

Sidling almost against her, Page said, "I hate thinking what would have happened had he walked in on me with the repeating rifle and caught me unawares."

Erin only gazed out, avoiding Page's eyes. The outlaw reached over with a dark chuckle and pushed a strand of long red hair from her cheek with his fingertip.

"You weren't going to leave me in a lurch, were you, little darling?" he asked. "After all I've done for you and your snakebit brother?"

"No, Mr. Page," she said, "I wasn't going to do that. I was on my way to tell you—"

"*Shhh*, of course you were," Page said, cutting her off with a flat grin. "How many times do I have to tell you? Call me Matten." He reached a hand out behind her and let it rest at the small of her back. Her skin crawled at his touch.

To detract his attention from her, she nodded out at the approaching Ranger.

"What are you going to do if that is him?" she asked.

Page grinned and gave a quick glance out the loft door and back to her.

"Oh, I'll just walk down there, put a bullet or two in him before he even knows I'm there." He leaned close and breathed against her ear, "Then I'll get myself right back up here . . . to you." His hand tightened a little above the curve of her hips. "How does that sound?"

Erin couldn't answer, for a hard knot had suddenly risen in her throat. Her silence caused the outlaw to chuckle knowingly.

"You stay right here for me," he said. "I'll be back shortly, to take up where we left off." He gave a squeeze on the small of her back before turning her loose.

My goodness, she thought. How would she ever shed herself of such dire circumstances?

Chapter 2

The Ranger wore a faded black bandanna tied back over his head, the tails knotted and hanging on the back of his neck, beneath a battered brown vaquero-style sombrero. He wore a faded dark-striped poncho that flapped low and steadily in the hot dry wind. As he rode forward, he eyed the few horses standing at the iron hitch rails of the Perros Malos Cantina.

Two doves from the cantina had stepped out onto the boardwalk to greet the Ranger when he rode up the center of the street. The older of the two, an American from Chicago named Glory Embers, fluffed her hair with her fingertips and wet her painted red lips.

"This one is mine first, Tereze," the older dove said.

The younger dove, a raven-haired French-Mexican beauty, Sidel Tereze, only stared with a smile, a hand planted confidently on her rounded hip.

When they saw the Ranger turn the black-point dun to the opposite side of the street before stopping and stepping down, though, both women recognized trouble. He raised his Colt from his holster, checked it and held it down his side.

"Damn it, never mind, Tereze," Glory whispered to the younger dove beside her. "You'd best go tell the Frenchman that a gunman has come to Wild Roses."

The younger prostitute only turned and stared at her with uncertainty.

"Go and tell him *now!*" the older woman insisted in a stronger tone. "Henri will know what to do."

Sam watched as the younger woman turned and hurried back inside the cantina from across the dusty stone-tiled street.

Sam knew the reputation of the Perros Malos—Bad Dogs—Cantina and its French owner, Henri "Three-Hand" Defoe. He unhurriedly laid the horse's reins over the hitch rail and examined the animal a little, making sure the young woman had plenty of time to tell Defoe he was here. Then he peeled off his finger-less right leather glove, stuffed it down behind his gun belt, turned and walked across the empty street.

Glory Embers stepped forward and gave him a welcoming smile, hoping to stall him long enough for Tereze to get to the Frenchman and warn him.

"Hello, stranger," she called out from a few feet away. "Care to buy a thirsty gal a drink?"

Sam realized what she was doing and didn't slow his pace.

"Not today, ma'am. I'm here on business," he said, gazing straight ahead.

Glory had started to move in closer, but gauging his demeanor, she decided it was best to keep her distance.

All right. She shrugged as he walked past her toward the cantina's open front doors. She had done what the Frenchman expected from any of his girls. She had sent Tereze to warn him. She drifted cautiously to the side as the Ranger walked into the cooler shade of the cantina.

At the far end of the bar, Sam set eyes on the younger woman. Beside her stood Henri "Three-Hand" Defoe, who stuck a large, fresh cigar between his teeth and tried to look as if he hadn't been caught by surprise. Behind the bar, a bald, thick-necked bartender hurriedly lowered a sawed-off shotgun down out of sight, thinking no one had witnessed the move.

From the stony look on Sam's face, Henri's smile faded away. He decided quickly that there was no room for pretense.

"Well, well, *monsieur,*" Defoe said with a trace of a French accent. "The little lady here tells me you stood your cayuse all the way across the street. I've never known that to be a friendly gesture. . . ." He let his words trail. He held his hand to his cigar, keeping his other arm hanging loosely down the side of his long, tan swallow-tailed coat.

"Especially when we have so much room for your horse out front," he said, giving a nod toward the half-empty cantina.

Sam didn't reply. Instead he stopped less than ten feet away and stared at the big, dapper Frenchman.

"Tell your bartender to take his hands up away from the hogleg," he said bluntly. "I'm not here looking for either of you."

"Oh?" The Frenchman eyed him up and down,

noting the big Colt hanging in the Ranger's right hand, beneath the edge of his dusty poncho. "And who might you be here looking for?"

"We'll get to that," said Sam. He cut a sharp sidelong glance at the bartender.

"Freddie," Defoe said without taking his eyes from the Ranger, "bring your hands into sight. You make the gentleman uncomfortable."

"Whatever you say, boss," said the bartender, Fred Loopy. He let down the shotgun hammers, set the gun on a lower shelf and brought his thick hands up slowly, resting them along the bar's edge. He stared at Sam with a sour expression.

Defoe gave a shrug and a flat, mirthless grin. His curly black hair hung damp on his sweaty forehead.

"These are dangerous times in which we live, eh, *monsieur*," he said to Sam. "A man must always prepare to protect himself and his chattels—"

"I'm looking for the Torres brothers and any of their Gun Killers," Sam said, cutting him off. As he spoke, he let his gaze move about the cantina. Men were staring from the far end of the bar, from three tables along a wall and from a half-open side door where a man stood with an arm around a woman's waist.

"As you see, *monsieur*," Defoe said with the same flat grin, "no one shoots you and no one runs for the door. The Perros Malos is a beacon of light in this harsh Mexican frontier." He gestured toward the Colt hanging in Sam's hand. "Anything else?" he asked.

"You can take your other hand from under your coat," Sam said matter-of-factly.

"My *other* hand . . . ?" The Frenchman turned a

puzzled look to his bartender, as if for clarification. Then he turned back to Sam as the bartender gave him a bewildered look.

"I know who you are, Henri 'Three-Hand' Defoe," Sam said. The hammer of his Colt cocked at his side. The barrel tipped up toward the big Frenchman. "Now, how do you want to do this?"

Defoe studied the intent eyes staring into his. Finally he let out a tight breath.

"You appear to have me at a disadvantage, *monsieur*," he said. With his left hand poised at his cigar and his right hand hanging down his side, he extended a third hand from beneath the right side of his swallow-tailed coat. He spread his fingers wide, showing Sam that his *real* right hand was empty. "There, now, are you satisfied?" he asked in a chilled tone.

Sam gave a short nod, stepping forward, and reached behind Defoe's coat to pull a small ornate Lefaucheux pistol from a slim-jim side holster. He laid the pistol on the bar top.

"Who the hell are you, mister?" the bartender blurted out.

"I'm Arizona Ranger Samuel Burrack," Sam replied, again cutting a glance around at the faces in the cantina. "I'm after the Torres brothers and their gang."

A sly grin came to Henri Defoe's rough, pitted face.

"My, my, Ranger, you've overshot the border by a long ways," he said, looking relieved that the Ranger had not mentioned any charges against him. "Out of curiosity," he continued, "have you any authorization from the Mexican government?"

"Yes, I do." Sam uncoiled a little himself. He

lowered the hammer on his Colt and eased the gun back down to his side. "I would not be here otherwise."

"Where is your badge?" Fred the bartender asked.

Both Sam and Defoe gave him a look, and Fred looked embarrassed by his own question.

"Just curious," Fred said.

The Ranger had taken off his badge his first day out of Nogales. He carried it in his shirt pocket.

Sam turned his eyes back to Defoe.

"Have the Gun Killers been through here?" he asked, knowing the answer to his question before he'd asked, but wanting to see if he could get any cooperation out of Three-Hand Defoe.

"Hmmm, let me think . . . ," Defoe said. He raised a hand from behind his coat and scratched his chin, feigning serious contemplation. "No, Ranger, I'm certain they have not."

Lying, just as I thought, Sam thought, staring at Defoe—a man whose reputation was so bad he had to keep an arm hidden behind his coat in case his past ever caught up to him.

"I'm afraid you made a mistake coming to Wild Roses," Defoe said. He grinned slyly, sucked on his thick cigar and blew a pointed stream of smoke upward. "Too bad," he lamented. "What a terrible waste of your time."

"I'll find a way to make up for it," Sam said, keeping his flat stare at Defoe. Ignoring the Frenchman's goading sarcasm and a chuff of laughter from the bartender, he backed away toward the front doors, his Colt still in hand.

On the boardwalk, Glory Embers stood to one side

and gave him a smile, as if he were still welcome in spite of the tension he'd left hanging in the air.

"You come back and see me. I promise *I* won't be a waste of time," she said.

Sam only touched the brim of his sombrero respectfully, stepped down from the boardwalk and walked across the dusty street.

Sam was well aware that riding to Wild Roses and approaching the Frenchman about the gang was not a waste of time. He picked up the dun's reins, leading the thirsty animal toward the large, stone-encircled village well.

He'd learned from experience. In hunting a gang as large and powerful as the Gun Killers, the next best thing to knowing where they are is knowing where they would run to when hard pressed by the law.

Oh yes, the Gun Killers had been here; he was certain of it. He'd come upon the tracks of many riders moving together across the windswept ground. The gang appeared to rotate in a long loop covering the Mexican desert and hill country from the border, stretching as far south as Mexico City. They hadn't broken up and gone in separate directions after they realized he was on their trail.

They had left men behind to kill him, plain and simple. This told him a couple of important things. The Torres brothers had yet to split up the money from the banks and payrolls they had raided and robbed across the Arizona Territory border. *Wise thinking on the part of their leaders,* he thought. It was hard to hold a group of killers together when they had pockets full of stolen money to spend.

It also told him the Torres brothers didn't mind leaving a few men behind to kill him, knowing if those men never made it back alive, it only meant more money for the rest of the gang.

Some things were not hard to figure, he told himself. Like how close this Frenchman and the Torres brothers must be, for him to lie on the gang's behalf, when he knew their horses' hoofprints led right to his cantina door.

So much for that, Sam thought. He'd remember Defoe, Wild Roses and the Bad Dogs Cantina.

Places like this were a safe haven for men like the Gun Killers Gang. When and if the time came, he would ride back here and find them—some of them anyway. That was how the job worked: gather information from every source along their trail. Sooner or later, the Gun Killers would raise their heads, and when that time came, he'd be ready and waiting.

Chapter 3

At the well, the Ranger stood beside the dun while the thirsty animal drew water from a runoff trough. As the thirsty horse drank its fill, Sam took down three canteens hanging from his saddle horn, uncapped them and held them under the water until they where full.

When he'd recapped the canteens and hung them back on his saddle horn, he pushed his sombrero back, letting it hang down his back, pulled the black bandanna from his head and plunged his face down into the cool water.

He took a long swig, swished his face back and forth and raised it. Slinging his wet hair back from his eyes, he stuck the black bandanna under the water for a rinse, wrung it out and fitted it back atop his head. He wiped his wet face with both hands and looked warily back and forth at the empty street.

He gazed off along the trails leading into the village for any sign of rising trail dust and saw none, indicating that no one from the cantina had gotten nervous and decided to leave on his account. He took in a long, refreshed breath, let it out and pulled his sombrero up onto his head, atop the cool wet bandanna, enjoying it while it lasted—which wouldn't be long in the scorching heat.

Across the empty street, Matten Page crept around the corner of an alleyway, out of the darkened shade and down behind the low remnants of a crumbling adobe wall. He peered up over the edge of the wall, Winchester rifle in hand, and watched the Ranger adjust his sombrero and snug the string up under his chin.

Here it is, Page thought, steadying his rifle atop the wall and gazing down the rifle barrel. He had the Ranger in his sights. He had the sun in the Ranger's face; he had the wall for cover. He had every element of surprise, and this was all the edge he needed. He cocked the hammer back quietly. Five seconds from now, he would be the man who killed *the Ranger*—and it was about damned time, he told himself. He squinted his left eye shut and took fine aim with his right.

"Mister, *look out!*" Erin Donovan cried out in a voice that was nearer to a scream.

What the—! Page turned his eye from the Ranger and stared in bewilderment at the woman running fast along the middle of the empty street, her long dress causing a flurry of dust. She screamed at the Ranger at the top of her lungs, "It's an ambush! He's going to kill you!"

An ambush? Page looked stunned. *No! No! Don't tell*

him that! he shouted to himself, staring wide-eyed, startled, confused. *Damn it to hell!*

What's she doing? He stood in a crouch at the back of the protecting adobe wall.

"Behind the wall!" Erin shouted, seeing the Ranger turn toward her from where he stood, ready to step up into his saddle.

Sam saw her finger pointing toward the adobe wall as she ran toward him, her long red hair streaming back on a hot wind.

Jesus! She's gone nuts! Page swung his eyes away from the woman, back toward the Ranger, knowing he had only a second to make his move now that he'd been exposed.

"Damn it!" he shouted angrily at himself. "I knew it! I knew it!" He never should have trusted this jack-potting wench. He took quick aim and squeezed the trigger.

From the window of the cantina, Three-Hand Defoe turned to the bartender and frantically shouted orders. "Freddie, get out there and help him! The woman has given him up!"

Drinkers hurried to the open window, the open front doors and slipped out onto the boardwalk as Page's rifle shot resounded along the empty street.

Thanks to the woman, Sam had seen Page swing the rifle at him. In that split second, instead of going into his saddle, he kicked himself away from the dun's side just in time to feel the bullet slice past him, mere inches from his chest.

The dun reared slightly as Sam hit the ground and

rolled away, another rifle shot kicking up dirt behind
him. In the middle of the street, the woman shrieked
and dived to the ground at the sound of the rifle fire.
Sam stopped rolling and lay prone on his stomach,
facing the rifleman with his Colt out arm's length,
cocked and aimed.

A third rifle shot hit the dirt beside him as the big
Colt bucked in the Ranger's hand. Sam aimed again,
watching through the veil of dust rising around him.
He saw that his shot had hit the crouched gunman in
his right shoulder, the impact strangely forcing him
to a stand.

Page let out a painful yelp, slinging his rifle to the
side, offering the Ranger his exposed chest as a target. Sam made the second shot and saw it knock the
gunman back a step. The third shot hit only inches
from the second. The fourth shot did the same.

Page slammed against a rough sun-bleached plank
wall, leaving a smear of blood glistening in the stark
white sunlight as his body slid down the barrier. A
few feet away, a donkey bucked and brayed, managing to break free from a hitch rail. It ran bucking and
braying out of sight down a darkened alleyway.

In the dusty street, Erin rose onto her knees, dirt covering her face, strands of her long red hair and the
front of her gingham dress. She stared, blinking her
eyes in disbelief at the long smear of blood running
down the plank wall, at the drift of dark rifle smoke
looming in the dust-filled air.

"Stay down, ma'am," Sam said, running to her in a
crouch, his Colt still smoking and still poised toward

the downed gunman. Coming to a stop kneeling beside her, he placed a protective hand on her back. "Are you all right?" he questioned. His eyes scanned the street both ways, then snapped back to the body lying slumped against the plank wall.

"Ye—yes, I think so," said the woman. She pushed her red hair back from her face and stared toward Matten Page, seeing him suddenly give out a wet rattling cough.

"Stay here, ma'am," Sam said.

For some reason she wanted to grab his arm, not let him leave her side, but he was off and gone before she could act. *Wait!* she shouted silently, rising into a crouch herself and running along behind him in spite of what he'd instructed her to do. From the well, the dun loped closer to the Ranger, stopped a few feet away and stood watching.

The Ranger loomed over Matten Page, his Colt pointed down at the mortally wounded outlaw.

Page coughed up a spray of blood, his right hand gripping his chest where three of the bullet holes had struck in a tight pattern, the fourth wound bleeding freely a few inches away.

"Well . . . lawman," he said in a rasping bitter tone, "do you . . . think you shot me enough?"

"Maybe not," Sam said, "you're still alive."

He leveled the Colt down toward Page.

"Wait," Page pleaded. "Don't you want . . . to question me . . . about the Torres brothers?"

"No," Sam said flatly.

"Jesus," Page mustered, "you just want to kill me. . . ."

"That seems to be the way it is," said the Ranger,

"and we both know you wouldn't have answered me if I did question you," he stated flatly.

Page shook his head. "Probably not," he rasped, blood running from his lips.

"Then there you have it," said the Ranger. He started to squeeze the trigger. Page closed his eyes tight in anticipation.

"Mister, *look out!*" Erin shouted again, this time from only a few feet behind the Ranger.

"*Holy Mother* . . . she's like a guard dog," Page groaned as the Ranger spun away, setting eyes on Fred the bartender.

Seeing the smoking Colt pointed at him, the bartender dropped his sawed-off shotgun as if it were red hot.

"Don't shoot!" he pleaded, wide-eyed, throwing his hands up chest high in surrender. "I wasn't going to shoot you, I swear it."

"Watch out!" Erin warned. "He's got a gun behind his back!" She stood at an angle that allowed her to see the bartender's broad back and a big Remington shoved down in his belt.

"Step away from the shotgun and turn around," Sam said to the bartender. "Let me see your back." He held the Colt out at arm's length, cocked, ready to fire.

"She can't stop *jackpotting* . . . ," Page said. His words trailed; his head fell to one side. "I should've killed her . . . first thing . . ."

"I wasn't going for it, lawman!" the bartender said. "So help me, I was only carrying it just in case."

"Aye," the woman said in a scorching tone, "just in case you lost your shotgun?" As she spoke, she stepped in closer to the bartender. "He meant to kill you, mister," she said to Sam, staring coldly at the bartender's worried face.

"Stand back from him, ma'am," Sam said sharply, reading what was about to happen in the bartender's eyes, but his warning came too late.

Fred jumped to the side, putting Erin between himself and the Ranger as his hand went behind his back and jerked out the big Remington. At the same time, he grabbed the woman and tried to swing her around in front of him as a shield.

The Ranger saw a narrow opening and took it. His Colt bucked in his hand and sent the bartender flying backward, his hand losing his hold of the woman. The bullet sliced past Erin's ear and nailed the bartender in the heart. The Remington flew to the ground and fired wildly, thumping into the side of a plank and stone building.

"Jesus . . . I've seen enough," Page moaned in a failing voice.

"Ma'am . . . ?" Sam asked, the Colt still in hand, fresh smoke curling from the tip of its barrel.

"I'm all right," Erin said, rubbing her wrist where the bartender had gripped her tightly. She stepped back from the body lying bloody on the ground.

"I'm sorry I had to shoot with you standing so close," Sam said, still scanning the street for any more guns that might be pointed at him. "I saw I only had a second. I had to take the shot."

"I—I understand," Erin said, appearing not too badly shaken by the sudden turn of events. "He might very well have killed me if you hadn't shot him when you did." After a moment's pause, she added, "I owe you thanks for saving my life."

"Ma'am, it's *I* who owe *you* the thanks," the Ranger said, lowering the Colt as he thumbed bullets from his gun belt to reload. "The bartender might have killed you. But it's certain either one of these men would have killed me had you not warned me both times."

The two turned from the dead bartender and looked down at Matten Page. The outlaw lay dead, his eyes wide-open, staring down at the dirt as if engrossed by the spreading puddle of blood beneath him.

"I take it you know this man," Sam said.

"Yes, I do—or I did know him," Erin corrected herself. "He rode with the gang you've been trailing. He's one of the Gun Killers." She stared at Sam, wondering what to expect from him.

Sam began to recognize that something had motivated her warnings.

"Go on," he said, encouraging her to continue.

She started to speak, saying, "My brother, Bram, has been trying to ride with the gang—"

"No, wait," Sam said, cutting her off as soon as he saw Three-Hand Defoe and several other men step out of the cantina and start walking their way.

"I see them," said Erin, her eyes following Sam's toward Defoe. "Can you take me away from here, to the livery barn? My brother is there."

Sam looked at her warily. The dun plodded up closer and stopped beside him.

"Am I going to have trouble with your brother?" he

asked Erin. He had reloaded the Colt and kept it in his hand.

"No, he's unconscious," she said. "He's snakebit. I'm keeping him in the barn loft until he's well enough to ride."

Sam didn't need to consider it any further. He reached around with his empty hand, took the dun's reins and brought the horse around in front of them.

"Hop on," he said to her. "I'm right behind you."

Defoe stopped in his tracks when he saw the Ranger swing up behind Erin Donovan, the big Colt still in his right a hand, a wooden rifle case under his bedroll between himself and the saddle. Defoe eyed the rifle case. *A sharpshooter rifle . . . ?*

"Easy does it, everybody," he said over his shoulder. "Let him clear out of here."

"What about him killing Freddie?" a Mexican asked with a hard stare toward the Ranger as the dun turned and bounded away along the dusty street. "Freddie was one of us, *nuestro amigo!*"

"Our friend?" questioned Defoe, shooting a hard stare at the Mexican. "I'd hardly call Freddie a friend. Did you ever smell him?"

"Yes, he was an odorous man—it is true," said Hector.

"That's putting it mildly," said Defoe.

"I will not speak ill of the dead," Hector said, "especially one of our dear amigos."

"Freddie Loopy tended bar for me, Hector," Defoe said bluntly. "Let's not make him out to be more than he is—or *was*," he added, gazing toward the bloody body lying in the dirt.

"Still," said the Mexican, "do we let this man ride in and shoot one of us down?"

"This lawman will get what's coming to him soon enough," said Defoe. "If you're just itching to do something, go get your horse. I'll pay you to do an errand for me."

"Yes, right away," Hector said, keeping his excitement at bay. He'd been hanging around in Wild Roses for a week trying to find a way to earn some money. It looked as if Freddie's death might be just the break he needed.

Chapter 4

As the Ranger rode the dun off the street and along an alleyway to the livery barn, Henri Defoe and some of the men from his cantina stood staring down at the two bodies. Meanwhile, Hector Pasada ran back to the cantina and unhitched his big paint horse from the iron hitch rail.

"Where's the Frenchman got you running off to, Hector?" Glory asked. She and three other doves were lounging on the boardwalk, watching with curiosity.

"Mind your own business, all of you *putas!*" the Mexican said over his shoulder to the giggling women. He ran along the street, leading his horse behind him.

"Hector," Glory called out, "if you're in a hurry, why don't you ride that cayuse?"

In his excitement, Hector almost stopped in his tracks and climbed up onto the horse, but hearing the doves giggle louder behind him, he stared back with an angry, embarrassed look on his face and kept running.

When he and his horse stopped beside Three-Hand

Defoe, the Frenchman looked back at the laughing doves out in front of the cantina.

"What is so funny to those whores?" he asked Hector.

"It is nothing," Hector said, out of breath from running in the pressing heat. "What do you want me to do?"

"I want you to ride out to High Pass," said Three-Hand, his dummy right hand always stuck down into his coat pocket, his real right hand resting on his holstered Lefaucheaux.

"Pase Alto?" Hector said. "That is an overnight ride from here."

"Yes, it is," said Defoe, "so you'll need to get going right away." He gave a thin smile. "Tell Sonora Charlie to get himself back here fast, pronto, extra-hurry. Tell him it's important."

"Sonora Charlie, the *asesino*? How will I find him?" Hector asked. "Where do I look?"

"Don't let me down on this," said Defoe, wondering for a brief moment if he'd made a mistake. "You won't have to worry about finding him. All you must do is show up in High Pass. He and his man Clyde will find you."

"All right, I go," Hector said. Then he stalled and added, "But will I not need some food to take with me, some coffee, something?"

"*Damnez-le*, Hector!" said Defoe, cursing in French. "Must I do this myself?" He stared pointedly at the Mexican. "You see that Freddie is dead. I need someone I can count on to take his place. Are you the man who will do that?" As he spoke, he leaned down and picked up the discarded, sawed-off shotgun from the dirt. Wiping it off, he thrust it into Hector's hands.

"*Sí*, I am that hombre," Hector said, looking down at the shotgun, seeing the leather reload pouch hanging from its stock by a short length of rawhide. As he spoke, he turned to his horse and climbed quickly up into his saddle.

At the livery barn, Sam stepped down and reached a hand up to assist Erin out of the saddle.

She appeared almost taken aback, unused to such a courteous gesture, but then she smiled, took his hand and swung down beside him. She straightened her dusty, disheveled dress.

"Why, thank you, Mr. . . ." Her words trailed.

"Samuel Burrack, ma'am," he said, his Colt still in hand. "*Arizona Territory Ranger* Samuel Burrack, that is," he added. He tipped his sombrero with his free hand.

"I am happy to make your acquaintance, Ranger Burrack," she said. "I'm Erin Donovan. Please call me Erin."

"I'd be honored to, ma'am—I mean, *Erin*," he said correcting himself. "Feel free to call me Sam."

She smiled. "Sam," she said, as if testing out the sound of it. "I like that."

They walked into the barn, the Ranger leading the dun behind him, his Colt still out, should he need it.

"He's up there in the hayloft," Erin said, lowering her voice a little, as if afraid she might disturb her brother. She stopped at the ladder to the hayloft, turned to Sam and said, "Bram can be difficult, Sam, especially with the snakebite keeping him so feverish and ill. I hope you can overlook any rudeness?"

"I'll certainly try," Sam said, staring up the ladder toward the hayloft.

"Thank you. That's all I ask," Erin said. She climbed the ladder ahead of him. With good manners, the Ranger looked away until she had stepped over into the hayloft. Then he followed, Colt in hand, eyes upward.

Standing side by side with the Ranger on the hay-strewn plank flooring, Erin gestured a nod across the loft toward a banked pile of loose hay where her brother lay partially visible on a worn blanket. His two bare feet stuck out, one purple-veined and the color of old ivory, the other one swollen over twice its size, the purple-green color of fruit gone bad.

"Bram . . . ?" she called out quietly. "It's me. I have a lawman with me. But he's our friend. Please don't shoot."

She looked at Sam and squeezed his forearm reassuringly.

"Don't worry. I don't think he can even lift a gun," she whispered.

Sam caught the smell of fever and sickness as they stepped forward.

They stopped and looked down at the young man's pale drawn face and saw a fly crawling across the tip of his nose. Erin immediately threw her hands to her mouth and let out a muffled gasp.

"Oh no, Bram . . . ," she whispered into her cupped hands.

Sam saw the big Starr revolver lying close to the

side of the young man's head, his right hand lying near it. He saw the streak of blood and brain matter lying splattered across the hay and on the plank wall three feet away.

He put an arm around the grieving woman's waist and gently turned her away from the grisly scene.

"Stand over here, Erin," he said in a lowered voice. "I'll cover him up."

He stepped toward what was left of the young woman's brother and pulled enough of the blanket from under the body to lay it over the dead man's face. Reaching down, he lifted Bram's gun hand away from the side of his head and tucked it to his side. Then he picked up the gun, checked it and shoved it down into his belt.

When he stepped back over to Erin, he glanced out through the open loft window and saw Defoe and his band of drinkers walking toward the barn, but he saw no raging anger in their demeanor. Their leader, Henri Defoe, knew that gunfighting in the street was bad for business. He must have decided to settle the men down before more trouble erupted.

That's good, Sam thought. The woman would need some time to bury her dead brother properly. Riding out after the Gun Killers would have to wait until tomorrow. Until Bram Donovan was in the ground. He sighed to himself and lowered his Colt into its holster. Behind him Erin cried quietly into her hands.

All right . . . he could do that, for the woman's sake.

The Ranger and Erin met Defoe and his drinkers at the barn doors. Defoe held his real right hand hidden inside his coat on the holstered Lefaucheux pistol. His false right arm hung loosely down his right side.

"Here he is, men, just like I thought," Defoe said as the Ranger and Erin stepped out of the barn.

"Back off, Defoe," Sam said menacingly. He wanted peace, but he didn't want to appear that he had to come asking Defoe for it, hat in hand. "The killing is over in Wild Roses, unless you've come looking for more."

Defoe noted the Ranger's Colt standing at rest in his holster.

"The only killing here has come from your hand, Burrack," Defoe said. "If you want more we can certainly see that you get it."

Sam knew the Frenchman would posture a little for the benefit of his cantina crowd, but he saw no danger now that everybody had taken some time to cool their tempers and take their bark off.

"I came here looking for the Torres brothers and their Gun Killers, Defoe," he said. "I drew a Gun Killer out and I killed him. He tried to ambush me."

"You also killed poor Freddie Loopy, a man who worked for me—a man greatly admired by all, both *Americano* and *Mexicano* alike," Defoe said, pointing at Sam with his right finger from beneath his swallow-tailed coat, taking his hand off his gun in doing so.

Sam caught the gesture. Yes, the trouble was over, he thought. *For now anyway.*

"He came upon me with the double-barrel, Defoe," Sam said, "the same gun he was ready to pull on me in your cantina. If I were to think on it long enough, I might decide that you put him up to it." He stared hard at the Frenchman.

Defoe stared ahead, not backing an inch. The Ranger had let him know it was over. Now it was up to Defoe to look good for his followers. Sam would give him that much.

"But I don't have time to think on it," Sam continued, gesturing toward Erin, a step behind him to the side. "Her brother is lying dead up in the loft. Is Wild Roses going to see to it she gets him buried proper?"

Defoe continued to stare at the Ranger for a moment, as if in consideration.

"Yes, of course," he said finally, letting out a sigh. Behind him, the men appeared to settle down even more.

"Miss Erin," Defoe said, reaching up and taking off his battered silk top hat, "you have my deepest sympathy."

"A snakebite is a terrible way to die," a crusty old Texan in buckskins cut in. "I've seen men's tongues turn inside out, blacken and burst before they can—"

"That's enough, Yancy," Defoe said, cutting the old border rat off. "Why don't you and Zerro go bring the poor fellow down and take him to the barber?" He glanced around and asked, "Where is Walden anyway?"

"The barber was with one of the doves a while ago," said one of the villagers.

Defoe chuffed. "If it has been over a few seconds, he is all finished. Someone go get him. Have him meet Yancy and Zerro at his tonsorial shop." He turned back to the Ranger with a smoldering glare.

"Obliged," Sam said, on behalf of Erin.

"Yes, thank you, Mr. Defoe," Erin said in a grief-stricken voice. "I will find a way to repay you and the town of Wild Roses someday, when I get on my feet."

"Oh . . . ?" Defoe studied her face for a moment, her eyes reddened by her tears. "Are you looking for work, then, young lady?"

"I—I don't want to—"

"She's not looking for that kind of work, Defoe," Sam cut in sharply.

Ignoring the Ranger, Defoe tipped his silk hat toward Erin.

"Pardon me for asking," Defoe said. "But that is the business I'm in, coarse though it may appear to some."

"I understand," Erin said, humbly. "Thank you for asking. But I'll be going back to Ireland as soon as I can find a port and make passage. I still have kin there."

"I see," said Defoe. He turned to the Ranger and said, "So, you and I are going to try to be civil to each other, for the sake of this grieving young woman?"

"Yes, as far as I'm concerned," Sam said. "I have no problem with you, unless you're a part of the Gun Killers I'm hunting." He gazed evenly at Defoe, convinced that the shifty Frenchman was on good terms with the gang, if not actually a member.

"As you can see, I run a cantina here in this Mexican hellhole," Defoe said, spreading his hands, his right hand still behind the lapel of his long dusty coat. "But you have my word that this is *all* I do."

Sam nodded, pretending to be satisfied, but he knew better. He'd already seen too much for Defoe to convince him otherwise. Besides, how could he take the word of a man who wore a third arm in order to shoot someone by surprise?

Chapter 5

⸺

Hector Pasada didn't stop until the sun had sunk completely out of sight behind the mountain line to his right. Luckily, just before dark his horse had whinnied and veered away from a large bull rattler as the deadly reptile coiled up and let out its spine-chilling warning.

Quickly getting his horse under control, Hector spotted the big snake as it continued making its presence known, its tail standing erect.

"You fat *diablo*, you!" Hector shouted, shaken by the snake's sudden appearance. "I will pick my teeth with your fangs!"

As the snake uncoiled and made its way toward deep rocks on the other side of the trail, Hector jerked the shotgun up from across his lap and fired, before the snake managed to slide out of sight.

"There," he said in a spiteful tone as the blast sent the big snake flopping and falling limp on the ground. "That will teach you to frighten my *caballo*." He patted the settled horse's withers and stepped down from his saddle. Retrieving the dead snake, he held it at arm's length and looked all around the rugged terrain for a good place to make camp.

"And now, to cook and eat you, you *diablo gordo*," he said aloud to the blood-dripping snake.

By the time darkness set in, Hector had cleared himself a campsite amid a stand of tall rocks and built a fire of dried mesquite brush and downfall juniper. With the big rattler skinned and impaled on a long stick, he roasted it above the flames until it was ready to fall apart. Then he stripped the white meat off the stick onto a flat rock he'd dusted off with his palm.

Sitting beneath a large, yellow, three-quarter moon, he ate half the snake, washing it down with tepid canteen water. Before he'd finished his meal, he heard the horse chuff nervously, and he eased up into a crouch and sidled over beside the animal.

"What is it you hear out there, *mi amigo*?" he whispered close to the horse's muzzle. He rubbed its nose with a calming hand and examined the shadowy terrain.

In a moment, he spotted a dark wispy silhouette moving slowly toward him beneath the purple starlit sky. Whoever it was, they were in no hurry and they didn't mind showing themselves in the grainy night. Silently, he slipped over and picked up his freshly loaded shotgun, eased down beside a rock for cover and waited.

When the silhouette was close enough, he rose slowly and raised his shotgun to his shoulder.

"Whoever you are, you must be a fool, riding up

on my camp this way without first announcing yourself!" he called out to the grainy darkness.

He heard no reply, just the steady plop of slow-moving hooves, which turned eerie after a moment of tense listening.

"I am warning you," Hector called out, a chill tightening up his spine. "You do not want to fool with me. I am not afraid of you . . . even if you are some demon from below the desert floor."

A demon from beneath the desert floor? Santa Madre! he thought. Now even his own words spooked him.

He crossed himself with a nervous hand. It dawned on him that he never liked being alone out in the desert at night. What in the name of God had ever made him offer to do this?

The dark silhouette had stopped a few yards outside the circle of his campfire—he should never have built the fire, he reprimanded himself. But what else was he to do, eat cold raw snake? He didn't think so, he reasoned. Beside him his horse chuffed and whinnied low under its breath toward the animal standing silently in the grainy purple night.

"What is wrong with you! Why do you not answer me?" Hector shouted toward the dark apparition-like silhouette, seeing it look almost translucent through a wispy flicker of flames.

Was it a ghost? *Oh God! No!* He heard the tremble in his voice, nearly a sob, he realized.

"*Por favor*, tell me something," he said at length, sounding submissive, almost pleading. "I do not know who you are or what you—"

His words stopped short as he felt the edge of a

long knife flat across his throat, an inch below his chin. A strong forearm tightened around his forehead and pulled his head back at a sharp angle, giving him a clear but shaky view of the yellow moon, the purple sky and the endless stars.

A warm breath moved across his ear from less than an inch away.

"What are you doing in our desert?" a voice whispered.

"I—I—!" Hector found it impossible to speak without gagging with his head at such an angle. Having lost all control of his hands, he let his shotgun fall to the ground.

"He can't talk, Clyde," another voice said, this one coming from atop the dark silhouette as it moved into the circle of firelight, its rider straightening up in the saddle. "You've got his Adam's apple in a knot."

The tightened forearm loosened a little on Hector's forehead, enough for him to gasp and swallow and form words. The long blade stayed against his throat as if to remind him who was in charge.

"Please, *señors*!" he gasped. "I am Hector Pasada . . . from Rosas Salvajes!"

"*Hec-tor*," said the man at his throat. "You look more like a Pancho to me."

"Please," begged Hector, "I am only here to find a man . . . to deliver a message to him!"

As soon as he'd spoken, the forearm tightened again, drawing his eyes back up to the starlit sky. He'd caught only a glance of the dark figure swinging down from his saddle.

"Oh, from Wild Roses," said the man.

"Is that why you smell so sweet?" the man with the knife to his throat said into his ear. He sniffed around Hector's collar.

Smell so sweet . . . ? Sante Madre!

The other man walked his horse over and stopped near the fire. He stooped down, picked up a piece of rattlesnake and put it into his mouth. He sucked on the bite of warm snake flesh. Then he spit it out at his feet. "This *rep-tile* needs something. Pepper . . . ? Sage . . . ? Something . . . ," he said.

"What?" Hector managed to gasp hoarsely.

"He's saying you can't cook for shit, *Pancho*," the man behind him whispered in his ear, his grip still tight.

At the fire, the other man stood and wiped his fingertips on his ragged, blackened doeskin coat.

"And who is this man you're looking for?" he inquired.

The arm loosened for a second, long enough for Hector to reply.

"Sonora Charlie . . . Charlie Ring," Hector said quickly, knowing the forearm would soon cut him off again. "The Frenchman sent me from Rosas Salvajes to—"

The forearm tightened.

"*I* am Sonora Charlie Ring," the man by the fire said. He wiped snake from his fingers onto his trouser leg.

The forearm loosened.

"You—you are Sonora Charlie?" Hector gasped.

"What did I say?" the voice said coldly.

The forearm tightened instantly, then loosened. "Listen up, *Pancho*—"

Hector gasped. "You said that you are—"

The forearm tightened again. The knife blade pressed just hard enough to keep Hector terrified.

"I *know* what I said," said Sonora Charlie.

"Please, *señor*—" Hector rasped again in spite of the knife against his throat.

Sonora Charlie looked the terrified man up and down, seeing the dark streak of urine that spread down both of his trouser legs.

"Clyde, take your pigsticker from Wet Hector's throat, turn him loose. Let's hear what the Frenchman wants."

"You mean you don't want me to cut Pancho open?" the voice behind Hector asked.

"Maybe later," said Sonora Charlie. "We'll see."

"Aw, hell!" Clyde Jilson shouted in disappointment. He turned the Mexican loose suddenly, shoving him from behind. Hector flew forward and landed at his horse's hooves, gasping and clutching his throat for a moment to make sure it wasn't laid open from ear to ear.

Thank God! Thank God and all of his holy saints . . . !

Sonora Charlie stepped over, reached a hand down to Hector and pulled him to his feet. Hector stood stunned as Charlie brushed his hand up and down his chest and even straightened his shirt collar for him.

"What does the Frenchman want with me?" he asked.

Hector collected himself and swallowed hard, lowering his hand from his throat. He looked at the short, stocky buckskin-clad Clyde Jilson, who stood inspecting the discarded shotgun as if he'd never seen one before.

"He—he wants you to kill someone," Hector said, "but it is he who must talk to you about it. I only bring his message. He said I would find you in Pase Alto."

"As you can see, I'm not there. I'm here," said Sonora Charlie. He spread his hands, as if to give Hector proof of his whereabouts. "It so happens I am on my way in the direction of Wild Roses anyway."

Clyde stepped forward and handed Hector the shotgun, butt first.

"So you were lucky, Pancho," he said with a wide grin. The top of his head was bald, but hair surrounded the sides and hung down to his shoulders like dirty curtains. "If you came into High Pass acting this way, we would have killed you and fed you to our dogs."

"Acting *what* way?" Hector looked back and forth between the two men, a baffled expression on his face.

"Never mind," said Sonora Charlie Ring. "We can see that you're young and probably haven't been with the Frenchman long."

"*Sí*, it is true. I have only started working for Three-Hand Defoe," said Hector. He spread his hands. "But tell me, *por favor*, what have I done wrong?"

"A lot of things," said Sonora Charlie. "We won't go into it all right now." He and Clyde Jilson looked at each another.

"You'll learn soon enough," said Clyde, "else you'll be dead and gone." He gave Hector a flat grin. "This desert will tolerate no man who does not respect it and give it its proper dues."

Hector felt his temper suddenly flare, but he kept himself in check. Who the hell were these two gringos, to tell him about *this desert*?

"My people have lived in this desert for hundreds of years," he said before he could stop himself. "I know every—"

"*Shhh!*" said Sonora Charlie, cutting him off. He raised a finger an inch from Hector's face. "This is *our* desert now. Mine and Clyde's. You have *nothing* here. Don't press the matter."

Hector just stared at the two.

After a pause, Charlie Ring let out a tight breath. Looking Hector up and down, he said quietly, "Go fetch your horse, Clyde."

Then he turned to Hector and added, "Go dry your trousers by the fire. Clyde's going to go get his horse and boil us up a pot of coffee."

"We're going to Wild Roses as soon as your trousers are dry," Clyde said, stepping away to get his horse from where he'd left it hitched outside the firelight. "We'd better not find out you're lying."

Lying? Lying! Why would I be lying? What the hell is this man talking about? Hector raged on in silence. He wanted to ask them both what the hell was wrong with them, but this was not the time or the place to say anything. This was a good time to keep his mouth shut, lest he get himself killed.

These were two bad hombres, he'd already decided. Bad and loco too, he told himself. *Sí, muy loco!* Very crazy *indeed*.

Chapter 6

The Ranger and Erin walked out the side door of the tonsorial and stopped beside the black-point dun that stood at an iron hitch rail. Sam had taken the dun to the livery barn, watered and grained him and washed him down with a bucket of water. He'd wiped the animal off with a handful of clean straw and led him over to the tonsorial.

Beside the dun stood Bram Donovan's roan gelding—a sturdy-looking desert barb that appeared too well cared for to belong to a man on the run.

"I can't thank you enough, Ranger Burrack," Erin said, her arms folded across her bosom, a thin shawl around her shoulders even in the heat of the day. "I will never forget everything you've done for me and my poor brother, Bram."

Sam noted that she called him *Ranger Burrack* in spite of the fact that he had given her permission to call him by his first name.

"All I did was make arrangements with the barber," he replied softly. "Thank Wild Roses for providing the box and the plot of ground."

"I—I could have paid," she said in a lowered voice. "But in doing so I would have cut my ocean fare short."

"I understand," Sam said. They had talked earlier and agreed that she would ride with him as far the nearest location where she could take a coach on to the Port of Tampico.

"It's most considerate of you to help," she said, "considering that Bram would have been riding with the Torres gang against you had he not met his end."

Sam didn't reply; he only looked at her and gave a slight smile.

" 'Tis fate that has us all in its pocket,' " she said. "It's an old Gaelic-Irish saying."

"I see," Sam said. He heard just a faint trace of brogue in her voice, and it seemed only to come forward when she allowed it.

"Will you be all right riding in that garb?" he asked, gesturing a nod toward her long gingham dress.

She gave him a look, as if to ask what choice she had.

"I have a pair of denims and an extra shirt in my saddlebags," he offered. "Did your brother own a hat? You'll need one while you ride—that is, if you're comfortable wearing it."

"I have his hat, and I have his trail coat and gun belt as well," she said. "They're tucked under some hay up there." She nodded toward the livery stable. "Bram would want me to get use of them." She looked at Sam and added hesitantly, "May I . . . have his gun?"

"Certainly," Sam said. "I only picked it up out of habit. He reached behind him, took Bram's Starr revolver from his belt and held it out for her.

Erin accepted the big Starr in her small hands and looked at it, hefting the weight of it.

"My, it is heavy," she said.

"Do you know how to use it?" Sam asked.

"No, not very well," she said. "Bram had me shoot it in case I ever needed to. But I never learned to aim and hit anything." She paused, then added, "Perhaps you could show me while we are on the trail?"

"Yes, I'll be happy to, first chance we get," Sam said. "Now, let's get some coffee beans while the barber gets your brother ready. As soon as we have him properly buried, we'll need to get some riding in before nightfall."

"Yes, that's a good idea," she said. A hand went to her midsection. Her eyes closed for a moment.

Sam saw her swoon slightly as if on the verge of fainting.

"Erin, are you all right?" he asked, reaching for her forearm to steady her. As he did so, he took the heavy Starr revolver from her hand.

"Oh yes, I'm fine," she said, seeming to catch herself and make an effort to stand straight. "I just felt weak for a moment, too much excitement, I suppose."

Sam looked at her closely.

"How long since you've eaten?" he asked, slipping the Starr behind his back and tucking it into his belt.

"Yesterday evening," she said. "I'm fine, though. I'm a light eater."

"Yes, well, I'm not," he said. "Why don't we eat something here before we pick up supplies?"

"If you feel we should," she said. "But not on my account."

"No, I'm hungry," he said. "I'm hoping you can eat something yourself. It's not good, traveling the Mexican desert on an empty stomach."

"All right, I can eat a little," she said.

"Good," he said. "Now, where is a clean place to eat?" he asked, and quickly added, "Besides Defoe's Bad Dogs Cantina, that is."

"I know a place at the other end of town," Erin said. "It's Mama Maria's. She cooks the best food in all of Wild Roses."

"Let's go there first," Sam said, a smile spreading across his face. He could see she was hungry, but her frugality, as well as her pride, would not allow her to say so. Would she have tried to put off her hunger until they were on the trail, where it would be only natural that she share the evening meal with him?

Probably so, he thought. If it was indeed hunger making her weak.

"Lead the way, please," he said.

Was he allowing himself to get too close to this young woman? he asked himself as he watched her brush a strand of hair from her cheek.

No, I'm not, he quickly thought in his defense.

Erin Donovan was a woman alone who had just lost her brother. She was frightened, and unaccompanied, and a long way from home, he reasoned. What else was he to do but help her?

Leading both horses by their reins, they walked along the edge of the street, noting the eyes of a few onlookers turn to them as they passed the line of plank and adobe buildings along the way.

Out in front of Defoe's cantina, Glory Embers and two other doves followed the Ranger and Erin with their eyes.

"Hmmph," said Glory, cocking a hand on her hip, "it looks like the little Nordic princess has finally stuck her hooks into something worth hanging on to."

"She's not Nordic, she's Scots-Irish," a young blond Dakota dove named Hopper Truit said, correcting Glory. "Her brother told me."

"Nordic, Scottish, Irish—what's the difference?" Glory said with a bored shrug. "I was betting she'd end up humping her butt along with the rest of us once the snakebite knocked her brother down."

"It must be the luck of the Irish," Tereze said, the three of them watching Erin and the Ranger turn a corner toward Mama Maria's.

"Yeah? Well, too bad her brother didn't catch some of the luck," Glory said. "Maybe he won't be getting his ass sewn shut to keep the maggots out." She turned with the final word on the matter, flipped her cigar away and walked back inside the cantina.

"Oh my God, Hopper," Tereze gasped, "does the barber really *do* that?"

"Do what?" Hopper asked.

Tereze said, "You know . . . what Glory said, about sewing his—"

"Damn, Tereze, how the hell would I know?" said Hopper, cutting her off. "I've seen a few I wouldn't mind sewing shut. Maybe a few days in that state would teach them some manners."

Tereze stared off with a pained expression. "I hope it's not true. I hate to think of poor Bram lying down in the ground like that."

Hopper stared at her with a bemused expression and shook her head. "Yeah, if it started itching, he wouldn't be able to scratch it?"

Sidel Tereze looked sickened by the thought.

"Jesus . . . ," said Hopper. She put her arm in Tereze's arm and said, "Don't listen to Glory. She's apt to say most anything. How would she know what the barber does to a corpse before he buries it?"

"Well," said Sidel Tereze, "I'm glad for the mick gal. I hope she never ends up here, like we all did."

Behind them, Defoe stuck his head out of the cantina doors and shouted above the den of cursing and laughter coming from the bar, "Hey, you whores. Are you going to work today or what?"

"We're coming, Henri," said Hopper. "By the way, your Ranger pal and Erin Donovan just turned the corner down there."

"Yeah? Where'd they go?" Defoe asked, stretching his neck out for a better look.

"How do I know?" Hopper shrugged. "There's nothing around there but Mama Maria's. Maybe they went for some roasted goat and frijoles. It's getting to be that time of day. Want me to keep watch and tell you when they come back?"

Defoe looked off across the desert floor toward the distant hill line in contemplation.

After a moment he said, "No, get on back to work. It'll be evening before they get her brother buried. They won't get far from here tonight."

After a meal of beans, roasted goat and red pepper gravy, the Ranger took out a gold coin and laid it on the table to pay for the meal.

"You must allow me to pay for my own meal, Ranger Burrack," Erin said, her eyes downturned.

"I invited you, remember?" Sam replied.

She raised her eyes and gave him a faint and obliging smile.

"Yes . . . and thank you *again*," she said.

They both stood and walked out of the restaurant and back along the dusty street. Returning to the side door of the tonsorial, they were met by the town barber, Walden Reed, who ushered them inside a small viewing room.

Sam stood at Erin's side as she leaned over the edge of a pine-plank coffin sitting atop two sawbucks.

"He looks so at peace now," she said, almost in a whisper. She touched his waxy rouged cheek. "It's as if he's only sleeping."

Sam gave the barber a slight nod of approval. He could still make out indentations on either side of the dead man's head where the entrance and exit wound had been covered with scraps of hair matching Bram's as closely as possible, but this was not the time to be picky, Sam thought.

"Yes, Erin," Sam said quietly, "he looks real good."

With the barber's help, Sam loaded Bram Donovan's coffin onto the back of a small buckboard wagon sitting outside in the alley. Then they rode in silence to the cemetery at the edge of town, their horses hitched to the rear of the buckboard.

Two Mexican gravediggers helped Sam unload the coffin and lower it by rope into a freshly dug grave.

When they'd finished, Sam stood beside Erin, his sombrero in hand and his head bowed, while she said a short prayer. Then he watched as she scooped up a handful of dirt, held it out above the grave and let it pour down on the coffin below.

Sam backed away as she stood in silent reflection for a moment. Making certain he was out of her sight, he tipped the Mexicans and thanked them for their help.

"When you finish filling the grave," he said quietly, "take the buckboard back to the barber, *sí*?"

"*Sí*," the two replied in unison. They stood aside and waited, shovels in hand, until Erin finally turned away from the grave and toward the Ranger. In moments, the Mexicans watched the woman and the Ranger mount their horses and ride away. Then the gravediggers set about filling the grave.

From a window of the Perros Malos Cantina, Three-Hand Defoe watched Sam and the young woman ride past.

"*Le fils d'une chienne*," he cursed to himself in French, almost whispering.

"What did you say?" Behind him, Sidel Tereze

stood buttoning her dress and straightening it down her midriff.

"I call him a *son of a bitch*, this lawman from No-gales," said Defoe. "Is that all right with you?" he added with sarcasm.

Tereze shrugged and dismissed the matter. She didn't care.

"I only asked because I heard you speaking French," she said. "It sounded like my father."

"*Oh*, then I remind you of your father?" asked Defoe. "Did he have you dance naked on the backs of his hands too?"

"I didn't mean in that way," Tereze said. "I meant the manner in which you speak French reminds me of him." After a pause, she asked, "Is there anything else you want from me?"

Defoe looked at the redness on the backs of his hands and rubbed them together, knowing they would bruise.

"All I want is to see someone kill this lawman," he said bitterly. "But now he has left, so I am *disappointed*."

He stood with his tie loose and hanging on his chest, his hair disheveled, his shirt unbuttoned halfway down his chest.

"But you are not disappointed in me?" she asked, pouting a little.

"No, no," said Defoe, "that was good." He rubbed his hands together more vigorously.

"I can kill him for you," Tereze suggested, taking a step closer to him from behind. "I could kill him in my *own* way . . . ," she whispered, letting her words trail.

"Go!" Defoe demanded, cutting her short. He pointed to the door. "If I want someone to stand on his hands, I will come get you."

"Whatever you say, Henri," Tereze said with another casual shrug of her shoulder.

Chapter 7

Sam and the young woman rode on well after the harsh sunlit terrain had succumbed to a purple blanketing darkness. Having eaten the good meal at Mama Maria's in the afternoon to hold them over, and having amply grained and watered both animals before preparing them for the trail, neither of them saw any reason to stop and make camp right away.

That suited the Ranger just fine, he thought, looking back over his shoulder from time to time, checking their back trail. He'd wanted to get across the rolling flatlands and take shelter in the rocky cover of the low foothills. The farther they rode tonight, the deeper they would be inside the hills come morning.

To be honest, he told himself, he'd enjoyed the woman's company and was hesitant to put the night to an end. He breathed deep and let it out slowly, savoring the feel of the night surrounding them, as if somehow the shadowy purple darkness drew them closer.

Did she feel the same way? He believed so. Of

course, it was not something he could just ask her. He straightened a bit in his saddle, having let himself relax in his thoughts. Anyway, it had been a good ride, and he hoped she felt the same.

Not that they had spoken to any great extent. In fact, their conversation had been sparse. Yet the presence of someone riding beside him other than a prisoner in handcuffs had felt nice for a change. *But enough of that—to the business at hand*, he told himself, straightening again and riding on.

When they did finally decide to stop, owing to the absence of moonlight in the deep blackened ravines, it was past midnight. The Ranger could have ridden farther—indeed, he could have ridden all night. There was the scent of the cooling desert below, the looming crispness of mesquite, of budding rock cactus and gusting night air, spiky and fresh and even heady with the faintest scent of the woman beside him.

Stop it, he told himself, feeling akin to a man on a first-time courting call. He smiled to himself, wondering how long it had been since he'd passed a night in this manner, a large yellow Mexican moon overhead, visions of wildflowers looming just out of sight.

"This is nice, out here," Erin said softly, as if she'd somehow read his thoughts. She raised her brother's flop hat from her head and shook out her hair. The two sat atop the horses, gazing into the shadowy darkness ahead of them. To their right, where the trail broke away, they looked above the ground and into the starry sky surrounding the hill line, as if it had risen from the flatlands below.

They turned their standing horses to the edge of rock and sky.

"Yes, it is," Sam said, hearing only the quiet creak of tack and saddle as the horses settled beneath them.

"I have spent many nights outdoors this past year, but none as peaceful or as beautiful," Erin remarked quietly, as if not to disturb the night and its sounds and feel. "It's enough to make one forget one's troubles." She paused, then added in a more solemn tone, "*Almost* anyway . . ."

"Yes, almost," he offered quietly.

They sat for a moment in silence.

Finally Sam stepped the dun forward and gazed down into the greater darkness, seeing only short traces of the silvery trail meander out of sight across the rolling flatlands below them.

"Come morning we'll be able to see our back trail from here," he said. "This is a good place to get some rest."

"I'm not even tired," Erin offered, but her voice said otherwise. "I mean, I could rest, or I could ride farther, either way."

"I'm not that tired either," Sam said. "But this is a good spot. The horses could use a rest before we head down tomorrow afternoon toward Pueblo de Ruinas."

"Where I'll take a land coach to . . . ," Erin said, hesitating, asking for help.

"To Jerez," Sam said. "From Jerez to a half dozen other towns. Then you'll be able to take a train in the San Luis Potosi region all the way to Mexico City."

"Then on to the Port of Tampico," Erin said as if

tiring just thinking of the long journey that lay ahead of her. She knew she still had a long way to go before even embarking on her sea trip back to Ireland. She shook her head in the moonlight.

"It's a far place you're heading to," Sam offered.

"Yes, but it's *home* I'm headed to," she replied, "and home is never too far." She turned a curious look to the Ranger. "And where is it that you call home, Ranger Burrack?"

Home . . . ?

Sam had to think about it for a second before he could answer.

"Owing to trouble along both sides of the border, my home is now Nogales . . . the Ranger outpost."

Erin smiled.

" 'The lawman from Nogales,' is what the Gun Killers call you."

"I bet that's not all they call me," Sam replied.

"No, it's not," said Erin. She followed his gaze out across the wide purple sky. A shooting star streaked in and out of sight. She thought about the Gun Killers, about her dead brother, Bram, Matten Page and the Torres brothers. She thought about Luis and Teto.

Teto . . .

"We are both a long way from home, Ranger Burrack," she said.

Sam pondered her statement. He was certainly not as far from home as she, but to him home was much the same as the present surroundings. Home for him was the weathered plank and adobe Ranger barracks. He was used to tall saguaros in a rocky valley carpeted sparsely by mesquite, hedgehog and barrel cactus.

"I'm at home *here*," he said in reflection.

"Here?" Erin questioned, looking around the rugged Mexican hillside. "Forgive me for saying so, Ranger Burrack, but Mexico isn't even your country."

"I know," Sam said, and he swung down from his saddle, offering nothing more on the matter.

He presented her with his gloved hand. Erin took it and swung down beside him.

"How does a body get so far from home, Sam?" she asked, as if he might actually have an answer to such a question.

Sam looked at her in the moonlight, realizing she had things she needed to say.

"I don't know, Erin," Sam said quietly. "You tell me."

She paused, then lowered her face and said in a voice that failed to hide that she was bordering on tears, "Ranger Burrack, I'm afraid I am not the person you think me to be."

Moments later, over steaming cups of hot coffee, the Ranger listened as Erin told him about the past three years of her life, and those of her brother, Bram's.

Theirs was not the story of two orphans coming to the United States to escape poverty or servitude. Their father had died and left them enough of an inheritance to get them both to America—the land of freedom and opportunity, she had told Sam as she held the warm tin cup in both hands.

"I offer no excuse for anything my brother and I have done," she said.

Sam only studied her face in the soft flicker of firelight.

Her brother, Bram, had fallen in with the wrong crowd almost as soon as they had stepped off the ship in the New York Harbor. As for her, rather than try to stop her brother from pursuing a life of crime, she had allowed herself to be swept into it. Lured by fast money and fast living, she'd gone along for the ride. And now . . .

"And now the ride is over," she said at length with a sigh, staring into the low flickering flames. Tears welled and glistened in her eyes.

The Ranger reached over with the coffeepot and refilled her nearly empty cup.

"I—I feel as if I've misled you somehow, Ranger Burrack," she said. "In spite of all your kindness, I feel I have let you down."

"Don't feel that way," Sam said. "You haven't let me down."

That wasn't quite true, he admitted to himself. He did feel disappointed. But he'd get over it, he reminded himself. "I would have done the same for anyone in your situation," he said, which was true.

"My brother and I are wanted in Texas," she said without looking up from the fire. "We took part in the robbing of a mine payroll with Luis and Teto Torres."

"Oh?" Sam was a bit taken aback by what she said. He didn't know what surprised him more, the fact that Erin had taken part in a robbery, or the fact that she had admitted to the act so openly. "What part did you play?"

She didn't answer; she couldn't seem to look him

in the face. He reached over and tipped her chin up gently.

"Don't tell me you shot somebody," he said, wanting to lighten the gravity of what he could see was clearly bothering her.

"No, nothing like that," she said, managing to face him now even as he withdrew his hand. "I didn't even realize what had happened until it was over. I waited up the trail for them with fresh horses," she said. "But I felt just as guilty as I would have had I shot someone."

Sam nodded and said, "Under Texas law, you *are* just as guilty."

She said hesitantly, "Are you—going to take me into custody?"

"No, ma'am," Sam said, sounding more business-like now than before. "I'm here for the Torres brothers. If Texas wants you, they'll have to come settle up with you themselves."

"Will you have to mention to anyone that I'm here?" she asked.

"Only if someone asks," Sam said. "But if you're in Ireland, it doesn't matter anyway. Does it?"

"No, I suppose it doesn't," she said quietly. She looked away and across the shadowy purple night, letting Sam know that she was finished talking about the robbery for the night. "Anyway, I only want to get home to Ireland and put this part of my life behind me."

Sam nodded. He suspected there was more she wanted to tell him, but it would wait until she was ready, he thought, leaning back on his blanket against his saddle, which rested on the ground. Above him a million stars shone all around, but they had lost some of their sparkle. Sam only watched the stars for a moment; then he closed his eyes and listened to the cry of a lonesome coyote somewhere across the rugged hills.

Chapter 8

━━◆━━

At the first sight of sunlight on the distant horizon, Erin awakened to the aroma of boiling coffee and sat up on her blanket. A few feet from her, the campfire crackled beneath a fresh mound of dried mesquite brush and downfallen scrub oak.

"Ranger Burrack?" she called out quietly, looking over at the bare spot where Sam's blanket and saddle had been.

Hearing no reply, she started to call out again. But before she could, Sam stepped forward into the fire-light leading both horses, saddled and ready for the trail.

"I'm right here, ma'am," he said, stopping a few feet away, the horses right behind him. "I thought we'd make our way out of here before daylight, so that we can get across the flats and into some hill shade before the worst heat of the day."

"Yes, I understand," Erin said, rising from her blanket. "I'm ready if you are." She ran her hands down herself and straightened the trail clothes she'd put on before they'd left Wild Roses.

"There's fresh coffee, ma'am," Sam said, letting her know he wasn't pushing to leave. "I have some jerked elk and hardtack in my saddlebags, for breakfast." He posed his words as an invitation.

"Thank you," she said, "but I can't eat a thing this early in the morning."

He'd called her *ma'am*? Not Erin like before?

"Coffee, then?" he said. He dropped the reins to the horses and stepped toward the pot sitting in a banked pile of glowing embers. "You're going to need something in your stomach—"

"Excuse me, Ranger," she said, cutting him off, as if something he'd said disagreed with her. "I told you in Wild Roses that I eat like a bird."

Sam watched her step over to her horse. She took down a canteen hanging from her saddle horn and walked away into the grainy morning darkness.

He pushed his sombrero up and looked down at the coffeepot for a moment. Then he stooped and filled both of the tin cups he'd set out for them.

He stood up moments later, his cup in hand, when Erin returned and hooked the canteen strap over her saddle horn. She stepped over to the fire, stooped down and picked up her cup of coffee.

"On second thought, coffee sounds good," she said.

Sam looked at her, seeing that she'd washed her face, pulled her hair back and tied it in place with a strip of rawhide.

Nothing like a clean face, Sam thought, seeing how

both her spirits and demeanor appeared to have lifted, brightened.

"How about that elk and hardtack now?" he asked.

She looked up at him, and smiled over the tin cup of steaming coffee. Before she could reply, Sam stooped beside her and took off his sombrero, leaving on the black bandanna tied back over his head. He looked into her eyes and took a breath.

"How far along are you, ma'am?" he asked.

"How far along—?" She stopped short with a stunned look on her face. "What on earth are you talking about?" she asked.

"Nobody eats *like a bird* crossing these Mexican hills and desert planes," Sam said. "Maybe back in Wild Roses," he added, "but not out here."

"How dare you, Ranger," Erin said, denying the matter as far as she could.

"Please, ma'am. You're with child," Sam said with finality. "I would call it none of my business, except that we're crossing some awfully rough country together. I need to know what condition you're in. So, begging your pardon . . . *how far along are you*?" he asked again.

She looked away, let out a breath and turned back facing him, her eyes welling with tears.

"Please don't think me a harlot, Ranger," she said.

"I don't, ma'am," Sam said. "I just think you're in trouble, you're scared and you don't know who you can trust. So you're holding back from telling the truth, thinking that lying is going to help you some way."

She stared back into his eyes and nodded slightly as if weighing what he'd said.

"If I am correct, it has been eleven weeks since I first missed my time," she said at length.

"Three months . . . ," Sam said, considering her condition and gauging her ability to withstand crossing the rough hill country that lay ahead of them. Not to mention the country that led to Port of Tampico, where she was headed.

"Please don't think me a loose woman, Sam," she said. "I fell in love with the wrong man. When he found out I was carrying a child, he left me." The tears welling in her eyes broke free and ran down her cheeks. She did nothing to stop them.

"Ma'am, you don't have to explain yourself to me," Sam said quietly. "My only concern is getting you safely to Jerez."

But she continued as if she hadn't heard him.

"After he left me, I learned that he'd been killed, robbing a train across the border in Texas," she said.

Sam looked at her closely.

"Was he one of the Gun Killers?" he asked.

"No," she said. "He rode with them for a while. Then he went on his own way." She wiped her eyes, collected herself and raised her chin. "Would you like to know his name?"

"Only if you want me to know it, ma'am," Sam said.

"I suppose it makes no difference," she said, dismissing the matter. "Now you know why I find it important to get home to Ireland. I want to bring my child into this world surrounded by people I have known all my life."

"It's usually a mother's wish that their child be born in the United States and become an American. But in your case . . ." He let his words trail.

"In my case, I am wanted by the law," Erin said with an edge of bitterness in her voice. "Yes, you're right, Ranger Burrack," she added, "and in the case of myself and my poor brother, Bram, America has not been the paradise we'd thought it to be."

"I'd never call my country paradise," Sam replied, "but I call living here a struggle in the right direction."

Erin considered his words for a moment.

"Perhaps I would feel differently had things gone better for us," she said.

"No matter how things turned out for you," Sam said, "there was an opportunity for you to rise or fall on your own. I expect that's the best we can ask of any place."

"Yes, I suppose it is," said Erin. "But you have to admit, there's much injustice in America—wrongs that need to be made right."

"I admit there's plenty of injustice for everybody," Sam said. "But the only way I know to make things right is to follow the word of the law and keep it headed in the right direction." He offered a tired smile. "My being a *lawman from Nogales*, that's all I know to do about it."

She returned his slight smile and watched him stand and walk to the saddlebags atop the copper-colored dun.

"There's lawmen from everywhere down here,"

she said to him, "from Texas, Arizona . . ." She shook her head slowly. "I don't understand how things work down here."

The Ranger gave a slight smile.

"Neither does anybody else, truth be known." He sipped his coffee. "That's how it's always been on the border. I don't look for things to change anytime soon."

When he returned, he stooped beside a flat rock he'd placed near the fire and laid out a knife and a shank of jerked elk for breakfast.

"Let's get you fed, ma'am," he said. "We've got a long ride ahead. In your condition, you'll need all your strength."

Erin moved over beside him and reached out for the knife handle.

"Let me do that," she said. "You sit down and enjoy your coffee."

"Yes, ma'am." Sam nodded. He picked up his coffee cup, but instead of sitting, he stood up and sipped his coffee while he picked up her blanket, shook it out and draped it over his shoulder. Then he picked her saddle up from the ground and walked it over to the roan.

With the knife in her hand slicing the elk meat, Erin turned enough to watch Sam set his coffee down and saddle the roan for her.

"I'm able to saddle my own horse," she called out.

"I know that," Sam said, his back turned to her.

She watched him roll her blanket and place it behind her saddle. She looked down at the knife in her hand, turning it back and forth, examining it for a moment. Then her eyes went to Sam's black-point dun, and to the wooden gun case beneath his bedroll.

"What's in the case?" she asked.

"A gift from a friend," Sam said. Then, realizing that she already knew it was a gun, he added, "It's a Swiss rifle, a gift from a former marine sharpshooter—a Cuban named Dee Sandoval."

"Oh, it's what they call a long-shooter?" she asked.

"Yes, it is," Sam replied.

"You—you'll be using it on the Gun Killers?" she asked hesitantly.

"I'll have to see how things go," Sam replied, not wanting to put her off, but not really wanting to discuss the matter.

Seeing his reluctance, Erin changed the subject. "Will you be teaching me to shoot Bram's gun today?" she called out.

"As soon as we get across the flats and back into the hills," Sam said without looking around at her. "There's an old mission ruins higher up. We'll take a good rest there and get you shooting in no time. How does that sound to you?"

Erin smiled to herself and went back to slicing the jerked meat.

"That sounds just fine to me," she said. "I see you're not carrying the Starr in your belt."

"No, I put it away in my saddlebags," Sam said. "When you almost fainted on me in Wild Roses, I took it back. I didn't want you to drop it on your foot."

"Yes, I understand," Erin said.

"Do you want it back now?" Sam asked.

"No, not right now," Erin replied quietly, still slicing the meat. "But once we're across the flatlands . . . when the time comes." She looked back around at him with a smile.

"Yes, when the time comes," Sam said, almost to himself.

PART 2

PART 2

Chapter 9

———

Sonora Charlie Ring and Clyde Jilson had ridden a few feet behind Hector Pasada all the way back to Wild Roses. Knowing that Clyde Jilson was behind him made Hector's skin crawl. He couldn't wait to get away from these two madmen. Theirs was not the action of normal men, of that much he was certain.

He thought of what had happened last night while he dried his trousers by the fire. The thought of it caused his anger to rise again. It took everything inside him to keep from turning in his saddle and emptying the shotgun into Clyde Jilson's face. But he managed to ride on in silence. Soon this would be over. He'd have done the job Defoe sent him to do, he told himself, nudging his horse on toward Wild Roses.

By the time the three rode onto the main street of Wild Roses, a thin line of sunlight wreathed the jagged horizon in the east. Three-Hand Defoe stood on the low boardwalk out in front of the Perros Malos Cantina. A cigar hung from the forked fingers of his real right hand; a cup of coffee steamed in his left.

Beside him three doves lounged with steaming coffee of their own.

"Hopper," Defoe said to the dove nearest him, "go tell old Margo we've got three more coming for chuck."

As the three rode up and stopped in front of him, Defoe had handed his cup of coffee to Sidel Tereze and stood with his right hand inside his coat on the butt of his pistol. Even to people who knew him, it was hard to tell if the arm at his right side was real or artificial—which of course was his whole intent, he thought with a faint smile.

"You made better time than I anticipated," he said up to Sonora Charlie.

"We were headed this way anyway," Sonora Charlie replied. "We came upon Wet *Hector* camped out along the trail."

"Wet Hector?" said Defoe, his cigar still in the forked fingers of his left hand. He eyed Hector as he spoke.

"Yeah," said Sonora Charlie. He chuckled. "We scared him so bad he pissed himself."

"Just like a young schoolgirl might do," Clyde Jilson put in. He gave Hector a wide grin.

Hector gritted his teeth, fighting himself to keep from grabbing up the shotgun and killing them both.

"Pissed his britches . . . ," Defoe chuffed in disgust. He shook his head and turned back to Sonora Charlie. "There's a hot breakfast around back for you."

"Obliged," said Sonora Charlie. "While we eat, you can tell Clyde and me what you want us to do, and why you're in such a hurry for us to do it."

"Will do," said Defoe, ushering them with an arm

toward the rear of the cantina. Turning to Hector, he flipped a coin up to him. "Good work, *muchacho*."

Boy? He calls me a boy? Hector raged in silence.

Containing himself, he looked at the gold coin in his palm.

"*Gracias*," he replied cordially. "If it's all the same with you, boss, I will go visit my woman while her father is driving cattle to Mexico City." His fist closed tight around the gold coin.

"Yeah, go on, Hector," said Defoe. "But get back here as soon as you've uncrossed your eyes. I need you on the job here."

"Tending bar?" Hector asked hopefully.

"Among other things," said Defoe.

Hector's chest swelled a little. He was taking over Freddie Loopy's job. *Thanks to the holy saints!*

"Yes, boss, I will hurry," Hector said, already turning his tired horse toward the far end of town.

Defoe and the two gunmen watched as Hector rode away.

"Where'd you find that squirrel?" Sonora Charlie asked Defoe. He and Clyde swung down from their horse and led them around the side of the cantina as he spoke.

"Didn't he tell you?" said Defoe. "Freddie Loopy is dead. Hector is the only man I had handy that I could send out to get you."

"Is he going to be taking Freddie's place, working for you?" Sonora Charlie asked.

"I need a gunman who can protect my interests," said Defoe. "Hector is all right to carry messages and whatnot, but he's high-strung like a cat. Too much to ever make a gunman. He would get jittery and shoot his toes off."

"Can we have him?" Clyde Jilson asked Sonora Charlie with a dark chuckle.

"What do you two want with him?" Defoe asked as they approached a long table set out for breakfast.

"I don't want *anything* with him," Sonora Charlie said flatly, "but Clyde wants him. He likes him."

"I like having fun with him," Clyde said with a wide grin.

Defoe just looked at the two. He pulled out a chair at the head of the table and sat down.

"Is that all right with you, Three-Hand?" Clyde asked.

Defoe gave a shrug and said, "If he wants to go with you two, it means nothing to me. Mexicans are a dime for a dozen in Mexico."

"But I'm thinking you could tell him he *has* to go with us," Clyde said, "in case he doesn't want to."

"Whoa, hold on, Clyde," said Charlie. "Let's hear who it is Henri wants us to *assass-inate*. We might take Wet Hector as part of the deal."

Defoe waited until an aging dove with a white cloudy eye and a missing ear ambled over from a smoking *chiminea* carrying a platter of sizzling meat and a large bowl of beans and peppers. She set the food on the table and ambled away.

"I want to hire you to kill a man for me and for the Torres brothers."

"Oh?" Sonora Charlie eyed him closely. "Teto and Luis are with you on this?"

"Of course they are *with* me," said Defoe. "Do you think I would use their names if they were not?"

"Who do you—I mean *they* want us to kill?" Sonora Charlie asked. Cutting a bite of steak with a sharp knife from his boot well, he shoved the sizzling piece of meat into his mouth and chewed it vigorously.

"The lawman from Nogales who is causing such trouble for everyone," Defoe said. "His name is Burrack. He is a Territory Ranger from Arizona. He rode out of here with a young Irish woman, headed south."

Sonora Charlie stopped chewing. So did Clyde, following his lead.

"You're talking about Samuel Burrack," said Sonora Charlie, "the sumbitch who killed Junior Lake and his pa."

"His whole gang," Clyde put in.

"Does that bother you?" Defoe asked.

"Nope. Does paying double bother you?" Sonora Charlie countered. "'Cause that's what it'll cost for this Ranger's demise."

"Yep, twice as much for the Ranger," Clyde put in.

"Twice *what* amount?" Defoe asked.

Sonora stared at him as he began chewing again. He took his time swallowing his food.

"The Torres brothers know my price," he said. "Just double it."

"And give us Hector," Clyde cut in.

Defoe looked back and forth between the two wild-eyed gunmen for a moment.

"I saw a wooden gun case tucked under his bedroll. Does it matter if he's packing a long-shooting rifle?"

"Nope." Sonora Charlie shook his head.

"Can we count on quick work from you?" Defoe asked.

"Dig a hole," Sonora Charlie said.

Three miles outside Wild Roses, Hector Pasada stepped down from his horse and spun its reins around a hitch post out in front of a small dusty adobe. He leaned the shotgun against the post. Across a rocky yard, a skinny goat looked at him and let out a long bleat.

At the sound, a young boy peered out the window. Seeing Hector, he bounced down barefoot into the yard and ran to him in a rising puff of dust.

"*Papá* is home! *Mamá! Mamá! Papá* is home!" the boy shouted as he ran.

"*Pequeño hombre!*" Hector called out as the excited child bounded through the dirt and leaped into the air.

Hector caught the boy and swung in a full circle with the child pressed tightly in his arms.

When he looked at the doorway and saw the young dark-haired woman staring out at him, he set the boy down.

"Ana!" Hector called out as he hurried toward the woman, a broad smile spread across his face. "It is about time I have come home to you, eh?"

She accepted his kiss on her cheek coolly. Staring into his eyes, she said flatly, "I have prayed that you were not dead, shot down by one of the *criminales* you now call your amigos."

"*Por favor, Ana,*" Hector said. "They are not my amigos. But they are who I must be with when I am gone to make a living for you and my son."

At their sides, the boy hugged both Hector's and his mother's leg with both small arms. Ana Pasada looked down at the boy, then back up at Hector, expectantly.

"*Sí*, look what I have made working for the Frenchman!" He pulled out the gold coin. "Enough for flour and frijoles and perhaps even—"

"Hector!" Ana Pasada cut him off, gasping at the sight of the gold coin glittering in her husband's hand. With a hand to her mouth she said in a hushed tone, "Who pays a man this much money? What did you have to do to earn it?"

"These *Americanos* pay well, Ana," Hector said. Pressing the coin into her free hand, he added, "And do not worry, I have broken no law. I only delivered a message for the Frenchman, Defoe." He held her close.

She smiled intently at the glittering coin as she turned it in her small hand, as if it were her salvation.

"These gringos who have come to our border lands bring so much money," Hector said. "They throw it around like a handful of sand. I will take all of it I can get, for you, and for our *hijo*." He placed his hand down on the boy's head.

"But the Frenchman, the Torres brothers, the Gun Killers, are they not all lawbreakers, desperados, thieves, murderers?" Ana asked.

"Look at me, Ana," Hector said. "If I must break laws to put food in our mouths, to keep us alive, who will judge me. God? Man? I don't know. But if a law starves a man and his wife, what kind of man will live by that law?"

"These men ride both sides of the border, robbing and killing," Ana said. "Will you cross the border with them when that time comes?" She stared into his dark eyes, the coin still in her palm.

Hector closed her hand over the coin and said quietly, "I must go back to the cantina now. When I am gone, take the boy and walk to the old store at the edge of town where this one will not see me and call out to me." He looked down at the boy's large dark eyes and smiled.

Ana said, "It is not good that a man must keep his wife and son a secret because he is afraid of what his *compañeros* will think of him."

"You are right it is not good," Hector said. "But for now it is how things must be. I do what I *must* do, to keep us fed."

"*Sí*, to keep us fed. Life is hard for the poor, isn't it?" she said.

"It will not always be so," Hector said. "I swear by the saints that someday I will take this world in my fists and make it my own." He clenched his fists tight as he spoke.

"*Sí*, someday," Ana said with finality, and she looked away toward the distant hills, as if they held a secret for her.

Chapter 10

Hector watered his horse at a small trough and kissed Ana good-bye, pulling both her and his son in to his chest.

"This time I will be gone a little longer," he said. "But when I come home, I will have more money for us." He tapped the side of his head with a finger and said, "I will make Defoe see the value of having me as his right-hand man."

"Oh? And what will you be doing for the Frenchman?" Ana asked.

"I will start by tending bar at the Perros Malos Cantina, but I am prepared to do whatever the Frenchman will have me do for him," Hector said, the shotgun hanging in his hand now that he was ready to mount up and ride.

"The Perros Malos," she said with contempt. "What sort of man names his cantina that?"

"A loco man, that's what kind." Hector gave a tired smile and said, "But for now, I work for him. His Bad Dogs are my Bad Dogs, eh?"

Ana managed a thin smile and pushed a strand of hair from her face.

"Tell me, husband, do the *putas* at the Bad Dogs Cantina offer themselves to you?"

"Now that I am the bartender, of course they will offer themselves to me," Hector said. "But I will turn them down."

"Are you sure?" Ana asked.

"The day that I cannot look you or my son in the eye, you will know that I have taken what the *putas* offer me," Hector said. "But that is enough talk," he added. "Now I must go to work."

From the front of the adobe, Ana and the boy watched Hector ride away, back toward Wild Roses. The boy stood at his mother's side, her arm down around his thin shoulders holding him against her leg.

"Why is *Papá* leaving so soon?" the boy asked.

"He goes to attend his job in Wild Roses," Ana said, waving as Hector looked back from a hundred yards away.

"Will he come back soon?" the boy asked.

"Yes, he will come back," Ana said. "But we will not be here when he returns."

"Where are we going, *Madre*?" the boy asked.

"We are going away with your other *papá*," Ana said with determination, watching Hector ride out of sight over a low rise and disappear in a swirl of trail dust.

"*Papá segundo?*" the boy asked, looking up at her.

"Yes, your second papa," Ana said. "The one I have told you about. He will be your *first* father, your *real* father. He will be your only father from now on—as well he should be."

"I do not understand, *Madre*," the boy said.

"Someday you will, my little man," Ana said, still clutching the coin in her fist, lest it somehow get away from her. "Now, you must help me pack our belongings. We will stop the land coach when it passes here. We have a long journey ahead of us."

On the trail, Hector breathed deep and tapped his heels to his horse's sides. As he rode, he thought about everything he and Ana had talked about in the short time he was home. He looked down at the small straw figure in his hand that his son had made and given to him.

"You will always have an amigo with you," his son had said, handing it to him.

Hector smiled to himself and gripped the tiny straw figure for a moment. Then he placed it in his shirt pocket.

Now to business, he told himself.

When he started tending bar, he must make sure to get off on the right foot with everyone, even the *putas*—the doves, he corrected himself. As a bartender, he knew it would be important that people take him seriously. Now that he had earned his position at the Perros Malos Cantina, it was important that people respect him the same as they had respected Freddie Loopy.

He ran the events of the past day and night through his mind, and his thoughts went to Clyde Jilson and Sonora Charlie. Thank the holy saints he would not have to deal with those two anymore—except to serve them whiskey from behind the bar, he told

himself. His hands tightened on the reins just thinking about what had happened between himself and
Clyde Jilson.

They had stopped in the night to rest their horses,
and Hector had stood looking out across the flatlands. Close behind him, Clyde had swished tepid
water around in a canteen and sipped from it. Then,
suddenly, catching Hector off guard, he'd stepped
forward with his finger bent and rounded a wet
knuckle into Hector's ear.

By the devil in hell . . . ! Hector still raged just thinking about it. What kind of loco, twisted son-of-a-bitch
gringo hombre did such a thing?

No one that he knew of, Hector replied to himself.
It was the sort of thing one prisoner did to another in
a place like Casa del Andar Muerto—Home of the
Walking Dead, or in Yuma Territorial Prison.

It was an act that not only showed disrespect; it
was a warning of worse acts to come should a man
not react with deadly and deliberate force against
such an affront.

Hector's ear still felt sticky as he recalled the inci-
dent, although he had dried it immediately on his
shirtsleeve and had continued wiping it throughout
the night as they'd ridden on.

He should have killed the filthy pig, he told himself.
He *would* have killed him had he not been convinced
that the two men had set him up and were waiting to
strike as soon as he touched the butt of his gun.

When he'd spun toward Clyde, the buckskinned
gunman had stood grinning and said, "I can see
you're going to have to get used to me."

Get used to him . . . ? Hector pictured himself shoot-ing him full of holes.

"Don't get your bark on, Wet Hector," Sonora Charlie had called out. "Clyde only stuck his finger in his canteen, not his mouth."

Not his mouth . . .

The information helped Hector a little, but *only* a little, he reminded himself, thinking back on it. Still, the idea of the pig thinking he could do such a thing kept Hector smoldering. He was glad to have gotten away from those two. After they rode off searching for the lawman Defoe wanted dead, he wouldn't have to look at their faces again. That suited him, he thought, nudging his horse up into a trot.

Inside the Perros Malos Cantina, Hopper Truit was behind the bar slinging mugs of beer and pouring whiskey for the midmorning drinkers. When Hector walked in, he stopped suddenly, taken aback at the sight of her as she pushed a strand of blond hair from her face and reached over and tugged playfully on an older drinker's long-handled gray mustache. She acted as if this was the work she would be doing for a long time to come, Hector thought.

"There he is now," Defoe said from his spot at the end of the bar where he stood with Sonora Charlie and Clyde Jilson.

The two gunmen looked at Hector over their shoul-ders and turned back to their shots of whiskey and mugs of foamy beer.

"Get over here, *muchacho*," Defoe called out, flag-ging the stunned Hector toward his end of the bar with his left hand. His real right hand rested on the gun behind his swallow-tailed coat.

Again he calls me boy?

Hector turned his face slowly to Defoe, seemingly stuck in his tracks at the sight of the dove Hopper doing what he was certain would be his job. But maybe he misunderstood what was going on here, he told himself. Maybe she was only tending bar until he returned to Wild Roses.

Yes, of course, that must be it, he told himself. He managed to walk toward Defoe's end of the bar, seeing Defoe's lips move, saying something to him, but Hector didn't hear a word of it in his numb, stunned condition.

"You missed a most wonderful breakfast," Defoe said as Hector approached. "What took you so long anyway?" Defoe gave a knowing grin.

But Hector didn't answer. Instead, he looked down the bar to where Hopper set up fresh mugs of beer for a group of Mexican *camioneros*, whose mule-killer carts sat out front at the hitch irons filled with copper ore en route from the Sierra Madres to Mexico City.

"You said I would be tending bar for you, boss," Hector said, his voice shaky.

"Forget that," Defoe said with a toss of his left hand. "As you can see, Hopper has a knack for slinging liquor." He grinned. "These men have to stand a foot farther back from the bar than they did when they got here, eh?" He chuckled at his own joke. When Hector and the other two didn't get it, he waved it away and said, "Never mind."

"But you said I would tend—" Hector started before Defoe cut him off.

"I said you would be tending bar *among other things*," Defoe replied sharply. "Besides, bartending is not a good job. What will you do if people stop drinking? You will be out of work, of course," he replied to himself.

Hector only stared at him.

"Anyway, I have a better job for you." Defoe said. He shrugged the matter off and looked Hector up and down. "But if you don't want it . . ."

"*Sí*, I must work," Hector said submissively, coming to accept his situation. "What will you have me do?"

"I'm sending you out with Sonora Charlie and Clyde," said Defoe. "Sonora has three twenty-dollar gold pieces I gave him to pay you."

Three twenty-dollar gold coins!

"What am I to do for them?" Hector asked, keeping his excitement in check. The prospect of putting three twenty-dollar gold coins in his hand forced him to put his ill feelings toward Sonora Charlie and Clyde behind him for the moment. He looked back and forth between Sonora Charlie and Defoe.

"Whatever they say," Defoe replied.

The two gunmen turned and faced Hector squarely. Clyde, who stood nearest, pulled Hector roughly to the bar beside him.

"Yeah, you're with me now, *Pancho*." Clyde grinned, sliding his empty shot glass and a bottle of rye in front of Hector. "Right now you're sort of my own *personal* bartender." He nodded at his empty shot glass. "Fill me up," he said close to Hector's ear.

Sonora Charlie smiled to himself and looked away. Inside his shirt, he carried a leather pouch filled with gold coins the Frenchman had paid him to kill the Ranger—half in advance, the other half payable when Charlie rolled the Ranger's head out on the ground in front of him.

Let Clyde have his fun with the Mexican, he thought. Reaching into his vest pocket, he took out the three gold coins and dropped them onto the bar in front of the young Mexican. What did he care? If Hector tried to duck out on them, all he had to do was shoot him twice in the head and take the coins back.

"This is for you, Hector," he said. "Call it payment in advance for doing what you're told."

Holy Madre! Hector stared at the coins in disbelief. Let the dove tend bar and shake her bosom in front of the drinkers. This was the kind of money that . . . well, *that men kill for,* he thought.

Chapter 11

————

At midmorning, Erin stepped back from the fall-away edge of the trail where she'd been perched looking back on the flatlands below. Behind her a few yards away, the Ranger stood up from inspecting the dun's hooves and watched her for a moment, seeing her eyes scan the distant hill line and trails on the other side. He looked away quickly as she turned toward him, her horse's reins in hand.

"Well, I'm glad that's behind us," she said, walking toward him and leading her horse.

Sam nodded.

"We made good time," he said.

"What now?" she asked, stopping, looking him up and down, the two of them feeling the cooler air of the partially shaded hillsides.

"Now we rest the horses a couple of hours, then head across this high trail and take it down the other side," Sam replied.

Erin looked past him toward a knee-high man-made wall of crumbled stone, beyond it a rocky flat courtyard and an ancient crumbling structure standing fifty feet high on the rugged hillside.

"These are the ruins you spoke of?" Erin asked.

A deep, thick blanket of flowering red vines covered much of the structure. The vines spilled over entranceways and windows and hung like heavy drapes.

"Yes," Sam replied, "this part of the country is full of old Spanish missions. Some say they built them this high up so the bell could be heard all the way across the basin."

Erin took a step forward and stood quietly for a moment, looking all around at the ruins. Ancient piñon, copal and calabash trees lined the short, crumbled wall.

"Is this where you'll be teaching me to shoot the gun?" she asked, glancing back over her shoulder.

"Yes, if you'd still like to learn," Sam replied.

"It's so peaceful and lovely here, I'm hesitant to disturb everything," she said in a lowered tone. Even as she spoke, a pair of doves rose from among the creeper vines in a flurry of batting wings and swooped away, out and around the hillside.

Watching Erin, Sam said in the same lowered tone, "Suit yourself." He continued watching her, the look of contemplation on her face suggesting that she continued to run the idea back and forth through her mind.

At length she said, "I suppose I should go ahead and learn while I have the chance. Do you think the shooting will be overheard by any of Luis or Teto's men?"

"Hard to say," Sam replied. "But it's no secret I'm trailing them."

"I wouldn't want to cause you any trouble," she said.

"You won't," Sam said. "I'll get the Starr out of my saddlebags and we'll get started."

Erin stood staring at the ruins. When Sam returned beside her and held the Starr out on his palm, she took it with both hands and looked it over good.

"Is it loaded and ready to shoot?" she asked.

"Just about," Sam replied. He took the reins to her horse, led both horses a few feet away and hitched them to a juniper tree.

They walked forward until the stone wall surrounding the ruins lay within fifty feet of them.

"Wait here. I'll set up some targets for you," he said, walking to a row of calabash trees.

He looked back at where she stood as he gathered an armful of fallen calabash gourds from beneath one of the trees.

"Isn't this a long way?" she called out as he set the hardened fruit shells up along the knee-high wall. Her raised voice sent a string of small sparrows careening away from within the Mexican creepers. A cloud of black moths rose behind the fleeing birds, then resettled.

Sam didn't answer her until he'd set up the last of the calabash gourds. As he walked back toward her, he noted the Starr still lying flat on her palms, its hammer cocked.

"I thought I'd see if I could pull it back for myself," she offered, seeing his gaze fall on the Starr's cocked position.

"Good idea," Sam said. He reached out and took the gun from her hand as he stepped around beside her.

Erin watched him uncock the Starr and recock it,

his eyes on hers as she realized he'd left the hammer lying on an empty chamber.

"Now you're all set," he said quietly. He held the gun out in front of her, its barrel pointed toward the row of dried fruit shells.

Erin smiled and reached both hands out around the butt of the big Starr revolver. She took control of the gun; Sam turned it loose in her hands.

"How do I aim?" she asked. She looked down the barrel as the weight caused the gun to slump toward the ground.

Sam reached out and lifted the barrel slightly.

"First few shots, don't aim," he said. "Shoot at the spot where you think the targets are. We'll see how good or bad your judgment is, then correct it if need be."

"Is that the way to learn?" she asked.

"Today it is," Sam said. "Squeeze the trigger, don't pull it," he added.

"All right." She steadied the revolver. Sam watched as she squeezed the trigger and the big gun bucked in her hands. She didn't flinch as the shot exploded and the distinctive after-clang of the Starr resounded out along the hillsides and basin floor.

The shot struck the rocky ground ten feet in front of the fruit shells.

"Oh my," Erin said quickly. "May I try again?"

"Go ahead," Sam said, noting she had already started cocking the Starr's hammer.

She fired, missed again and immediately recocked and fired a second time.

"I'm terrible," she said quickly. "May I try again?"

Sam only nodded, seeing her recock the hammer.

She fired and recocked, once, twice. She pulled the trigger a third time but the hammer landed on an empty chamber. Her shots fell short, but each one hit the ground a little closer to the gourds.

"I'm afraid I'll never get this right," she said, letting the gun slump down in front of her.

Once, twice, three times . . . , Sam noted silently.

"You got a little closer with each shot, and all without aiming," he said. "I can reload you if you like. This time, we'll teach you to take aim."

"I'm afraid I'm a little shaken up just now," Erin said. "Perhaps another time, farther along the trail?" She raised the smoking gun and pointed it loosely at Sam's chest.

"Of course, anytime," Sam said, reaching out, taking the big Starr from her.

"May I—" She hesitated, then said, "May I keep Bram's gun, Sam?"

Sam looked at the unloaded gun in his hand, then at her.

"Yes, ma'am," he said, handing the big revolver back to her. "And what about some ammunition for it?" he offered.

She took the gun quickly, as if afraid that Sam might change his mind at any second.

"Obliged, but I have some bullets in Bram's saddlebags," she said. She clutched the gun to her bosom and backed away toward the horses. "I know you'll be wanting to get under way shortly," she added. "So I'll be prepared to ride as soon as you are."

In the late afternoon, as the sun sank below the cliffs and rock juts behind them, Sam and Erin pulled off the trail again, this time beneath a sheltering over-hang, and made camp for the night. Sam gathered scraps of brush and dried piñon kindling and built a small fire far enough back under the rock ledge that it would not be seen from the surrounding hillsides. He ensured that the fire would burn down quickly. As an additional precaution, he banked stones up around the fire to keep its light contained until it reduced itself to a small bed of glowing embers.

In the circle of waning firelight, the two sat across from each other, sipping hot coffee after a modest meal of jerked elk and hardtack.

Talk had come easy for them both from the moment they had met, but not tonight, Sam noted, studying Erin's face as she gazed into the fire. She appeared to be searching for things to say.

"Will you always want to live this way, Sam?" she asked, glancing around beneath the shadowy over-hang. "I mean, *outdoors*, in the wilderness this way?" she added quickly.

"It suits me . . . for now anyway," Sam replied, watching how she carefully kept her eyes away from his for anything longer than a passing glance.

"But someday you'll be wanting a wife and family for yourself?" she asked.

Forcing conversation, Sam thought.

"Someday," he replied quietly, "if it works out that way," he added.

"Someday . . . ," she murmured, with almost a

sense of regret in her voice. She set her empty cup aside and adjusted her blanket on the rocky ground beneath her. "I bid you a good night, Ranger Burrack," she said. She pulled half of the blanket over her.

"Good night, ma'am," Sam said. He set his cup aside, adjusted his blanket and tipped his sombrero down over his eyes.

In the night, after the fire had burned out, Sam listened to the quiet sound of the woman stand up into a crouch, lift her saddle from the ground and move away toward the horses. From beneath his lowered sombrero, he watched her shadowy figure move around between the two horses, his black-point dun chuffing, threatening her as she moved close to unhitch him.

Rather than have the dun raise a fuss, Erin gave up and moved away from it. After a moment, she had quietly saddled her horse and led it away in the dark.

And that's that, Sam thought, hearing the click of hoof as somewhere down the trail Erin had climbed atop the horse and put it forward into the black-purple night.

Sam allowed himself to relax, pushing up his sombrero and staring at the starry sky. The trails were treacherous enough. He wasn't about to get too close behind her and cause her to hurt herself. Besides, he would have no trouble following her. With his boot knife, he'd scored a deep X on the tip of the horse's front right shoe while she'd heated the jerked elk and hardtack.

It had been nice having her with him, he had to admit, even though he had questioned her intentions from the very start. The gunshot signals had confirmed for him what he'd suspected all along. She was as much a part of the Gun Killers as her brother, Bram, had been. True, she had saved his life. But for good reason, he told himself—to protect herself from Matten Page, the gunman he'd killed in Wild Roses.

The man he'd killed for her, as it turned out.

He sat up on his blanket with a sigh and gazed out across the darkened land below. Now to give her a good start and follow her to the Gun Killers, he thought, with more than just a little regret.

Chapter 12

————

In the night, in a small plank and adobe hovel on the lower edge of a jagged hill line, a Gun Killer named Arthur "Big Chili" Hedden had stood up from his cot at the distinct sound of the big Starr revolver. He'd walked to the front doorway of the run-down shack and pulled aside a long, dirty canvas.

"There it is," he murmured to himself, gazing off into the darkness beneath the purple starry sky.

He walked to the other cot in the small room and kicked its frame soundly. "Wake up, Horn," he said.

A stream of interrupted snoring arose above a smothering odor of dirty feet. Hedden turned his head, repulsed, the odor worsening as the snoring gunman struggled to maintain his sleeping state.

"Good God, Horn," Hedden rasped, kicking the cot frame again. "Wake up, you lousy, stinking son of a bitch."

Robert Horn sat up with a start and grabbed for the big Remington lying in the holster on a short stool beside his cot. His hand felt all around the top of an empty holster.

"Here's your gun, *fool*," said Hedden, wagging the Remington toward the waking man.

"What's going on?" Horn mumbled, sounding like he had a mouthful of rocks.

"I heard a Starr pistol out there in the hills," said Hedden, gesturing in the direction of the black distant hill line.

"I gotta shave," mumbled the half-asleep gunman, rubbing his bristled jaw.

"Damn it, wake up!" Hedden shouted, kicking the cot even harder. "We've got work to do."

Horn snapped awake and sat on the side of the cot in his underwear and sock feet.

"The Starr . . . ?" he managed to ask, sounding more awake.

"Yes, it was," said Hedden. "There's no mistaking the sound of that Starr."

"The right signal?" Horn asked in a sleepy voice.

"Yep. I heard one shot, then two, then three in a row," Hedden said. "Just like the Torres brothers said."

"You figure Page killed that Ranger for us?" he asked.

"That's what I'm hoping," said Hedden. "If not, we'll do it ourselves after we meet up with Page and the Donovans."

"I'm not counting on meeting Bram Donovan back there," said Horn. "Did you see his foot before we left?" He stood up scratching and reached for his trousers lying on the stool beneath his holster.

"I saw it," said Hedden. "I figure Bram Donovan is

feeding worms or buzzards by now. It's the woman and Page signaling us."

"We'll go see," said Horn. He fumbled with his trousers and his holster belt, and nearly fell in his attempt to dress himself. "Damn mescal," he growled. He kicked an empty straw-wrapped bottle across the dirt floor.

Hedden shook his head and turned away.

"I'll go get our horses," he said over his shoulder.

When he returned from a plank lean-to behind the shack, he led both his dark bay and Horn's dingy gray horse to the front doorway.

Horn stepped out of the shack, his empty holster belt slung over his shoulder.

"I wish we had some hot grub before heading out," he said. "Some coffee anyway."

Hedden pitched his Remington to him. Horn caught the heavy gun as it thumped into his chest.

"Shoot yourself something along the way," Hedden said, turning and stepping up into his saddle. "With any luck, we can catch up to Page and Donovan before noon."

Horn cursed under his breath and shoved the Remington into the holster hanging from his shoulder.

"I don't remember how long it's been since I had a good full night's sleep," Horn lamented, stepping up into his saddle.

"Must have been the day you last washed your socks," Hedden said.

"The hell does that mean?" said Horn, adjusting his hat atop his head.

"Nothing," Hedden said. The two turned their horses and rode off along the dark rocky trail.

Erin had ridden hard the first two miles as she fled the camp. Yet, after stopping a couple of times, listening closely, and hearing no sound of the Ranger on the trail behind her, she had slowed the horse to a less dangerous pace.

She had to admit she felt bad running out on the Ranger in the middle of the night. He had been nothing but kind to her in every regard. But he was a lawman, she reminded herself. Their worlds were too far apart. Both her father and her brother, Bram, had taught her everything she would ever need to know about lawmen.

Lawmen might start out pretending to be your friend . . . , she could hear them both lecturing as one inside her head. Sooner or later he would've turned on her, she thought, completing the lesson for herself. She had learned early on to trust no one, and the practice had served her well.

Near the bottom of the hill line, she stopped, raised the reloaded Starr and fired it: one shot . . . then two . . . then three. As her ears rang, she reloaded the smoking gun, knowing it had been heard, resounding through the night in every direction.

She rode onto a trail weaving through a wall of boulders that had rumbled down the hillsides centuries past and spilled outward onto the flatter plane.

Halfway through the deep maze of rock, she felt the horse stall and tense up beneath her. She had to strong-hand the reins in order to keep the animal under control. She heard the slightest brush of paw and nail across the tops of boulders lining the narrow trail, and caught glimpses of black, ominous figures streaking from rock to rock above her.

My God! Wolves! she realized, a cold chill striking her and racing up her spine.

The large pack of night hunters had picked out the horse's scent on a wisp of air and followed it across the hillsides and saddlebacks until they found themselves loping along above it.

Erin didn't have to nail her heels to the horse's sides—it was all she could to hold on as panic overtook the terrified animal and sent it racing forward in a frenzied run for its life. Seeing the horse bolt away, the wolves streaked down from atop the rocks like black lightning, snarling, snapping at both horse and rider.

Erin felt a paw rip at her thigh as one of the ferocious hunters fell away to the ground. Even in her struggle to stay atop the horse, Erin grasped at the big Starr revolver at her waist. Yet, as soon as she felt the gun firmly in her hand, the earth seemed to collapse under her.

Whinnying loudly, bucking as it ran, trying to shed Erin's weight from its back, the horse stumbled on the hard rocky trail. Its forelegs folded back brokenly beneath it, the fleeing animal crashed to the ground, sliding and rolling in a spray of rock and dust as the predators launched themselves like spears from every direction.

Erin flew forward over the horse's neck. She hit the ground at a sliding angle and came to a tumbling halt at a pile of boulders heaped beneath the sloping hillside.

A young wolf growled and snapped at her heel as she crawled wildly away into the rocks, gun in hand. But the animal didn't pursue her. Instead, it turned and raced away, joining the fray of snarling wolves that had descended onto the downed and dying horse.

Erin heard the pitiful whinnying of the animal in the swirl of dust behind her, but she didn't stop— *couldn't* stop. She crawled and clawed her way deeper into the spilled boulders, the big Starr gripped tightly.

Her free hand frantically grappled the land-stuck boulders until she found a slim opening beneath two of them—just in time.

Oh my God!

She managed to wiggle her way down between the two boulders and pull her feet in behind herself. She heard a wolf growl; she felt its fangs tug powerfully at her shoe heel, but then release her and turned growling toward three more wolves that had bunched up around it.

Above the terrible feast going on in the swirl of dust, and above the horse's dying screams, Erin heard the wolf at her heels growling and scratching at the dirt, seeking entrance to what questionable refuge she'd found for herself.

"Damn you to *bloody hell!*" she raged, wiggling around until she could point the Starr down her thigh and cock it toward the snarling predator at her heels. *"Get away! Eat the horse!"*

She pulled the trigger, heard the explosion and felt the burn of powder down the side of her calf. At her heels, the wolf let out a loud yelp as the bullet scraped the ground past it and showered its flews with a blast of fiery powder and sharp particles of rock and dirt.

No sooner had she heard the sound of paws running away from behind her than she heard insistent whining and scratching in front of her, just above her face. She felt loose dirt fall down on her from between the boulders. She saw a probing paw break through the dirt and dig feverishly toward her face. She pulled back as far as she could from it without backing out and exposing her heels to the many fangs waiting behind her.

My God! Was she to be eaten alive, dragged from this lair like some varmint and torn innards from skin all over the bloody ground? She muttered a silent and mindless prayer.

She wiggled the Starr around from her side until she could point it up at the probing paw only inches from her face. She cocked the gun just as the wolf pulled its paw away. She waited until the paw was replaced by a sniffing nose. Hot saliva swung down into her face. When she pulled the trigger she closed her eyes to keep from blinding herself—the gun being so close to her face.

A back-spray of warm blood and meat tissue splattered into her face, back onto her shoulders as the shot exploded blue-orange into the wolf's drooling mouth.

Now what?

She dropped her face to the dirt and listened to the sound of feasting wolves on the trail behind her. The horse had fallen silent. Now the only sounds were that of ripping, slashing, chewing. An occasional threat resounded from one animal to another as they ravaged and fed.

Moments later, as the sounds of feeding waned, she heard more and more padded paws moving restlessly back and forth on the ground behind her. Above her blood-smeared face, she heard paws digging relentlessly only inches away. She even heard the whine of younger wolves, those only reaching hunting age. She was their meal for the night, she thought.

With a tight breath, she opened the revolver in front of her face and looked at the four remaining bullets in a sliver of moonlight.

All right, four shots left . . .

She cleared her head and tried to think rationally. She removed one of the four bullets and held it in her hand, lest she use it on one of the animals instead of herself when the time came to do so. She clasped her fist tight around the single bullet, closed the Starr and held it poised.

Outside, both in front and behind her, she heard the pawing, the digging, the whining grow more intense.

After a moment, she sighed and murmured to herself. "No, you may not. . . ."

She opened the Starr again, placed the bullet back inside and shut it with finality. She thought about the tiny helpless baby growing in her belly as she laid her face back down into the dirt. What manner of God brings life to something only to have it eaten from its mother's womb?

She lay silent and still, as if awaiting her turn—hers and her child's—to sate the hungry wolves.

Chapter 13

———

The Ranger had given Erin almost an hour's head start before he'd saddled the dun, ridden out onto the dark trail and started following her. Even in places where moonlight spilled onto the trail, it was still too dark to follow the X on her horse's hooves, unless he wanted to stop, step down and examine the dirt every few minutes.

No need, he'd told himself. There was no other way for her to go but down this trail until she reached the flatlands in the wide basin below.

He'd followed at a steady but checked pace, not wanting to get close enough for her to hear him behind her. Come daylight, he would find the marked horse's shoe helpful. Tonight, he told himself, he would lag back, take his time—

He stopped short, hearing the big Starr's distant twanging sound rise from the base of the hillsides. Listening closely, he made out the faintest sound of a woman's scream.

How far down? Three miles, five . . . ?

Faintly, he identified the baying and barking of wolves. Without hesitation, he booted the dun and put it forward back onto the trail. He rode on, listening as best he could above the clack of iron shoe on the hard rocky ground.

He'd gone over a mile when he reached a place in the trail that rounded to his right and gave an open view of the flatlands below. He stopped for only a moment, just long enough to look down and see the tiny black figures darting back and forth in the purple moonlight.

Drawing his rifle from its saddle boot, he gave the dun another tap on its sides, this time with urgency, as he heard another gunshot resound in the night

Burrowed in tight stone and earthwork, Erin could do nothing now but space out her remaining shots as far as possible and hope that when death came upon her, she would die quickly—she and her child.

Very quickly, she told herself, hearing the wolves snap and growl and fight among themselves over her.

She could hear the animals still pulling and tearing at the horse's carcass, yet the sounds had fallen from that of a feeding frenzy to a calmer, more selective picking-over of the bloody remains.

In front of her, a younger, smaller wolf stuck its head into the dug-away opening beneath the boulder and stared at her, panting, its face so close that she could smell its putrid breath. But as she raised the Starr and pointed it, the animal jerked its head back out of sight.

Her shot exploded from beneath the boulder and

sent a half dozen wolves scrambling away. A moment later, though, and they were back, a gathering of probing, digging paws that moved all about in front of her in the first pale glow of dawn.

Three shots left, she reminded herself, smelling the strong odor of burnt gunpowder in the tight area she'd enclosed herself in. Her cheeks and forehead were drawn and stiff, covered by a layer of dried blood. Her back and legs cramped. Her stomach ached deep inside. She wondered if the baby had even survived the spill from the saddle. If she thought for a minute that it hadn't, she might yet turn the Starr around in her hand, put the barrel to her head—

Stop it! she demanded, cutting herself off. She wasn't going to *do that*—she wouldn't allow herself to even *think* about it.

At her heels, she felt a paw rake at her. She tried to pull her foot farther inside the rock shelter, but this time the persistent animal managed to get a firm grip with both paws and pin her foot down until its jaws clamped onto her ankle and began dragging her backward.

Erin screamed, but as she did, she clawed at the ground and the rock in front of her with one hand and leveled the Starr down her side with the other. The gun was already cocked, ready to fire.

She pulled the trigger and heard the wolf jump back with a loud yelp. But the bullet had missed, done no damage, and the wolves were quickly losing their fear of the loud gunshots. In front of her, younger, smaller paws scratched at her hand as she clung to the bottom edge of the boulder to keep from being dragged out and eaten.

Two shots left. . . .

She hurriedly turned the Starr to the front of her, cocked it and fired. Fresh blood splattered Erin's face, but the wolves had grown more insistent with the coming of dawn. The pack had grown restless, impatient, bolder, more daring.

One shot left!

Behind her, the pair of larger paws returned with renewed vigor, digging at her heels, getting a grip on her left foot and pulling hard. This time she knew she couldn't stop them. Her hand, bloody from killing the young wolf, slipped away from the boulder.

As she cocked the Starr for her last shot, the wolves dragged her out from beneath the rocks. She felt more paws scraping at her, more fangs dragging her by her clothes, by her skin. She screamed and fired the last shot into the large mass of fur and fangs. A wolf flew away with a death yelp. But that wasn't going to save her. It was over now.

With a snarl, the big wolf slung her out onto the ground in the pale, morning light. As she caught herself in the dirt and drew the Starr back for a swing, she saw the wolves quickly back away from her and form a small, tight circle—too many of them to count.

The pack leader, the larger wolf that had dragged her from her stone sanctuary, stood a few feet back, crouched, ready to spring forward. The rest of the wolves waited, also crouched, poised, but giving the kill to their leader.

"You damned devil!" Erin screamed at the alpha wolf. She swung the empty Starr just as the big wolf pounced forward.

In midleap, she saw the leader's bared fangs, the open jaws thrust forward almost atop her. But then she heard the blast of a rifle shot and saw the animal crumple in midair and fall brokenly away.

Erin froze in the dirt as the pack of wolves scrambled away wildly—all but one. The remaining animal charged at her, but another rifle shot lifted the animal into the air, half spun him around and sent him tumbling across Erin. The wolf's warm, dead body flattened her to the ground.

Twenty yards away, the Ranger levered a fresh round into his rifle chamber, smoke curling from the big Winchester's barrel. He tapped the dun forward as the last of the wolves vanished into the gray swirl of morning.

He looked at the dead horse's remains as his dun walked past it to the spot where Erin lay motionless on the hard ground. Shoving the Winchester back down in its boot, he lowered himself from his saddle, picked the dead wolf up by the scruff of its neck and pulled it off her.

"Let's get you up from there," he said almost in a whisper.

Stooping down, scooping her into his arms, he carried her a few feet away and sat her against a rock. The dun tagged along close behind him, made wary by the dead wolves lying strewn on the ground, and the strong scent of them looming in the morning air.

Erin sipped the tepid water from the Ranger's canteen as he held it to her lips. She leaned back against
the rock without a word, lying in shock, neither con-
scious nor unconscious. She saw the Ranger as if from
behind a gauzy veil.

Sam had taken his bandanna from around his
neck, wet it and wiped dried blood from her face. He
had rolled the loose leg of her trousers up past her
knee, and wiped and inspected the claw marks on
her thigh. Then he'd examined the teeth marks on her
ankles, most of the damage deflected by her high-
topped leather shoes.

"Feeling better?" he asked quietly. He'd reloaded
the Starr revolver and shoved it down behind his gun
belt.

The world surrounding Erin was a shadowy dream,
yet one that she knew would soon pass. For now, she
only looked him up and down and nodded her head
slightly in reply.

Sam understood. He poured fresh water from his
canteen onto the bloody bandanna, squeezed it and
held it to her forehead.

After a moment, when her mind had cleared some,
she looked all around at the carnage in the silvery
light of dawn, as if she were seeing it for the first time.

Watching her fix her eyes onto the remains of the
dead horse, Sam tipped her face away from the grisly
scene and touched the tip of the wet bandanna to her
chin under the pretence of removing more dried
blood.

"Turn it loose. It's over and done," he whispered.

She stared at him, watched him up close as he touched the bandanna to her chin, to her cheek.

"You . . . followed me," she said, a questioning look on her face.

Sam only nodded. He turned, capped his canteen and laid it aside. Of course he'd followed her, he thought. What else would he have done? When he turned back to face her, the questioning look was still there.

"You left without saying good-bye," he said, looking into her eyes.

"I didn't mean to hurt—"

"You don't owe me an explanation," he said, cutting her off. "Riding with me was your free choice, ma'am. So was leaving, if that's what suited you."

"But you saved my life," she said.

"And you saved mine," Sam replied. "So I expect we're about evened up."

"But I had a reason to do what I did in Wild Roses," she said, a guilty look coming to her face.

"We all have our reasons," Sam said. He rolled her torn trouser leg down and stood up, as if dismissing the matter. Reaching a hand down to her, he asked, "Are you able to stand?"

She took his hand and rose to her feet. She dusted the seat of her trousers and took a deep breath, trying to settle herself after the ordeal she'd gone through.

"I—I want to clear the air, Sam," she said. "I wasn't riding to Port of Tampico in order to return to Ireland. I was *using you* to help me catch up to the Gun Killers." She stared at him, awaiting his reaction.

"I see," Sam said quietly. He took a step back, and

drew the big, reloaded Starr from his belt and pointed it up.

Erin flinched as he fired one shot, waited a second, fired two more, then three. He stared into her eyes as he pulled the trigger.

"You knew all along?" she asked.

The Ranger didn't reply right away. He stood in silence, smoke curling from the Starr.

"We understand each other, ma'am," he said finally, lowering the Starr, letting it hang down his thigh. "Let's get going. You're stuck with me until we can round you up a horse."

Chapter 14

In the morning sunlight, Big Chili Hedden and Robert Horn looked west, watching the black-point dun bound up into sight across the flatlands, a bellowing swirl of dust rising in its wake. They watched until the horse drew close enough that they could see it carried two riders, the one in front a woman, her long red hair whipping sidelong on the desert breeze.

"My, my," said Hedden, "look what we've got coming here. It's about time, after all the signaling we heard." He sipped a mouthful of water from a gourd dipper and spit it out in a stream.

"It's her, sure enough, Big Chili," said Horn. "Is that her brother riding behind her?"

"Naw," said Hedden. "I told you Bram Donovan is deader than hell."

Hedden lowered the water gourd from his mouth and wiped a hand across his wet lips. He laid the gourd on the low stone wall surrounding the well where they had stopped to water themselves and their horses. The animals stood hitched to an iron ring, water dripping from their mouths.

"Who do your think, then? Matten Page?" Horn asked.

"Most likely Page," said Hedden. "Whoever it is, they damn sure wanted us to know they were coming."

Horn grinned. "Yeah, it was that little Irish sugar-plum signaling," he said. His voice took on a lewd tone. "She got homesick . . . missing what she'd been getting, if you know what I mean."

"I don't recognize that horse," Hedden said warily, staring out, disregarding what Horn had said. "Who rides a black-point dun?"

"Tom Custer rode one, I heard," said Horn.

"Tom Custer? General George's brother?" Hedden said without taking his eyes off the horse and its riders.

"Yep," said Horn, "that's who I'm talking about."

"That is *not* Tom Custer, Horn," said Hedden, still staring intently.

"Well, hell, *of course* it ain't really Tom Custer," said Horn. "How could it be— "

"I'm thinking it's that damned Ranger," said Hedden, cutting him off. "The lawman from Nogales."

"The Ranger?" Horn questioned.

"Yeah, the Ranger," said Hedden.

"Damn," said Horn, more serious, paying more attention now. "That means Matten Page didn't kill him, Big Chili."

"Yep," said Hedden, "and that puts Matten Page's name on a long list of men who *didn't* kill him."

"Three of ours that I know of," Horn said.

Hedden paused for a moment in contemplation, then said, "If we keep getting whittled down by this lawman, the Torreses are going to get rich splitting our money."

"That's something to think about," said Horn. As he spoke, he lifted his Colt, checked it, spun it on his trigger finger and slipped in back into his holster. "Except they won't make nothing off me."

"Me neither," said Hedden. "Let's spread out. If that's the lawman, we're going to kill the sumbitch soon as he rides in."

Across the flatlands, riding behind Erin, the Ranger stared ahead at a place where two trails intersected on the rolling desert floor. He saw the two men moving away from each other in front of the public well. Behind the gunmen, timbers, sun-bleached planks and chiseled stone lay in rubble where a row of shacks and adobes had fallen to the ground.

"Sam . . . ?" Erin said over her shoulder.

"I see them," Sam replied. "Who are they?" As he spoke, he pulled his Winchester up from the saddle boot and laid it across his lap. The big Swiss rifle was still in its box, tucked under the bedroll between him and the saddle. It wasn't yet time to bring the rifle into play—better to keep quiet until the conditions were right.

"It's Art Hedden and Robert Horn," Erin said. "They're both top gunmen."

"Big Chili Hedden?" the Ranger asked.

"Yes," Erin said, staring forward, watching the two gunmen spread out in front of the well, taking position.

"That's who you were signaling?" Sam asked.

Erin didn't answer.

When they drew closer to the well and the two gunmen flanking it, Sam slowed the dun to a walk.

"Trade me places," he said quietly. Before Erin could respond, he lifted her from the saddle, shifted her around effortlessly and sat her behind him.

"Yep, the lawman from Nogales . . . ," Hedden murmured to himself, getting a better look at the gunman now that he sat in front of Erin. He began opening and closing his gun hand, loosening his fingers. "Get ready, as soon as he's in range, Horn," he called out. "We're not going to give him a chance to get the drop—"

A shot from the Ranger's Winchester cut Hedden short. He saw the shot lift Horn an inch off the ground and fling him backward.

"Je-*sus*!" Hedden cried out, turning and running toward the horses as the Ranger levered another round into his rifle chamber.

Watching over Sam's shoulder, Erin saw the fleeing gunman dive for cover behind the well's stone wall.

"He's—he's getting away," she said, seeing the gunman crawl up his horse's side, back the animal away and turn it to the trail lying low in his saddle.

"I know," Sam said, keeping the dun walking forward at a leisurely pace.

"You're just letting him go?" Erin asked, surprised.

"Yep," said Sam.

"But he'll ride straight from here to the Gun Killers," Erin said. "He'll tell them you're coming."

"I know," Sam said. "I figure it'll save your bullets."

Erin let the remark pass and said, "You want them to know you're coming?"

"They *already know* I'm coming," Sam said. "I'm just letting them know how far back I am . . . and who's with me," he added.

Moments later, when Sam stopped his dun at the well, Art Hedden and his horse were only a small dot in a sheet of dust on the horizon.

"There's your new mount, ma'am," Sam said, reaching around and helping Erin down from behind him. Looking down at her, he said, "You're free to do as you please."

Horn's horse looked at them from the iron hitch ring. Erin unhitched the animal and turned to the Ranger as he swung down from his saddle.

"As I please?" she said. "Then, I can ride on with you, if that suits me?"

Sam only nodded, turning the dun to the well, where one of the gunmen had left a bucket sitting half-full of water.

As the dun drank, Sam walked over to where Horn lay dead in the dirt. He stooped down and looked the gunman over. When he stood up, he saw a thin little man walk from out of the rubble toward the well, a long, tin bathing tub hooded over his bowed back.

The Ranger walked back to the well as the man rolled the bathing tub from his back and set it upright in the dirt. Horn's horse and the dun shied back a step.

"*Hola*," Sam said quietly. "What can we do for you?"

"*Hola, señor*," the man replied. He wagged a thin finger and said, "It is not what you can do for me. It is what I can do for you." He gestured a trembling hand toward the galvanized tin tub, then toward Erin, her torn trousers, her dirty bloodstained shirt. "For the *señora . . . Bañese?*"

Sam said to Erin, "He asked if you want to take a bath."

Erin looked at the Ranger. "Do we have time?"

"We'll take the time," Sam said, noting her condition. He looked all around, then turned to the little man and said, "Where will she take the bath?"

"Right here," the man said. "I fill the tub, no?"

Sam and Erin looked at each other.

"I *could* do with a bath," she said with a shrug.

"I understand," said Sam. He reached down inside his trouser pocket and pulled out a coin. To the little man he said, "*Sí, por favor*, fill the tub."

It was late afternoon when Hector Pasada, Sonora Charlie Ring and Clyde Jilson followed the dun's hoofprints across the rolling flatlands to the ghost town's public well. They had ridden past the sparse remnants of Erin's horse and the bloated bodies of the dead wolves strewn about, roasting in the harsh desert sun.

At the well, the three stepped down and looked at the dried blood and the drag marks of Horn's bootheels in the dirt. The marks led off into the rubble where the little man had taken the body, stripped it and covered it with stones and loose broken planks. At the well, the tin tub leaned against the low stone wall, having been cleaned after Erin had used it. A small puddle of water lay in its lower end.

"A washing tub, out here?" Clyde said, thumping his finger on the tin as if to make sure the tub was real.

"Yes," said Hector, "I have seen this bathing tub before, and the man who hauls it around with him."

"You mean *that* man?" Sonora Charlie said, nodding toward the little man who stepped into sight wearing the dead gunman's loose-fitting clothes and oversized boots. He shuffled toward them from the stone and timber rubble.

Seeing the little man clutching Horn's ill-fitting gun belt, keeping a big Colt from falling down around his ankles, Clyde shook his head and chuckled under his breath.

"Think I ought to shoot him before something bad happens to him?" he said.

Sonora Charlie laughed. But then he turned to the little man as he watched him stop and stand beside the tin tub, as if protecting it.

"We trailed a man and woman here," Sonora said flatly. "How long ago did they leave?"

"Much earlier," said the little man, "before the sun was straight up. The *señora* bathed. The man watered his horse—and he killed a man." He gestured a hand down the front of him. "I received these new clothes and boots."

"The woman bathed in *this* tub?" Clyde asked, staring at the tub with renewed interest.

"*Sí,* and they paid me for filling it," the little man said. He rubbed his finger and thumb together.

Clyde looked at Sonora Charlie and said in an urgent tone, "I want a bath in it too."

Sonora gazed off across the rolling flatlands,

following the two sets of hoofprints leading along the trail.

"It'll soon be dark," he said, judging the amount of time left before the sun slid down the western horizon. "I expect this is as good a place as any to make camp."

"Shall I fill the tub for you, *señor*?" the little man asked, his left hand still clutching the heavy gun belt at his waist.

"Damn right you can, little fellow," said Clyde, sliding down from his saddle, "and hurry it up." He looked around at Hector and said, "Help him, Pancho. I want in that tub, pronto, while it's still wet."

This bastardo. Hector looked at Sonora as he swung down from his saddle.

"You heard him, Pancho," said Sonora. "Help get that tub filled. I might even want to wash myself a little."

Hector stood seething, his jaw clamped tightly. But after a moment he realized that he had no choice but to do as he was told. He stepped over, leaned his shotgun against the stone wall, let out a tense breath and hitched his horse to an iron ring. Then he helped the little man turn the tub over and set it on the ground.

Chapter 15

Evening shadows had fallen long across the darkening land while the little well tender walked in a slow circle, turning a large pole connected to a well wheel. Pot after pot of water rose from under the ground and emptied into the stone reservoir.

"Hurry the hell up, little fellow," said Clyde, standing naked and filthy beside the tin tub that was still only half-full. His clothes lay in a heap in the dirt, his Colt lying atop them. "Why don't you have a donkey to turn the wheel?"

"I ask myself that same question all the time, *señor*," the little man said, pushing the long pole steadily in a circle. "Perhaps in another life, I myself was a donkey—"

"Don't start some religious craziness," Clyde said, cutting him off. "This bath is taking too damn long as it is." He picked a crawling bug from the hair atop his shoulder and flicked it away. Hector turned his head in disgust.

A few yards from the tub, Sonora Charlie had built a small fire and set a pot of coffee on it to boil.

"It's going to be half the night the way this is going," he said. "I'm getting some shut-eye." He said to Hector, "Pancho, wake me up when it's my turn."

Before Hector could even reply, Clyde turned to him, scratching his naked hairy crotch.

"Go to my saddlebags, Pancho," he said. "There's a rag down in there. Bring it to me."

Keeping his rage contained, Hector stomped over to the saddlebags lying in the dirt, stooped down and flipped back the leather flap. Reaching inside, he felt a leather bag filled with coins, but quickly pulled his hand away, as if he was worried Clyde might realize what he was doing. In the bottom of the saddlebags, he found a wadded-up cotton rag. He pulled the rag out, shook it loose and carried it to the naked gun man.

Clyde took the rag and stood grinning at him, still scratching his hairy crotch.

"Gracias, mi amigo muy especial," he chuckled in a lewd, joking tone.

His special friend? What kind of man was this, to say such a thing to him with his scrotum in hand? Hector turned away, his face burning, his jaw clamped tight to keep himself from grabbing the gun at his waist. More importantly, how little did this man think of him to dare make such a remark—to treat him in such a manner?

As Hector stomped away, Clyde stepped into the half-full tub of water.

"I ain't waiting any longer," he said to the little well tender. He sat down in the water and picked up a chunk of soap the well tender had laid on a rock beside the tub. "Keep bringing water over here," he said to the little man.

"*Sí*, I will," the little man replied. He stopped turning the wheel, hurried over with two buckets of water and poured them into the tub.

"Pancho, get over here," Clyde said. As he spoke, he looked over at Sonora Charlie, grinned and gave him a wink.

Sonora Charlie shook his head and leaned back onto his saddle, which was lying in the dirt behind him.

"Best leave that little squirrel alone," he warned under his breath.

Hector walked over to the tub and tried hard to keep the anger out of his voice.

"What do you want, for me to help him bring more water?" he said, barely under control.

"No," Clyde said. He pitched him the wet rag he had lathered with soap. "I want you to scrub my back real good for me."

At the fire, Sonora Charlie held back a muffled laugh.

"You are loco," Hector said flatly. "I wash no man's back. What do you think I am?"

"Come on now, Pancho," Clyde said in a mocking tone. "I'd do it for you."

"I will *not* do it for you," Hector said with determination. "I will not do it for any man."

"Hear that, Sonora?" Clyde called out, letting himself sink down into the tepid water. "Pancho is being plumb unfriendly."

Sonora Charlie shook his head and sighed under

his lowered hat brim. "Pancho, scrub his back. Don't make us think you're not going to do as you're told. You don't want to see us upset."

Hector gritted his teeth, his fists clenched at his sides. Across the well, the little man walked in a slow, steady circle, looking back, watching them over his thin shoulder. He had taken off the heavy gun belt and laid it nearby in the dirt.

"Give me the rag," Hector said, stepping forward.

"That's a good boy, Pancho," said Clyde. He handed the rag back to Hector, sat up and leaned slightly forward.

Hector avoided the well tender's eyes as he gritted his teeth and rubbed the soapy rag back and forth on Clyde's broad, hairy shoulders.

"Aw, that's good, Pancho," Clyde said, grinning to himself at having humiliated Hector. "I just knew you would make a damn fine back-scrubber once I got you started, once you applied yourself."

Hector swallowed a tight knot in his throat. It was not going to get any better for him with these two, he told himself. Not as long as this man was alive.

"You keep on doing such a good job," Clyde Jilson said, "I'll soon have you warming my back, these cool nights in the desert."

In a moment, Clyde noticed Hector had stopped scrubbing back and forth with the cloth.

"Hey, have you quit on me back there?" he asked over his shoulder.

"No, here I am," Hector said, stepping around in front of him with the cocked shotgun he'd picked up from against the low stone wall, his hands still soapy.

Clyde's eyes widened, staring into the deep black gun barrels only inches from his face.

"Oh, *hell*! Wait, Hector! I'm only jok—"

One shotgun hammer dropped. Clyde's face disappeared in a red bloody mist of fire, meat and bone matter.

"But I am *not joking*! What do you think of that, my *special friend*?" Hector said, leaning in close to the bloody, headless corpse lying slumped back in front of him, gray smoke looming above its chewed-off neck.

"*Jesus, Hector*! What have you done?" shouted Sonora Charlie. He'd sprung to his feet. In his stunned surprise, he'd left his gun in its holster lying on the ground beside his saddle. "Clyde's crazy, but he meant no harm! He was just funning you!"

Only when Sonora saw the shotgun swing toward him did he think about his gun on the ground near his feet.

"Oh, I see, *just funning*," Hector said. He gave a tight grin that flashed on his face, then vanished. "Did you see me laughing?"

As he spoke, he'd started stepping closer to Sonora Charlie, the second hammer already cocked, aimed and ready on the smoking shotgun.

"No, Hector!" said Sonora Charlie. "It wasn't funny. Clyde took it too far! But you're not going to kill me, are you?" He stood ready to leap toward his gun at any second—but his seconds had run out.

"Yes, I think I am," Hector said calmly, his hands tightening on the shotgun, his finger starting to squeeze the trigger.

Seeing it coming, Sonora shouted, "Hector! *Hector*—!"

The other hammer fell; the shotgun bucked in Hector's hands. A blue-orange blast streaked across the seven feet of space between them, picked Sonora Charlie up and slung him backward in a spray of blood.

"Now it's *Hector*, eh? You son of a bitch," Hector said. He stepped forward and looked down at Sonora Charlie's mangled face and chest. "But I am no longer Hector," he said. "I am Pancho, remember?"

At the water wheel, the little man had stopped turning the pole and stood staring wide-eyed at Hector, the carnage and the looming gun smoke in the still night air.

"What are you looking at?" Hector asked him as he stepped toward Clyde's saddlebags lying on the ground.

Seeing Hector reach inside the bag and pull out the leather coin pouch, the little man looked over at Clyde's bloody, headless body, then back to Hector.

"Are you going to take a bath this night, Señor Pancho?" he asked meekly.

Hector thought about it for a moment as he stepped over and also pulled a coin pouch out of Sonora Charlie's saddlebags. He hefted the weighty pouch in his and smiled at it.

"*Sí*," he said, at length. "Dump this pig out of the tub and refill it." He tilted his chin up with pride. "Tonight, I will take a bath."

He looked off in the direction of Wild Roses and thought of his wife awaiting his return.

Tomorrow, I come home to you, Ana, he said silently to the black distant hill lines. He gripped the bag of money tightly. *You and my son will not go hungry again.*

Chapter 16

————————

Art "Big Chili" Hedden rode his dark bay long and hard throughout the night and most of the next day, stopping only long enough to rest the tired horse and keep it from dying on its hooves. At a settlement along the Rio Verde on the outskirts of the small village of San Felipe, he had stopped at a hitch rail and traded the blown and winded animal for an almost identical dark bay standing in a row of fresh *rurales'* horses out in front of a small, loud cantina.

In the cover of darkness and the sound of drunken laughter, guitars and castanets, Hedden traded saddles, bridles and saddlebags at the hitch rail. Atop the fresh horse, riding away, he looked back in time to see his own worn-out animal stagger sidelong against another horse, then collapse to the ground.

"Somebody's going to be a while thinking this one through." He chuckled darkly under his breath and rode on. It was not until the following day that he gazed ahead and saw the crumbling rooflines of

Pueblo de Ruinas across a stretch of pale wild grass and wavering heat.

At the town of Caminos, Teto Torres sat staring back from a high-backed stuffed chair on the stone porch of a sun-bleached adobe building. Six members of his and his brother Luis' Gun Killers gang stood gathered around him, all of them watching steely-eyed as the lone rider approached from the northwest.

"The lawman from Nogales?" asked Paco Sterns, a half Mexican, half Arkansan standing near Teto. "If it is, I will go kill him for you."

"No, it's not him," Teto replied without taking his eyes off the single rider. "It is Big Chili."

"Big Chili? Then where the hell is Bobby Horn?" asked another gunman, this one an *Americano*, Truman Filo, from one of the tougher street gangs of New York City.

"We will soon know," Teto said, still staring straight ahead. "If I were to guess, I would say Horn is lying dead somewhere in his own blood."

"Hell of a thing . . . ," said Filo, letting his thought trail on the matter.

A blue-black tattoo circled Filo's left eye and reached out onto his left temple in the form of a bird's wing. A large T had been branded onto his forehead years earlier, identifying him as a thief caught in the pursuit of his trade.

Behind the gunmen, in the open doorway of the adobe building, Luis Torres stepped forward and leaned against the doorjamb beneath a faded wooden sign that read TRABAJOS PÚBLICOS. He reached sideways, struck a match and held the flame to the black cigar in his lips.

"I don't know that you should want the lawman dead just yet, Filo," he said, letting out a stream of smoke. "He makes money for each of us every time he pulls the trigger."

"Any lawman offends me, money or no," Filo replied. He spit to the ground, staring out at the lone rider. "Anyway, I'm getting tired of staying only a step ahead of him. I'm ready to go rob something, else split up our booty and go make a party for a month or two."

A gunman from New Orleans named Bo Sapp gave a dark chuckle. "I have to admit that I myself am beginning to sway in that same direction. When are we going to fill our saddlebags?"

"Very soon," said Teto.

"Yeah?" said Sapp. The gunmen's expressions perked.

"Take it easy, all of you," said Luis Torres. "We're circling back to pick up the money we stashed in Wild Roses. Now that we know there's only been this one lawman dogging us, it's time we get back to town, split the cake and everybody take their slice."

"Suits the hell out of me," said Sapp.

"Damn right," said Filo, all of the men nodding in agreement.

"I knew that would make all you freebooters happy," Luis said. He stepped forward from the doorway with a smile, watching Hedden draw closer, up onto the dirt street into town.

From his overstuffed chair, Teto said, "One of you go lead Hedden over here, make him feel important."

"I've got him," Sapp said, stepping onto the dirt street, walking toward the approaching lone rider.

When Hedden and his tired, stolen horse walked up to him, Sapp took the animal by its bridle and looked up at Heddon as he turned it toward Teto and the others.

"You look like the devil's run up your back with his spurs on," he said with a grin.

"It ain't no laughing matter what I've been through, Sapp," said Hedden.

"Well, now, you just tell ol' Bo here all about it," Sapp said in a mock fatherly tone. Looking around he asked, "Where's that privy-house rat, Horn?"

"Don't call him names, Bo," said Hedden. "The poor sumbitch is dead."

"Damn," said Sapp.

"Yeah, so grind on *that*," Hedden said, jerking his horse away from him and kicking it on toward Teto and the others.

The men stepped to the side as Hedden rode on and stopped out in front of Teto in the overstuffed chair. Teto sat with a long cigar, one leg hiked up over a chair arm, a bottle of rye perched between his thighs.

"Start talking, Big Chili," Teto said.

"I will," said Hedden, "soon as you introduce me to your friend there."

Teto raised the corked bottle and pitched it up to him.

The men watched as Hedden pulled the cork and took a long gurgling drink of rye.

"I remember you now," Hedden said to the bottle, lowering it, corking it and tossing it back down to

Teto. The Mexican outlaw looked at the half-empty bottle.

"We got ourselves lured in hands down by that blasted lawman," Hedden said in a whiskey-strained voice. "Horn got himself nailed by a Winchester shot before that snake even rode into pistol range."

Teto just stared at him.

"What did you do?" Sapp asked, walking up from the street and standing beside Teto.

"Hell, I turned and cut out of there, is what I did," Hedden said grudgingly, answering Teto instead of Sapp. Luis Torres watched and listened from the open doorway.

"You couldn't turn and shoot him down?" Sapp asked. The rest of the men stared, hanging on every word.

"Who am I answering to, Teto?" Hedden asked harshly. "*You*, or this scornful prick?"

"Shut up and let him talk, Bo," Teto said to Sapp.

"I couldn't shoot back at him," Hedden said to Teto, tossing Sapp a scorching glance. "He had the Irish gal in front of him. He used her as a shield."

"Erin?" said Teto, sitting up a little. He looked around at Luis, who now stepped forward with interest.

"Bad as I hated to, I figured I best turn tail while I could, else I'd take a chance on killing her," Hedden said, lying straight-faced. "Did I do wrong?" He held a fixed stare on Teto.

Teto gave a slight shrug.

"Did Erin look to be this lawman's prisoner?" Teto asked.

"It didn't seem like some kind of afternoon frolic,"

Hedden said, "if that's what you're asking." He looked at Luis, gauging how well his words were being received by them both.

The two Torres brothers only stared at him.

"Fact is, she looked like she'd been rode hard and beaten to sleep with a bag of rocks."

"This pig of a lawman," Teto whispered, gripping the chair arm tightly.

"Did she give you the gun signal?" Luis asked. He raised a cautioning hand toward his brother as if to settle him.

"Yep, she gave us the gunshots, *twice*, in fact," said Hedden. "That's what had us riding her direction in the first place. We made it as far as the well in El Pueblo Fantasma. That's where he struck us. With Erin in front of him, we never had a chance."

"Are you saying Erin Donovan might be on this lawman's side?" Teto asked. As he spoke, he set the bottle of rye on the porch beside his chair and lifted a big Colt lying alongside him.

A worried look came upon Hedden's sweat-streaked face.

"*Huh-uh*, Teto," said Hedden, "I'm not saying any such thing. I'm only saying we got hit in a way that we couldn't fight back without hurting her. I'm not making any more of it than that."

"That's good, Big Chili," Teto said, the Colt tipping over to rest on his thigh. "For a minute I was concerned that you were saying something *ugly* about her." He offered a smug grin. "I am glad we cleared that up."

"Now that you *have* cleared it up, let's get our horses and get out of here," Luis said.

Hedden looked back and forth between them, a worn-out expression on his face.

"I just got here," he said.

"You could have saved yourself the trouble and stayed in your saddle," Teto said. Then he looked at his brother and asked, "You want all of us to finally meet this lawman head-on and kill him?"

"No, we continue the same way with him," said Luis, "only this time we leave men who have *cojones* enough to kill him." He ended his words with a critical stare at Hedden.

"Leave me behind, Luis," said Hedden. "I'll kill the lawman this time, else you can nail my *cojones* to a plank and sell them for a child's toy."

"*Ouch*," said Teto.

"I mean it," said Hedden. "Now that I know what kind of sneaky, backstabbing sumbitch this lawman from Nogales is, I'm ready for him." He looked all around, then added, "Only, leave a good man with me that I can count on."

"You couldn't count on Bobby Horn?" Bo Sapp cut in. "Come on, Big Chili," he said skeptically.

"I won't answer that, Sapp," said Hedden. "But if you'll wager your *cojones* too, we'll soon see who's got the bigger pair."

Sapp looked at Teto and Luis and said, "Let's make sure we understand one another, hombres. I'm not wagering my balls to be nailed to a plank, neither as a child's toy nor for a general conversation piece. But I'll stay back with Big Chili and kill the lawman, if that's all we're talking about." He gave a Hedden a look. " 'Nailed to a plank for a child's toy'?" he murmured in disdain.

"I've seen it done," Hedden said in his defense.

"Stay behind and kill him," Teto cut in. He rose from his chair and walked back inside the seized public building where a hound stood with a leg cocked over a strewn pile of paperwork spilled from atop an overturned desk.

"This Nogales lawman will kill them both," Luis said matter-of-factly behind him.

"I know," said Teto, "and our share of the stolen money only continues to grow. Dead gunmen are like bank interest to us." He gave a short grin.

Luis shook his head and said, "You have used that joke too much for it to still be funny, *mi hermano.*"

"Who said I was joking?" Teto said.

PART 3

PART 3

Chapter 17

Hector Pasada noticed something was wrong as soon as he reined his horse to a halt and stared across the last fifty yards of sandy flatlands toward the small adobe where he'd left Ana and his son. As he jerked the lead rope and brought Sonora Charlie's and Clyde Jilson's horses to a halt beside him, he saw two coyotes race away from the rear of the house.

Uh-oh. . . .

He gave his horse a sharp gig with the Mexican spurs he'd taken from Sonora Charlie's body and sent it racing forward, the two dead outlaws' horses running along beside him. At the front porch, he slid his horse to a stop and jumped from its back, shotgun in hand, and bounded across the porch into the empty adobe.

"Ana . . . ?" he called out, looking all around, relieved to see no sign of a struggle, or of any act of violence. Yet, he was disturbed and puzzled that the house stood empty—empty long enough that coyotes had grown bold and wandered inside.

"Ana . . . ?" he called out again as he crossed the floor and looked inside the small, empty bedroom he and his wife shared. On an empty crate beside a straw-filled pallet on the dirt floor, he saw a letter lying beneath a blackened candleholder.

He picked the letter up and read it silently to himself.

"Oh no, Ana . . . ," he whispered to himself, shaking his head in disbelief. As he continued reading he began repeating over and over, "On no, oh no, oh no," his words growing louder and more painful with each repetition until they ended in a long, mournful cry.

Outside, across the stretch of flatlands, the old well tender heard Hector's long, loud plea to heaven. The sound caused the little man to stop in his tracks, roll the tin bathtub off his crouched back and straighten enough to stare toward the weathered adobe.

Three times, he heard Hector cry out in an anguished voice. With each wail, he saw the horses stirring about nervously in the dusty yard. On the third cry, the little man nodded to himself, as if knowing that some terrible pain had now been overcome. He picked up the tub and continued walking on toward the adobe, following the horses' tracks as he had for the past three days, since they had left the public well at El Pueblo Fantasma.

As he approached the adobe, he saw Hector standing with the letter gripped tight in his fist through an open window. Hector stared out at the little man with reddened eyes and a sick, bitter expression on his face.

The old man stopped beneath the widow and rolled the tin tub from his back like some strange desert beetle shedding its shell. He stared at Hector without offering a word.

"My wife has left me," Hector said in a tight voice, struggling to keep his emotions from showing.

"Oh . . . How can this be?" the well tender whispered. "A man's wife cannot leave him. It is forbidden. It is an act against the law of God's divine province."

"Do not tell me about God's law, Bent One," Hector said venomously. "My Ana has left me. She has taken my son. She goes far away to live with another man."

The well tender raised a gnarled finger and shook his head.

"Then you must exercise your right to hunt her down and kill her—not only her, but the man as well. No woman can take a man's son away from him and *live*."

Hector stared off across the sandy, rolling flatlands and watched a dust devil stand up as if arising from sleep and spin away in flurry of dust.

"My son is not the blood of my blood, Bent One," he said as if confessing himself to the well tender. "He is the blood of the man my wife goes to live with. When I married my Ana, the boy was still waiting to be born. When he was born, I welcomed him and vowed to raise him as my own—"

"Stop," the little man said with a wince. "I must hear no more." He held up a hand toward Hector, as if to keep any more information from leaving his lips. "Why do you tell me these things?"

"I don't know," said Hector. He looked away, out across the empty, desolate land. "Why do you follow me here, all the way from the Ghost Town well?"

The little man shrugged his crooked shoulders.

"It was time for me to pick up my tub and leave Pueblo Fantasma," he said. "It is not good for a man to live only among the dead. I only stayed because of the tub. It is not easy to carry a tub in this land."

"Oh?" Hector stared back down at the little man. "Yet, when I offered you one of the horses to pull your tub, you turned me down. Instead you have walked behind me all this way."

"*Sí*, and I have made it here without the horse's help," he said proudly. "I have carried my tub to this spot, on my own, from the town of the dead with help from neither man nor beast."

"Good for you," Hector said dismissively. He spit and stared off in the direction he knew his wife and the boy had taken.

"You will go after her?" the little man asked.

Hector didn't reply.

"To kill her, or the boy's father, or to bring her back with you?" he asked, staring up at Hector's troubled face.

"She was a good wife," Hector said. Then, as if talking to himself he said, "She could not bear this life that was forced upon her. How could I kill her for being weak when it is I who brought the weakness out of her?"

"So, you kill the man?" the well tender asked quietly.

"I cannot kill the man without hurting Ana. I cannot kill Ana without hurting the boy. I cannot destroy one without destroying all three, and I cannot destroy all three without destroying myself."

A silence set in beneath a whir of hot wind. After a moment of contemplation, the little man scratched his head and looked back up at Hector.

"So, you do nothing?" he said. "You do not seek vengeance for what has been done to you?"

"What has been done to me has been done by everyone in this world I live in," Hector said. "I cannot blame one without blaming all."

"Ah . . . I see," the little well tender said, almost in relief. He gave a crooked grin. "And one cannot destroy the entire world in which one lives, eh?" He gave a short chuckle.

But Hector didn't share in either the sense of relief or the humor of what the little man offered. Instead, he stared down at him, the shotgun still in his hand.

"Don't sound so sure of yourself, little man," he said.

Inside the Perros Malos Cantina, Three-Hand Defoe stood with a cigar in his right hand, cigar smoke curling up the lapel of his swallow-tailed suit coat. His artificial right hand lay inside his coat pocket. His left hand lay wrapped around a shot glass atop the bar.

"Here comes your Mexican squirrel," Hopper

Truit said across the bar as she wiped a damp bar towel in a circle.

Defoe looked toward the open doorway as Hector walked inside and crossed the floor toward him, a look of determination in his dark eyes.

"Well, well, my boy, Hector," Defoe said with a superior grin. "I wasn't expecting you fellows back so soon."

"I am alone," Hector said in a clipped tone. He stood in front of Defoe, noting the cigar in his right hand, seeing him adjust the cigar in the fork of his fingers.

"Oh?" said Defoe. "Then where is Sonora Charlie and Clyde Jilson?"

"They are both dead," Hector said flatly.

Defoe looked stunned for a second.

"The lawman killed them both?" he said.

"No," Hector said, "I killed them both." He stared at Defoe as he rapped his knuckles on the bar for Hopper Pruitt to pour him a drink.

Along the bar, several drinkers stopped talking among themselves and turned their attention toward the two.

Defoe gave Hopper a nod; she set up a shot glass. Hector wrapped his fingers around the glass as she filled it with rye.

Defoe grinned. He watched Hector raise the glass to his lips and empty it. He chuckled under his breath and gave a glance at the faces lined along the bar.

"For a second there I almost took you serious, Hector," he said. "Where are they?"

Hector set the empty glass down hard on the

bar top, his shotgun in his right hand tipped slightly up.

"They are both in hell," he said. He raised his left boot and raked the butt of his shotgun across the rowel of Sonora Charlie's Mexican spur, spinning it.

"Whoa . . . ," the Frenchman whispered, realizing no one would be wearing those spurs if Sonora Charlie were alive. He reached his right hand out to lay his cigar in an ashtray atop the bar.

But Hector raised the tip of the shotgun barrel toward him, stopping him. Drinkers along the bar backed away, seeing a fight in the making.

"Keep all of your hands out where I can see them," Hector said to Defoe. "I have a question for you."

Defoe stopped, keeping his cigar in his fingers. "I can see that you have something stuck in your craw, Hector. What can I tell you?"

"You had Sonora Charlie give me three twenty-dollar gold pieces to help him kill the lawman from Nogales. How much did you give him and Clyde Jilson?"

"All right, I gave them a *little* more, Hector," Defoe admitted.

"You gave them *much* more," Hector corrected.

"That's true," Defoe admitted. "But they were more experienced. They're the best two—"

"They are *dead*. . . . I killed them," said Hector cutting him off.

"All right, I paid them more than you," said Defoe. He offered a tight smile; a bead of sweat glistened on his forehead. "But the fact is, a Mexican just does not need as much money as an—"

"Bad answer," said Hector, cutting him off. The shotgun bucked and exploded in his hand.

Defoe's body flew backward in a spray of blood. His fake arm flew up out from his coat pocket and spun like a pinwheel until he hit the floor. Half of his face and skull splattered on the far wall and stuck there.

No sooner had Hector pulled the trigger than Hopper Truitt made a move for a large pistol lying beneath the bar—but Hector swung the cooked shotgun around an inch from the tip of her nose.

Raising her hands chest high, she shouted, "Don't shoot, *Squirrel*—I mean, Hector—I mean Señor Pasada!" Her face turned ashen in fear. "I mean, *whatever* you want me to call you."

"Call me Pancho," Hector said. He stretched over the bar top, reached down and raised the big Colt from beneath it.

"I—I was scared, *Pancho*!" Hopper said. "I didn't know what I was doing. I swear it!"

"Don't worry, Hopper," said Hector. "I am not going to kill you." He stuck the Colt down into his belt. "If I killed you, I would be without a bartender."

One of the onlookers stepped forward and said warily, "Are you taking over the Bad Dogs Cantina?"

Hector turned facing the drinkers.

"That's right, I am taking the cantina for my own." He looked back and forth, his shotgun poised and ready. "Everything that belonged to Three-Hand Defoe now belongs to me—unless there is one among you who steps forward and kills me and takes it for himself." He looked all around searching for such a person who might try to defy him. "Is there such a man among you?"

The drinkers milled nervously in place. In a far corner, a quiet outlaw named Bud Lowry sat nursing a glass of rye whiskey, having watched everything that went on. But he only looked down at his rye and kept his mouth shut as the young Mexican's dark eyes passed over him.

Hector gave a hard smile to all the drinkers and waited for a moment while his challenge hung in the smoky air.

"No takers, eh?" he said at length. "In that case, I invite all of you to join me at the bar." He raised the shot glass from the bar top as if in a toast. "Drinks are *on the house.*"

The drinkers trampled toward the bar whooping and cheering loudly. From the side door, Glory Embers, Sidel Tereze and a plump young dove named Lynette squealed and laughed and pushed their way to the suddenly crowded bar.

But as they passed, Hector snatched Tereze by the forearm and pulled her to his side.

"You, come with me," Hector commanded. "Show me around my new property."

Tereze looked repulsed at first, but she caught herself quickly and presented a warm smile as she hooked her arm in Hector's.

"I was hoping you'd ask, Hector," she said. "Why don't I take you to Defoe's sleeping quarters?"

"Call me Pancho from now on," he said. He

waved a hand at Hopper Truit, who stood busily tending bar.

"Two bottles of tequila for us," Tereze called out when Hopper looked up from slinging mugs of beer along the bar. "It's about time you and I got to know each other, *Pancho*," she whispered close to his ear.

Chapter 18

The midmorning sun had climbed high in the east when the Ranger and Erin Donovan followed Big Chili Hedden's trail into the settlement alongside the Rio Verde. The hoofprints of Hedden's dark bay still showed clearly in the dirt from the night before.

As the pair rode onto the dusty street, they saw two mounted *rurales* riding their horses toward them at a walk, dragging Hedden's dead horse on ropes behind them. On the street behind the two *rurales*, the rest of the armed men stood watching, standing among their horses at the hitch rails.

Spotting Hedden's horse as the pair of horsemen dragged the animal past him, Sam raised a gloved hand.

"Hola," he called out in Spanish. "Where's the owner of that horse?"

"Hola yourself," said one of the armed *rurales*, neither of them stopping now that they had the dead animal's weight scooting along behind them.

"He is back there," said the other man, gesturing a

nod over his shoulder toward the hitch rails. "He is the one without a horse."

Sam stared ahead, seeing one of the men standing in an empty space at the rails, his hands on his hips. A saddle and bridle lay at his feet. He stared out at Sam. A wide dragline in the dirt reached from the hitch rail to the dead horse being pulled along the street.

"That's not Big Chili Hedden," Erin said quietly to Sam, staring ahead at the man by the hitch rails.

"No, but I'm betting this *is* his horse," Sam replied as the dead horse scraped along in a low stir of dust. He nudged his bay forward.

The two rode on and stopped at the hitch rails. As they approached, the armed men spread out a little. The horse's owner stood glaring at the Ranger.

"*Hola, señor,*" Sam said, bringing his horse to a halt. Erin stopped beside him. "Are you the horse's owner?"

"*Sí,* do you wish to *buy* him?" the man said with a sarcastic snap. Fire smoldered in his dark eyes.

Sam ignored the question. He returned the man's stare.

"Did you look him over good, *señor*?" Sam asked.

"I did not check his *fucking* pulse, if this is what you ask," the man snapped. "But, *sí,* I look him over. Why do you ask me this?" His intense stare turned more suspicious than malevolent.

"Watch your language," Sam said without hesitation. He gave a slight nod toward the woman beside him.

The Mexican looked Erin up and down, as if determining whether or not she was indeed a lady. Then he gave her a curt nod as a form of apology.

"I ask because I've got a notion it's not your horse," Sam said.

"No *shit*," the Mexican said, the contempt returning to his voice. "Do I look like some *yanqui* imbecile to you? Like a man who cannot see when a horse has been ridden to death?"

"*Ninguna ofensa*," Sam said respectfully. He touched the brim of his dusty sombrero. "But I'm not going to mention the language again," he said quietly, but in a tone that held a warning.

"Excuse me, *señorita, por favor*," the Mexican said to Erin. He drew a breath, settled himself a little and said to Sam, "No offense taken. I have had a hard night. . . ." His words trailed. "*Mi amigos* and I have a few drinks last night," he said to Sam. He gestured a hand toward the other men, who stood nodding in agreement.

"*Sí*, a few drinks . . . ," one of them confirmed.

"We come out and all of the horses are fine, except for *mine*!" The Mexican pounded himself on the chest. "Which is dead—"

He stopped himself short, realizing he was telling his misfortune to a stranger. "Who are you?"

"Territory Ranger Samuel Burrack, from Nogales. I'm trailing the Gun Killer who swapped horses with you."

"The lawman from Nogales . . . ," said the Mexican. "I have heard of you. I am Ernesto Merino." He gave another gesture toward the armed men. "I lead this *tropa*—this volunteer posse of local citizens. We also hunt the Gun Killers—we hunt all desperados who ride across our border to rob and kill and take what is ours." He looked around proudly for support from the other *rurales*.

"I understand," said Sam. He'd already started to back his black-point bay and turn the dusty animal. There was nothing for him to learn here about Arthur "Big Chili" Hedden. The fleeing gunman had ridden through during the night, stolen a horse and kept riding.

But the posse leader wasn't through talking.

"My country does not need more *Americanos* sticking their noses into our business." He raised his voice to make sure the other men heard him. "We will take care of our side of the border. You take care of yours."

"Sounds fair to me," Sam murmured to himself. He touched the brim of his dusty sombrero. "Adios," he said, he and Erin turning their horses onto the street.

"Wait! I did not mean for you to turn your back and leave!" the posse leader called out, seeing the Ranger wasn't going to sit still while he put on a show for his men. "I want this man who stole my horse. We will ride with you!"

"You don't have a horse," Sam called back over his shoulder, not wanting to waste time with this man or his posse.

"I have one coming," the leader called out. "As soon as it arrives, we will ride together," he called out as the Ranger and Erin moved away on the empty street. "Together we will stick this man's head on a pole, *you and me*! His blood will flow like water in the streets and gutters, eh, Ranger?"

"Follow my trail," the Ranger said under his breath. "You'll see all the blood you want."

When the two had ridden out of the small settlement town and on toward Caminos, Erin turned to the Ranger.

"Thank you for considering me," she said. "But you really didn't need to correct his language on my account."

Sam only nodded and offered no reply.

Erin said with a forced smile, "I mean, look at me, a woman living in the outlaw world . . . an outlaw's child growing inside me. You hardly need consider *my* values or defend my virtue."

Sam looked at her.

"*Virtue* needs no defending," he said. "What *values* I consider are my own."

"Then why did you say anything?" Erin asked.

"He was too upset for his own good," the Ranger said with a trace of a smile. "I saw he needed boundaries—I helped him set them."

They rode on in silence for a few moments as Erin thought about it.

"What about me?" she said finally. "Is that what you're doing with me—helping me set boundaries for myself?"

Sam looked at her.

"I'm hoping you do," he said. "But it's your business. You have to decide for yourself what to do, what not to do."

"I'm still free to go my own way?" she asked.

"Nothing's changed," Sam said. "You're still free to go." He paused, then added, "Just be careful of the wolves."

He nudged the bay forward, picking up its pace.

Erin stared ahead at him for a moment; then she touched her heels to her horse's sides and rode up beside him.

From the overstuffed chair sitting out in front of the adobe building in Caminos, Art Hedden squinted through the wavering heat and saw the Ranger and Erin appear out of the dust on the horizon. Noting the two were no longer riding double, he grinned to himself, his hand tightening around the stock of a repeating rifle in his lap.

"We've got the sumbitch this time," he said to Bo Sapp, who stood a few feet away in the shade of an alleyway alongside the public building.

Standing halfway up from the hot, dusty chair, Hedden levered a round up into the rifle chamber.

"Stay back out of sight," he said to Sapp, who had started to take a step forward.

"You want my help or not?" Sapp asked sharply. Not liking Hedden to begin with, Sapp especially resented taking orders from the big gunman.

"Your *help*?" Hedden chuffed. "So far I haven't seen any *help*. All I've seen you do is hang in the shade like some locked-out house cat."

"Keep it up, Big Chili," Sapp said, calling his nickname with contempt.

Hedden ignored the warning in Sapp's tone. He shook his head, spit and looked away toward the two riders drawing closer to town.

"I'm not needing any of your *help* from the looks of it," he said. "Just try to keep yourself out of my way."

He stepped over and kneeled down behind a water barrel sitting on the edge of the porch.

Sapp gritted his teeth, fighting the urge to raise his Colt and put a bullet in the back of Hedden's head.

"Watch how I pick this fool's eyes out," Hedden said. "Maybe you'll learn something." He laid the rifle down across the barrel top, watching the Ranger and Erin ride closer, a rise of dust billowing up behind them.

Sighting down along the rifle barrel, Hedden saw the two ride down out of sight on the roll of the land.

"There went your target," Sapp said, also watching the two riders from his spot at the corner of the building.

"Yep," Hedden said confidently, "and as soon as he rides back up into sight, he's not going to know what hit him."

Sapp stood staring out, his neck craned slightly.

Hedden relaxed for a moment, his finger still on the trigger of the cocked rifle. As soon as the Ranger and Erin rode back into sight, he would take his shot at a hundred and fifty yards. Not a hard shot at all for him, he reminded himself.

A few tense moments passed.

"All right, where is he?" Sapp finally asked. He drew his Colt up out of his holster as if he might need it real soon.

Damn! Hedden stared out, seeing neither Erin nor the Ranger reappear.

"Something ain't right!" he said to Sapp.

"You're telling me," Sapp said, stepping onto the street, edging closer to where their horses stood at a hitch rail. "Hell, he's no idiot. He knew some of us would be waiting to kill him!"

"Where do you think you're going?" Hedden asked, seeing Sapp unhitch his horse and start to swing up into his saddle.

"He's too bashful to ride in," said Sapp. "I expect I'd better go out there and get him."

"Wait up, I'm going with you!" Hedden said, sounding worried. He looked all around warily as he stood in a crouch and hurried over to his horse.

"It's been over fifteen minutes. No sound of hooves—*nothing*," he said, unhitching his horse with a nervous hand. "This ain't normal, I'm telling ya!"

"Jesus, Big Chili," said Sapp with the same contempt in his voice. "Don't wet yourself. He's out there. He's just scared, hiding, waiting until he sees us and knows where we are." He swung his horse toward the far end of town.

"Hey! You're going the wrong way," Hedden said even as he turned his horse beside Sapp.

"No, I'm not," Sapp called back over his shoulder, his Colt still in hand, cocked and ready. "I want to meet this sumbitch face-to-face on *my* terms, not his."

Chapter 19

While Big Chili Hedden and Bo Sapp had waited for the Ranger to ride into Caminos, Sam and Erin had ridden around the small empty town at an easy gait and taken cover beside a half-collapsed plank and adobe shack. Sam stood beside his horse watching the street in the direction of the two gunmen until he heard hooves thundering around a long turn in the street and come galloping into sight.

"Sam, be careful," Erin whispered sincerely as she saw him drop the dun's reins to the dirt and step out into the dusty street.

Be careful . . .

Sam looked at her, thinking it odd that she should say such a thing—these being two more of the men she and her brother had allied themselves with here in this badlands desert plane.

Yet, Sam touched the brim of his sombrero toward her.

"Obliged, ma'am. I will," he said, his Winchester hanging in his left hand, his big Colt in his right.

Less than fifty feet away in the empty street, facing him through a swirl of dust, the two gunmen gave each other a heated glance.

"On your terms, huh?" Hedden said to Sapp in anger and disgust.

"Shut up, Big Chili, damn it!" Sapp shouted. "He slipped around on us! I'm not a damn mind reader!"

The two jerked their horses quarterwise toward the Ranger, rifles coming up from across their laps, ready to charge.

Sam waited, watching, his feet spread shoulder-width apart.

"What the hell is it with you, Burrack?" Hedden called out. "You've got no damn business down here, butting your nose in! All you're doing is killing people! It ain't right! It ain't fair!"

The Ranger stood staring in silence.

Sapp turned to Hedden with a strange bemused look on his face.

"Jesus, Big Chili, are you through?" he said.

"Damn it, yes, I am," Hedden said, staring toward the Ranger in disgust.

"Good," said Sapp, "because I don't think he's wanting to discuss matters." He slid down the side of his horse and slapped its rump. "Let's shoot this sumbitch and get on down the trail."

But Hedden wasn't through talking. He stepped down from his horse and shoved it away. "Get ready," he whispered sidelong to Sapp. He took one slow step after another toward the Ranger, his rifle in both hands, ready to swing it up to his shoulder and start shooting.

"I want you to tell me, Burrack, who is it you think really gives a damn what goes on in this bowl of sand? The Mexican government? The American government?"

"People care," Sam said flatly.

"Ha! Don't make me laugh, Burrack. You two-bit lawman from Nogales!" He gripped the rifle tight. So did Sapp, a few yards to his right. "If people care, where the hell are they?" he shouted. "I don't see them, I don't hear them!"

Sam saw the move coming; he didn't wait.

"They're standing right in front of you, Big Chili," he said, raising the Colt, firing it on the upswing.

The Ranger's shot hit Hedden dead center, picked him up and slung him backward like a rag doll. Sam immediately swung the big Colt toward Bo Sapp, cocking it, pulling the trigger.

Bo Sapp had managed to get a shot off with his rifle while Sam's Colt took Hedden down. But the rifle shot went high left and off center, slicing a deep gash across Sam's left shoulder as Sam's second shot nailed his chest, dead center.

The deep bullet graze on Sam's shoulder nicked the bone and caused the Ranger's Winchester to fall from his hand. Blood flew.

"Sam!" Erin cried out. She ran into the street to him and stopped short two feet away, seeing his smoking Colt cocked and pointed toward the badly wounded Bo Sapp, who lay struggling to raise his rifle for another shot.

Blood ran down the Ranger's forearm and dripped from his hand holding the Winchester.

"Drop it," he called out to the downed outlaw.

"Or . . . what?" Sap said in a strained, grave voice. "You'll . . . shoot me?"

"Count on it," Sam said.

The outlaw hesitated; Erin saw the look of determination on the Ranger's face.

"For God's sake, Bo," she called out, "drop the rifle. It's all over!"

"What the hell . . . do you care, woman?" Sapp said to her as the Ranger stalked closer, one slow step at a time, the Colt still raised and ready.

Sam gave her a questioning glance.

"No, it's not him," Erin said, easing along beside him, seeing the downed outlaw's rifle barrel drop to the ground, then seeing the rifle fall from his grip.

"Not . . . me?" Sapp said, hearing Erin as the two stopped and looked down at him. "What do you mean . . . not me?"

Sam kicked the lowered rifle away from Sapp's bloody hand.

"It's nothing, Bo," Erin said quietly, seeing the gaping hole in his chest, knowing his life was spilling out of him with each beat of his heart.

Sapp gripped his bleeding chest and gave Erin a harsh look.

He rasped, "What would . . . Teto say if he . . . knew you were riding with this damn lawman . . ." His words trailed to a whisper and stopped.

"From Nogales," Erin said. Ending his words for him.

Teto . . . Sam repeated the dying outlaw's words to himself, but he wasn't going to mention the matter to Erin. If she wanted him to know, she'd have to tell him.

They stood in silence for a moment. Sam opened his smoking Colt, dropped the empty cartridges to the ground and replaced them with bullets from his belt.

"Two more down," he murmured under his breath. Shoving the Colt down into his holster, he turned to the dun. Erin moved along beside him.

Within moments, they had mounted their horses, directed them to the rocky trail and ridden away.

As far as Pancho Pasada was concerned, his old self, *Hector* Pasada, was dead—*and good riddance to his stupid pitiful soul*, he told himself. He kicked empty tequila bottles away from the edge of the bed with his bare feet.

He raised a tall bottle of tequila to his lips and drank deeply. Strange, he thought, that for the past three days he had drunk more tequila than ever before in his life, yet it barely fazed him.

Always before, it seemed that only a small amount of the fiery liquor reduced him to a thoughtless fool. He ran the back of his shirtsleeve across his wet lips and stood up from the dead Frenchman's dirty bed. Now the tequila, the mescal, the rye whiskey, even the ground cocaine powder that Sidel Tereze had shared with him, seemed to straighten out tangles inside his mind and leave his thoughts clear and deliberate for the first time in his life.

He looked around at Tereze lying naked and asleep on the Frenchman's bed—his bed now. His cantina, his bed, his woman . . . one of his women anyway. All of the doves belonged to him now. What money they made, they made for him. Everything was his—the *world* was his!

He smiled to himself, corked the bottle and set it down on a small table beside the bed, where, like the naked young dove herself, it would be waiting for him anytime he wanted it.

This is how a man lives, he told himself, *if he is a real man, and not some timid, stupid squirrel,* such as he had been. Yes, he had heard them call him a squirrel. But they would not call him that again. They knew better.

A picture of Ana and the boy came to his mind, but he quickly shut them out. Although, he had to admit, he wished she could see him now, what he had done for himself, how he now lived. But enough of that. He picked up the bottle, took another swig of the tequila and set it back down. That was all in the past, when he must truly have been as stupid as the Frenchman and the rest of the world had thought him to be.

Not anymore. . . .

It had been his for the taking all along. Had he only known that the secret to having everything he wanted was to care for nothing, not even his own life. All he had to do to arrive here was to kill three men who were not fit to live anyway. How he wished he had known this sooner, he told himself.

How simple life could be. He smiled again to himself and looked all around the Frenchman's living quarters behind the Perros Malos Cantina.

Want a cantina? Take it! And now it belongs to you. He looked again at the young, naked whore. Before, this

beautiful woman would not spit on him. Now she
would do for him whatever he told her to do, without
question—and she would do it free of charge. Not
only was her body free to him, he reminded himself;
she would *pay him* two-thirds of what she charged
other men to lie down with her.

Oh, and the gold! he reminded himself.

He raised five shiny new gold coins from his trouser pocket and turned them back and forth in his
hand, examining them. All of the gold and the American greenbacks he'd found buried in the ground
beneath the plank floor—three hundred, four hundred thousand dollars?

He smiled and closed his eyes toward the ceiling,
making a tight fist around the coins. No one knew
about the gold but him. In the cover of night, he had
moved it to another hiding place.

Yes, all the gold was his, too.

In the blink of an eye, his fortune had changed. He
looked at himself in a long dusty mirror leaning
against the far wall.

This was what the old *padres* at the missions
must've meant when they had talked to him about
heaven.

Chapter 20

———

Bud Lowry had ridden hard all night and half the next day before coming upon the Torres brothers and their Gun Killers Gang. He'd first spotted the band of riders from the edge of a cliff on a trail high above them. From there, he'd ridden his tired horse down and met them on a rocky trail leading up into a rugged hill line toward Wild Roses.

"Lucky for us all I found you heading this way," he said as soon as he'd turned his horse quarterwise to Teto and Luis Torres.

At the head of the riders, Teto and Luis stared hard at him.

"You'd better have a damn good reason for leaving Rosas Salvajes," said Teto. "Your job was to stay there and keep an eye on things."

"Three-Hand Defoe is dead," said Lowry. "Got his face shotgunned all over the wall." He paused, looked from one to the other and said, "Is that a *damn good enough* reason?"

Teto and Luis stared at him.

"Shotgunned?" Luis asked in disbelief.

"At the Perros Malos?" Teto asked.

"Yep, standing right there at the Bad Dogs on his favorite spot," said Lowry. "Half his big ole face is stuck there on the wall, 'less somebody has peeled it down by now." He gave a black-humored chuckle. "I've got to say, it looks strange as hell."

Neither Teto nor Luis returned his dark smile.

"Who shotgunned him?" Luis asked as the rest of the men crowed up closer to listen.

"The Mex who always hung around looking for work," said Lowry. "The one the whores all called a squirrel."

"*Hector* Pasada killed Three-Hand Defoe?" Luis asked in disbelief.

"Deader than hell," said Lowry. "His third hand didn't help him a bit. He could have had a dozen hands—that shotgun didn't care."

"*Hector Pasada . . . ?*" Teto said again, having a hard time accepting it. "The squirrel?"

"He's not a squirrel now," said Lowry. "He's not Hector either. He's got everybody calling him Pancho. Turns out this Mex is nobody to take lightly. He killed Sonora Charlie and Clyde Jilson too."

"Jesus," said Teto, "the squirrel killed Sonora Charlie and Clyde Jilson? You saw this?"

"Deader than hell," Lowry repeated. "No, I didn't see it. But I heard him tell Defoe he killed them. He's wearing Sonora's big Mexican spurs. That's proof enough for me."

"Yeah . . . ," said Teto, he and Luis both looking a little stunned by the news. "Sonora loved those spurs. I can hear them ringing yet."

"You'll be hearing them ring again in Wild Roses," said Lowry. "The squir—I mean, the Mex, *Pancho*," he corrected himself, "took over the cantina, everything else Defoe has there. Turns out he's a greedy, pushy little prick. Said anybody wants the Bad Dogs Cantina, they have to kill him to take it."

"Who the hell would want to take over the Perros Malos Cantina?" asked Truman Filo, he and Paco Sterns sitting atop their horses close to the Torres brothers.

Teto and Luis looked at each other.

"If he is bold enough to kill those three murdering *bastardos*," said Teto, "he is bold enough to take over the Perros Malos and do for us what Defoe has done."

"So, I did right coming out here looking for you?" said Lowry.

"*Sí*, you did right," said Teto.

"Now we deal with this *Pancho* the same way we dealt with Defoe," Luis declared.

"*Sí*," Teto said. "If our money is waiting as safely for us as it was with Defoe, I don't care who runs the Bad Dogs Cantina." He grinned and added to Luis, "So long as it is not *us*."

The men turned their horses back onto the trail and kicked the animals up into a gallop.

In the dusty alley on one side of the Perros Malos Cantina, the little well tender from Pueblo Fantasma had set up his tin bathing tub. He had strung a rope from the side of the cantina to the empty adobe next door, twenty feet away, and draped a blanket over it, providing privacy for his more modest bathers.

A crudely painted sandwich board stood in the dirt near the tub, reading on either side BAÑO, 25 CENTAVOS. A few feet away, the little well tender sat on a three-legged stool beside a small fire burning beneath a large kettle of water.

He stood up quickly as Hector walked up to him in the gray morning light, Sonora Charlie's big Mexican spurs ringing on his bootheels. A holstered Colt hung butt-forward from his left shoulder. He held his shotgun loosely in his left hand, a half bottle of tequila in his right.

"*Buenos días, mi jefe,*" the little well tender said, quickly adjusting the draped blanket on the rope.

"Good morning to you, little hombre," Hector replied. From the other side of the blanket, he heard the quiet splash of water on tin and a woman's voice humming softly in the grainy morning light.

"It is one of your women, *señor,*" the well tender said. "When she finishes with the men for the night, she comes here to my tub."

"Ah, it is *one of my* women," said Hector, liking the sound of it. He gave a short smile of satisfaction. "I have several women, little hombre." He pulled the blanket aside and looked down at the young dove, Lynette, sitting sprawled back in a bed of white sudsy water.

She sat upright and let out a little gasp of surprise as the blanket pulled away. But upon seeing it was Hector looking down at her, she relaxed back in the soapy water and managed a suggestive smile.

"Come on in, Pancho," she said, raising her open hands toward him. "This is perfume soap I've been saving since Omaha."

Hector looked down at her large rosy breasts bobbing atop the sudsy water.

"Another time, perhaps," he said. He looked at her a moment longer, then drew the curtain back in place.

"Is it good for you here?" he asked the little well tender.

"*Está bien . . . ?*" The well tender looked up at him.

"*Sí, está bien?* Is it good?" Hector asked, rubbing his thumb and fingertips together in the universal sign of greed.

"*Sí,* it is good here so far," said the little man, nodding, patting the lump of coins in his trouser pocket. "And it is a beautiful morning." He gestured a wary gaze toward the distant horizon and said, "But you know what the wise ones say. '*Cielo rojo por la mañana . . .*'" He left the words unfinished, gazing up at Hector.

"Red sky at morning," Hector translated. Then he completed the saying. "Shepherds take warning. . . ."

"*Sí, 'Los pastores toman la advertencia,'*" the well tender translated back to Spanish.

"But you must understand something, my little friend," Hector said, sounding irritated. "The saying means nothing to me. I am not a *shepherd.* I do not even *like* sheep."

"But you have become a *serious* man," said the well tender, "and when a serious man takes on his position in this world, he must decide how he will treat those around him. He can protect them as a shepherd, or devour them as a wolf."

"Stop it, well tender," said Hector. "I do neither. I took what I have from ruthless men . . . killers, thieves. But I do so only in order to live in peace, without hunger or need. I wish to *protect* no one—to *devour* no one."

"Then you should not have led me here," said the well tender. "You should have lived as a ghost in El Pueblo Fantasma."

"I did not *lead* you here, little hombre," said Hector. "You followed me to this place of your own free will."

"A shepherd, or a wolf," the little man said with resolve on the matter.

"Neither," said Hector. "As a man of position, I will *kill* in order to keep my position. But this is all I can say." He hesitated in troubled contemplation. "This is as far as I have thought things out. Who knows? Perhaps I will become both a *shepherd* and a *wolf*?"

The well tender only stared blankly at him.

Hector considered his own words and turned up his first tequila swig of the day. He lowered the bottle and wiped his hand across his lips.

"Yes, both a shepherd and a wolf. I will *protect*, but only the things that are mine—the people and things that matter to me. I will *devour* only those who seek to take all that I have acquired." He paused, then smiled to himself. "This is what a *serious* man must do," he decided. "So, this is what *I* must do." He thumped himself on the chest with the sloshing bottle of tequila.

"*Sí*, perhaps you will," the little well tender murmured. He shook his head slowly and gazed off toward the distant horizon.

Hector raised a hand as if to say more on the matter. But instead, stuck for words, he only wagged his finger at the well tender. Turning, he walked back around front of the cantina, where a passed-out vaquero lay facedown in the street. Each snore from the vaquero's gaping mouth raised another short puff of dust.

Having forgotten the young dove soaking in the tub, the well tender jerked the towel back when he heard a splash of water.

"Oops, it's only me," said the plump, naked young woman, standing, water and suds running down her. She cradled her large breasts in her forearms.

"May I have a towel please?" she asked.

The well tender looked her up and down and gave here a fierce stare.

"What did you hear?" he said.

"Nothing, really," said Lynette. "Just a lot of foolishness that I could make no sense of."

The well tender's fierce expression changed. He cackled under his breath.

"*Sí*, foolishness indeed," he said. "What else is there for men to talk about?" He tapped his finger against the side of his head.

Lynette smiled and shrugged a wet, naked shoulder; she didn't know.

"A towel, *por favor* . . . ?" she reminded him.

Inside the Perros Malos, Hector stood at Henri Three-Hand Defoe's favorite spot at the bar and looked all around the empty cantina like a young king appraising some new and exotic empire.

Without being summoned, Hopper Truit appeared almost magically across the bar. She set down a heavy white mug in front of him and filled it with steaming coffee.

"Cigar, Pancho?" she asked.

"*Sí*—a cigar, *por favor,*" Hector said, feeling awkward. He did not even realize it, but it was the first time in his life he stood at a bar and had someone voluntarily pour him coffee, and offer him a cigar to boot.

"Coming up," said Hopper. She walked briskly away along the back of the bar, came back with a cigar and a long wooden match.

"*Gracias,*" Hector said, taking the cigar, sticking it between his teeth.

Hopper struck the match and started to hold it out. But before doing so, she stopped and smiled, staring into Hector's eyes as if it were the first time she had ever seen him.

"You know, Pancho, Henri used to say that when it came to *special things,* I was always his favorite among the doves."

"Oh . . . ," Hector said, "I must remember that."

"Yes, please do," she whispered, leaning forward with the match, touching the flame to the tip of his cigar.

Not bad for a squirrel, eh? he thought.

He lit the cigar, tilted his head, blew a long stream of smoke and watched it climb and curl to the ceiling.

Not bad at all. . . .

Chapter 21

In the late afternoon, when shadows stretched long across the simmering land, Teto raised a hand and brought the men behind him and his brother, Luis, to a halt. Ahead of them at a distance of a thousand yards, firelights in the town of Wild Roses had started to flicker in the gloom of evening. Oil lamp and candlelight glittered in open windows.

"Let us keep in mind, *mi hermano*," Luis said, sidling his horse up beside Teto's, "the lawman from Nogales is still on our trail."

"Yes, he is," Teto replied with a flat, tight grin, "unless our Erin has slit his throat in his sleep."

Our Erin?

Luis brushed his brother's remark aside. "My point is, we must waste no time here. We must keep moving as soon as we pick up our money." He paused, then said, "Unless of course we agree it is time to stop and wait for this lawman and kill him as soon as he catches up with us."

Teto glanced back at the riders gathering up closer to him and Luis.

"I think it is time we do just that, my brother," said Teto, keeping his voice lowered just between the two of them. "We get the money, but we do not split it up until we have killed this damned lawman."

"These men already have money on them," said Luis. "They will start drinking as soon as we ride in."

"Yes, but nothing whets the thirst like a large sum of money."

"We have all waited this long to kill the lawman," said Luis. "What is another day, or even two?" He studied his brother's face for a sign of agreement.

"That's what I say," said Teto, staring straight ahead toward Wild Roses.

"And what about the woman?" Luis asked.

"What about her?" said Teto.

"Now that her brother is dead, what will we do with her?" Luis asked. "This life we live has no room for a woman."

"Erin belongs to me," Teto said. "She stays with me until I say otherwise."

"It's not good to keep her with us," Luis said. "This is not the kind of life that allows you to follow what your heart desires."

"My heart is not the part of me that *follows* her, *hermano*." He smiled, gripping himself down low. "Must I explain to you how these things work, Luis?"

Luis looked away; his jaw tightened. There were things he wanted to say, but he stopped himself. This was neither the time nor the place.

"The woman is trouble, is all I'm saying," he replied tightly.

"*Sí*, she is trouble," said Teto. He booted his horse forward toward Wild Roses. "But she is trouble so sweet I can taste her even now."

Luis stared sullenly at his brother pushing ahead. He let out a tense breath and booted his horse along behind him. The rest of the riders followed suit in the darkening evening light.

Beside the Perros Malos Cantina, the little well tender looked down at the gray, dirty water that had bathed over a dozen travelers throughout the course of the hot, dusty day. He raised the big kettle of hot water, tipped it against the side of the tin tub and poured it in. Steam bellowed.

He set the kettle on the ground and churned a long stick around in the water to break up a film of grease and soap. On the three-legged stool sat a burning oil lamp, its wick already trimmed down to a glow. The little man reached over and trimmed the wick even lower, knowing it more economically sound to lower the light than to change the bathwater this late in the evening.

"The sun goes down, little hombre," Hector said behind him.

The startled well tender turned in his surprise and saw Hector sweep a hand to the west, where a red-purple glow simmered above a cauldron of melting gold beneath the dark Mexican horizon.

"As you can see, nothing bad has befallen us on this beautiful day," Hector said.

"Todavía no," said the little well tender. He turned his nose to the south and sniffed through the arid scent of sage, sand and creosote. Somewhere in the mix, he smelled horse, sweat and fine-stirred dust.

"Not yet, you say?" Hector chuckled and sucked down a quick drink of tequila from the bottle in his hand. His shirttail hung out of his trousers on one side. "Your old wives' saying meant nothing," Hector said, a little tipsy from the tequila, a little jittery from the cocaine Tereze had all but pressed upon him before he'd left her once again, lying naked on his damp, tangled bedsheets.

"There are horses in the air," the well tender said warily, yet so quietly that Hector had not fully heard him.

"I thumb my nose at any such warnings from now on," Hector said.

"Riders coming," the well tender said. This time his voice was a little louder, his warning more clear.

"What did you say?" As he asked, Hector turned and looked out at a rise of gray-yellow dust adrift like some foreign matter on the shadowy hill line.

"Riders coming," the well tender repeated. He turned toward Hector, but all he saw was the young Mexican's back. Hector had spotted the riders himself. He'd also felt the first throb of hoofbeats in the ground beneath his feet. Without hesitation, he'd turned and raced away around the far edge of the cantina toward the side door leading to his living quarters.

The well tender scratched his head, looked all around. He walked over and turned out the oil lamp. He jerked the blanket shut in front of the tin tub, picked up his hand-painted sign and walked away into the grainy darkness.

Inside Hector's living quarters, Sidel Tereze rose naked on the bed and looked over to where the young Mexican rummaged through his saddlebags and a dirty carpetbag that had belonged to Three-Hand Defoe.

"Pancho . . . ? What are you doing?" she asked sleepily. Brownish ground cocaine residue lay above her upper lip. Her nostrils were red-rimmed, as were Hector's. More residue showed across her bosom, evidence that she'd encouraged Hector to snort cocaine from her breasts earlier.

"Riders are coming. I get a bad feeling from them," Hector said without looking around from his feverish task.

"A bad *feeling* about riders coming to the Bad Dogs?" said Tereze, sensing right away that the powder he'd used earlier still danced wildly in his brain. "You should get a *bad feeling* when there are *no riders coming*," she offered, hoping to settle him down. "Come, lie down here with me."

Hector just stared at her.

She patted the tangled sheet beside her with one hand and reached for the leather bag of cocaine powder on the small table beside the bed with her other.

"I know what you need," she purred.

But Hector would have none of it, although he did stop long enough to take a deep breath.

"No," he said, "I must keep my head clear, to do what I must do."

"Are you running away, Pancho?" Tereze asked,

almost with a giggle—the same giggle he had grown used to hearing from the doves before he'd taken over the cantina.

Hector turned to her with fire in his eyes, shotgun in hand.

"Does this look like *running* to you?" he said to her, breaking the shotgun open.

He shoved two fresh loads into the barrels and snapped the gun shut. Without waiting for her reply, he tossed a bandoleer of shotgun ammunition onto his shoulder, then jerked his Colt from his holster, checked it and holstered it loosely.

Tereze sighed and relaxed back onto the damp sheets.

"It's probably just the Torres brothers and their gang," she said idly. "There's nothing to worry about. It's no big secret that Henri keeps their money hidden until things cool off after a robbing spree."

"*Worried*?" said Hector. "I am not *worried*. Perhaps it is the Torres brothers and their gang. I must still be prepared to protect what is mine." He turned and stomped out through the door of the cantina, the din of music and laughter rising and falling as he opened and closed the door behind himself.

Jesus. . . . Tereze shook her head. *The same squirrel after all.*

As darkness overtook the land, the Torres brothers and their Gun Killers rode on toward Wild Roses at an easy gallop. When they entered the town, Teto veered away from the others. He rode past the Perros Malos Cantina and turned at the far corner. Luis and

the others hitched their horses at the rails out in front
of the cantina and filed inside. As they entered, the
music stopped. Drinkers looked around, recognized
the dust-streaked faces and hurriedly began to empty
their glasses and mugs of beer, rye whiskey, tequila
and mescal.

By the time Luis Torres and the gunmen crossed
the floor, a wide empty space had been made for them
at the bar. Some drinkers only shied back away from
the Gun Killers; others left the cantina altogether,
grabbed their horses or donkeys and rode away.

As the sound of hooves fled away into the night,
Hopper Truit stepped up and stood across the bar
from the gunmen. She spread her hands along the
bar edge, giving them a good view of her cleavage
behind a low-cut gingham blouse.

"Evening, Luis . . . gentlemen," she said, nodding
in turn at the hard faces staring back at her. "I hope
you came thirsty enough to raise this joint and set it
down sideways," she said with a crooked smile.

Truman Filo let out a whoop and said, "You damn
well right we did—"

But Luis cut the excited gunman short with a
raised hand. The rest of the men fell quiet along the
bar. The remaining drinkers stood staring intently.

"I understand the Bad Dogs Cantina has changed
hands," Luis said. "We want to meet the new owner
before any serious drinking gets under way."

Before Hopper Truit could reply, Hector stepped
inside the front door, his shotgun cocked and leveled
in one hand, his Colt leveled in his other.

"*I* am the new owner," he said, stepping forward

across the floor. Some of the remaining customers now slipped out the side doors and the open rear window.

"Easy, amigo," Luis Torres said. "We came to drink and talk a little business with Three-Hand Defoe, nothing more."

"Three-Hand Defoe is there," Hector said, gesturing toward the drying, blackened residue of what was once Defoe's face still stuck to the wall. "Start talking."

The gunmen turned their heads as one and looked at the grizzly glob of flesh and bone fragments stuck to the wall. A single gold-capped tooth hung from the center of it, above part of Defoe's lolling tongue. Flies circled and whined.

The gunmen gave a dark chuckle, examining the remains.

"We heard you killed him," Luis said.

Truman Filo commented, "This looks like a vulture came flying through too low and too fast."

Ignoring Filo's remark, Luis turned from the disgusting death mask.

"*Sí*, I killed him," said Hector, not mincing words, "and I now own what was his. I will kill any man who tries to take it from me."

"I'm not interested in what was his, or what you think is yours. We only want what's ours," Luis said. He looked Hector up and down. "You thought we might show up seeking vengeance."

"The thought crossed my mind," Hector said flatly. Cocaine powder still bubbled and boiled in the back of his brain, but he kept himself calm, in check, ready to kill to protect his ill-gotten desert empire.

"Aren't you the one the whores call the squirrel?" Filo asked.

"Hey! We called him that with the utmost respect and affection," Hopper Truit cut in, Hector turning a scorching glared at her.

"That day is over," Hector said. "This day has begun." He gestured at the shotgun and Colt in his hands.

"No more *squirrel*, eh?" said Filo with a wide, taunting grin.

"Only if you wish me to hang your portrait beside Three-Hand Defoe's," Hector replied calmly.

Filo just stared at him.

"Easy, everybody," Luis said. To Hector he said, "The Bad Dogs is your place now. We call you whatever you want to be called, eh?"

"Call me Pancho," said Hector, his guns lowered slightly.

"Pancho it is," said Luis. He looked at Hopper Truit with a smile and said, "Pour all of us drinks now that we have met our new friend."

Hector let his guns lower a little more, but upon hearing the sound of boots enter the cantina door behind him, he swung around and aimed both guns at the man who entered—Teto Torres.

"It is not there!" Teto exclaimed to Luis, staring at Hector with a smoldering glare on his face. Behind Teto stood Sidel Tereze, wearing nothing but a wrinkled gray bedsheet.

The money!

Hector understood instantly. While Luis and these men had kept him talking, Teto had gone around and searched his living quarters.

Hector started to swing back around toward Luis Torres and the other gunmen, but before he could do so, Luis stepped forward and slammed his rifle butt into the back of his head.

The gunmen gathered around Hector as his consciousness spiraled downward and away.

As he went down, Luis kicked both of Hector's guns across the floor.

Filo raised his Colt, cocked it and said, "Want me to put a couple of hot ones in his head?"

"Back away, Filo," said Luis. "Your stupidity is starting to get on my nerves." He looked across the cantina as Sidel Tereze walked forward, her breasts cradled in her arms behind the bedsheet.

"What about it, Tereze?" he said. "Did you see him take the money?"

"I saw nothing," Tereze said, looking down at Hector. "I didn't even know the money was there until Teto came in and pulled up the floor planks."

"All right," Luis said to the men, "tie him to a chair. This squirrel wakes up, I don't want him getting away."

Chapter 22

The Ranger knew when Erin Donovan had once again left in the middle of the night. Like the time before, he'd lain quietly in his blanket and listened as she'd saddled her horse and led the animal away. When he was certain she was gone, he stood up, picked up his saddle and blanket and walked over to his dun. Seeing him step in closer, the coppery dun chuffed under its breath and sawed its head up and down.

"I know," said the Ranger, as if defending the woman's actions to the watching horse. "She's just scared—unsure of herself."

He rubbed the dun's muzzle and looked off in the direction Erin had taken down along the hill trail.

Rosas Salvajes . . ., he said to himself. *She's headed right back to where we started in Wild Roses.*

He couldn't say he was completely surprised, but it would have been good to see her do what she'd told him she was going to do—take a ship out of Tampico, go home to Ireland, put the Mexican badlands behind her.

Careful of the wolves . . .

He recalled his words to her when she'd first mentioned leaving. Maybe that was the only advice he had a right to give her, or anyone else here in this wild, merciless land.

But so much for that. . . . She was an outlaw's woman. What had he expected her to do?

Anyway, he reminded himself, his work was cut out for him in Rosas Salvajes.

He took the lead rope from the dun's muzzle and slipped the bridle up into place. Letting the reins hang free, he pitched the saddle up onto the dun's back and cinched it for the trail.

He hadn't pressured the woman into any particular direction; he had made up his mind early on not to butt into her personal business—not even to question her story any more than necessary for his own safety's sake. Where she was now headed, she was headed of her own free will.

To the father of her unborn child?

Yes, he believed so, he told himself. And from everything he'd heard and seen and discerned of her and her situation, that man was Teto Torres.

He let out a deep breath as he finished cinching the saddle and laid the stirrup down the dun's side.

He could make no sense of a beautiful young woman like Erin Donovan taking up with the likes of an outlaw like Teto Torres.

But who am I to say? he asked himself, picking

up his Winchester from where he'd left it leaning against a tree. Would life treat her any better had she chosen to spend it with a lawman, a man like himself?

Would the trail have been less rocky, the sun less scorching, the narrow line between life and death any less precarious had she taken up with a man like himself? How thin was the line separating an outlaw from the badlands and a lawman from Nogales?

Stop it.

He checked the rifle and shoved it down into his saddle boot—a little harder than usual, he noted. He didn't know why, but it bothered him somehow, her being gone. Even though there had been no suggestion of anything between them, it had felt good being near her. Her presence made him feel more like a *man* and less like a *lawman.*

Was that a good thing? he asked himself. *Here in this time, this place?*

He led the dun closer to the glowing ember remnants of the fire. Dropping the horse's reins, he walked over and rubbed the fire out with his boot. He stood staring out across the night sky in a silence as lonely as death until the dun ventured forward almost shyly in the darkness and stuck its nose to the side of his neck.

"I'm all right," he said, turning, adjusting his big Colt in its holster. He rubbed the horse's long jawline and patted the side of its head. He took up the reins from the dirt, swung up into the saddle and turned the dun toward the trail.

Erin kept her horse at a safe pace until she reached a wide, flat plateau stretching three hundred yards across the hillside.

"Please, Blessed Mother, no more wolves," she whispered to the dark sky, collecting the horse beneath her.

In the pale moonlight, she batted her heels to the horse's sides and brought the animal up into a gallop. With the night wind whipping her hair and clothing, she kept the quickened pace until she reached the other side and started down the trail leading into a steep, narrow canyon.

She brought the horse to an abrupt halt and sat for a moment staring into the mouth of the canyon. Raising the big Starr from her lap, she looked at it for a moment, knowing it wasn't loaded. Hefting the gun by its barrel, she weighed its value as a club.

It would have to do, she told herself. She lowered the gun back onto her lap, still grasping the barrel, and nudged the horse forward. She searched the darkness for the faintest sound of man or beast on the rock walls flanking her on either side.

She rode three miles deep into the canyon, hearing nothing but the slow, steady rise and fall of her horse's hooves.

From sixty feet above, on the edge of a rocky overhang, three of the Gun Killers lay in wait.

One of them, a gunman named Wade Carrico, sat up from against a rock and listened closely for a moment to make sure his ears weren't misleading him. When he heard the sound again, growing closer, he raised his rifle from across his lap.

"*Pssst*, wake up, Jete. Wake up, Nells," he whispered to two dozing gunmen lying a few feet from him, their hats tipped down over their eyes.

"What the hell?" said Brolin, coming awake startled.

"I hear a rider down there," said Carrico.

Jete Longley sat up too, tipping his hat up into place on his forehead.

"I hear it too," he whispered. "Sounds like only one horse, though."

"I don't hear nothing," said Brolin, rubbing his face.

"That's because you're half-asleep," Longley said critically. "Wake the hell up and pay attention."

"I'm awake, damn it, Jete," Brolin growled. "This ain't my first time ever covering our back trail."

"Then act like it," Wade Carrico snapped at him, still in a whisper.

The three rose into a crouch, rifles in hand, and slipped away to where they had left their horses hitched to a scrub juniper farther back away from the ledge.

"One horse means something," Carrico warned as they unhitched their horses.

"Yeah," Longley said with a chuckle, "it means one of them might have killed the other."

Carrico continued, saying, "It means we best keep on our toes, make sure we don't kill the woman by mistake. She's still one of us, don't forget."

"According to Hedden, she might very well be thrown in with the lawman," said Brolin.

"We're not the ones deciding that," Carrico reminded them both. "Teto said don't hurt her till we all see where she stands. We're playing this thing his way."

"Suits me," said Longley.

"Me too," said Brolin, grudgingly. The three mounted their horses and moved away toward a thin game trail leading down the steep canyon wall.

When they reached the narrow trail below, they spread out and took cover behind rocks, hearing the horse's hooves draw closer and closer.

"I'm moving in," Carrico whispered. "Get ready to fire when I call out to you." He slipped away from the other two and waited behind a tall boulder at a turn in the trail.

"What the hell is this?" said Brolin as he and Longley watched Carrico step out onto the trail in the moonlight as the horse clopped around the turn, its saddle empty.

"Stray horse," said Longley, already standing, his rifle lowering at his side.

In the middle of the moonlit trail, Carrico saw the empty saddle just as he raised his rifle to his shoulder. He'd started to issue a warning, but he stopped himself.

"Damn it," he said, feeling a little foolish. He took the horse by its bridle and halted it in the trail. "It looks like somebody got left afoot tonight," he called over to the other two gunmen.

Brolin and Longley both walked toward him.

"Hold up," Carrico said. "This could be the lawman's trick."

"Lucky for all three of you, it's not," Erin said, step-ping into sight from the other side of the boulder where Carrico had stood in hiding. "He would have killed the lot of you."

"Damn it, Erin," said Carrico. "We were being careful not to hurt you—here you come sneaking up on us."

"I heard your horses from farther up the trail," Erin said, grateful to have run into the three familiar faces. She lowered the big Starr she'd held out at arm's length until she'd recognized the three.

"You were going to start shooting at us?" Carrico asked.

Erin started to tell them the big Starr was empty, but she thought better of it.

"We'll never know, will we?" she said with a smile. She lowered the useless revolver and shoved it down into her trousers. "Let's get on to Wild Roses. I'm worn out from riding these hills."

"Can't do it," said Carrico. "Teto and Luis has us waiting here to kill the lawman as soon as he shows his face."

"We've got a dead-sure spot for an ambush up there," Brolin said. "We heard your horse from a long ways back."

"Yes, I see," said Erin. She gazed up along the ledge sixty feet above them. The gunman was right, she thought. This was the perfect place to kill Sam Burrack. As she thought about it, she saw his face, his smile—warm, easygoing, a little sad at times, she thought. She pictured herself the night the wolves had dragged her out from under the rocks like some varmint, for their dinner. And there was Sam, just in time. . . .

"Well, you can save yourselves the wait. He's not coming," she said. "At least no time soon."

"What do you mean?" asked Carrico. "Did you kill him in his sleep?"

"I would have," she lied, "but he was too smart to let himself get caught off guard. So I did the next best thing. I stole his horse—left him afoot."

"Afoot in country like this? Stealing his horse might be worse than cutting his throat," said Brolin with a grin.

"That's what I decided," said Erin, returning his smile.

Carrico looked all around, then said, "If you stole his horse, where is it?"

"I killed it and ate it," Erin said flatly.

"The whole horse?" Jete Langley said, his eyes widening.

"Just its lips, Jete," Erin said with the same flat tone.

"Jesus, just its *lips*?" Jete said.

Carrico and Brolin shook their heads and chuckled under their breath.

"*Damn it* to hell!" Jete said, embarrassed.

"I turned it loose along a high trail," Erin said. "There's wolves prowling everywhere. I thought the horse might draw them away from me. I was right. By now it's dead and picked clean."

Carrico looked at Brolin, then at Jete, who still stood shaking his lowered head.

"Like as not, so is the lawman," said Brolin, satisfied with her story.

"Then what are we waiting for?" Carrico said, also satisfied. "Let's ride."

At daylight, Hopper Truit walked in through the front doors of the Perros Malos Cantina and looked back at Teto and the Gun Killers, who stood gathered in a tight circle. At their feet, Hector Pasada lay covered with his own blood, tied to a wooden chair that had fallen over onto its side.

"Fellows, you've got company coming," Hopper called out.

Teto gave her a nod of acknowledgment. Then he stooped down and wiped the back of his bloody hand across Hector's torn and bloodstained shirt.

"Listen to me, Pancho," he said, moving in close to Hector's purple, battered face. "You have been a tough little *pinchazo*. But now the *easy* part is over for you. Now I turn you over to Filo, to carve on as he sees fit." He motioned for Filo to step in closer. The wild-eyed gunman did so, first drawing a long knife from his boot well.

"Not yet, Filo," Teto said quietly, raising a hand to hold the eager gunman at bay. He reached down, grabbed Hector by his hair and jerked his head around so he could appraise his cut and battered condition.

The thing he did not want was for the tough little Mexican to die just yet, not until he revealed where he'd hidden the money. So far, Hector hadn't admitted to knowing anything about the money, let alone hiding it.

But Teto was certain he was lying. And if he wasn't lying, it didn't matter. Once they finished with Hector and nailed his body to the front of the cantina, whoever had the money or knew anything about it would give it up when it came their turn for questioning.

"Start with his fingers!" Teto said to Filo, loud enough for Hector to hear him. He shook Hector by his hair, but Hector gave no response.

"He'll wake up once I commence cutting," Filo said, ready to get to work with his knife.

Teto dropped Hector's head in disgust.

"No, let him wake up first," he said. "Carry him back to the room. Give him some water. Let him have time to think about what awaits him."

"*Then* start cutting and hacking?" Filo asked hopefully.

"Yes, then start cutting," he said, "but be careful he does not die on us. For now, this *ardilla* is valuable."

"You're the *jefe*," said Filo, the knife hanging in his hand.

Teto stood up and walked to the front door, most of the men following him.

"All right, *Squirrel*," Filo said, reaching down and pulling the knocked-out Mexican's chair upright. "You heard him, no fingers lopped off until you're awake enough to know I'm doing it." He roughed the hair atop Hector's limp head. "Not everybody would be that nice, would they?"

A young Gun Killer named Ludlow Blake who, along with Teto, had done most of the beating, looked closely at Hector's cut and swollen face, assessing his brutal handiwork.

"Crazy sumbitch," he commented to Filo. "I like money as much as the next man, but damn! I'd given it up before I'd take a beating like this, wouldn't you?"

"I don't know, Lud," said Filo, "but why don't you shut up and help me move him? We can talk about it later."

Chapter 23

Out in front of the cantina, Teto and a group of Gun Killers stood watching as Erin and the three gunmen rode in a gallop, their dust trailing high in their wake. To the east, the sun had begun its climb upward into the breaking morning sky.

Teto smiled to himself. From around the edge of the cantina, Luis walked up and stood beside his brother.

"So, she comes back to us now," Luis said, the two of them staring out at the riders entering the town.

"She comes to *me*, my brother," Teto said, watching Erin bobbing easily atop the dingy gray. "Once a woman has been with me, she cannot help herself. She has no choice but to return for more, eh?" He nudged his brother with his elbow.

Luis backed away in silence.

"Look at you, my darling!" Teto called out as Erin slid the gray to a halt, slipped down from the saddle and ran to him from the hitch rail. They spun in an embrace. Luis looked away; the other gunmen catcalled and whistled as the couple's lips met in a fiery kiss.

Ending the kiss, Teto held her away from him at arm's length.

"Let me look at you, my bold and naughty Irish princess," he said. "What did you do to get the law-man to set your free? Or do *I dare* ask such a question?"

"No, Teto," Erin said teasingly, "perhaps you should not."

"Uh-oh, now I know I must kill him!" Teto said, feigning rage. "Unless you tell me he is already dead?"

"No," said Erin, "I can't say for certain that he's dead. But it's a good bet that he is by now."

"Oh . . . ?" Teto studied her eyes with a question-ing expression.

"She stole his horse, left him afoot in wolf country, Teto," Wade Carrico cut in with a dark laugh. He stepped down from his horse, the other two gunmen doing the same beside him.

"Did you hear any shooting?" Teto asked.

"No, but that doesn't mean much," said Brolin. "These Mexican *lobos* are known to jump a man so fast he can't even get a shot off."

"Don't tell me what a pack of *lobos* can and cannot do, Brolin," Teto said, glaring at the gunman. "I was born in wolf country. Were you?"

"Sorry, Teto," Brolin said meekly.

Teto continued to stare at the gunman with fire in his eyes.

To change the subject, Carrico quickly cut in, saying to Teto, "She damned near threw down on us with the big Starr when we surprised her on the trail."

After a tense silence, Teto turned his glare from Bro-lin and said to Erin, "You are a bad girl." He grinned, reached out and pulled the big Starr from her belt. He checked the gun, saw that it was unloaded but didn't question it.

"*Smart* too?" Erin asked, seeing that he understood why she'd done such a thing.

"Yes, smart too," Teto added, giving her a knowing look. He handed her the Starr.

She shoved it back down in her waist and gazed at Luis as he stepped forward. "Hello, Luis," she said. "Were you not going to welcome me back?"

"Of course, welcome back," Luis said in a restrained tone. He said to Teto, "So, what about the lawman now? Do we call him finished business, or do we send somebody else out to kill him?"

Teto seemed to consider it for a moment as he stared into Erin's eyes.

"Forget the lawman," Erin whispered up close. "We're back together now. That's all that matters."

"Yes, to hell with him," Teto said with a shrug. "If he is traveling afoot in wolf country, he is either dead or getting prepared to be."

"That's how I figured," said Carrico. "That's why we came on in with Erin. We figured you'd want her escorted, that time of night."

"You did well, Wade," Teto said to Carrico. He put his arm around Erin's waist and turned her toward the cantina. "Come, have breakfast. Tell me all about this lawman from Nogales."

As they walked toward the open cantina doors, Truman Filo and Ludlow Blake stepped out, holding Hector in the wooden chair between them.

"Merciful Father!" said Erin. "Who is this? What

happened to him?" She stepped aside as the two gunmen walked past her.

"That's Pancho Pasada," Teto said. "He used to be Hector Pasada, the one all of Henri's whores called Squirrel, remember?"

As he spoke, the two men carrying the beaten Mexican stopped to give her a look. Hector's head lolled, his eyes swollen almost shut, his lips hanging open, smashed and swollen twice their size. He tried to look up at her. A terrible sound gurgled in his throat.

"Hector, the squirrel?" said Erin. "Yes, I remember him. What has he done?"

"He killed Sonora Charlie, Clyde Jilson and Three-Hand Defoe," said Teto.

"All by himself?" Erin asked.

"Yes, with the help of his shotgun," said Teto.

Erin noted Teto's red, swollen knuckles.

"But why are you beating him, Teto?" she said. "I didn't know you were so close with Defoe or Sonora Charlie."

"I don't care that he killed them," said Teto. "But he stole all the money we left with Defoe for safekeeping."

"*All* of the money?" Erin said. "My brother Bram's share too?"

"Yes, everybody's share," said Teto. "So far, he is a tough monkey. He tells us nothing. But don't worry. When Filo is through cutting his fingers off, he'll give up the money."

Erin looked down at Hector's swollen face as he struggled to say something.

"Take him away," Teto told the two men.

Erin stood staring until they had rounded the

corner of the adobe cantina and headed back toward the living quarters.

"It's crazy beating him this way. What if he dies first?" she said. "Then we lose everything."

"Oh? What do you say we do," said Teto, "cook him a nice dinner? Serve him *café*, *puros*?"

"No, not dinner, or coffee and cigars," Erin said in an even tone. "But give me a pan of water and a wash-cloth and let me spend some time with him. I'll get him to give up the money."

"Oh . . . ?" Teto looked her up and down. He leaned in close and whispered, "Will you do all this with or without your clothes on?"

Erin returned his whisper. "What difference does it make," she said, "so long as we get our money?"

Teto laughed and shook his head.

"No, I want to let them cut on him some," he said.

"But we could lose all that money, Teto," Erin insisted. "At least let me try first. If I fail, you can always sic Filo on him."

"I am a jealous man," said Teto. "I want you all to myself." He guided her through the cantina door.

"Let her try, Teto," Luis said, walking in step behind them. "You know she's right."

Teto stopped and let out a long breath.

"All right, if it means that much to both of you," he said.

"I'll go make sure Filo and Blake behave themselves until you get there," Luis said to Erin.

But it was Teto who answered, saying, "Yes, you do that, my brother. She will be right along."

Luis turned and walked out.

"I warn you now, Erin, if you don't make him come around pretty quick, I will send in Filo and Blake to take up where we left off."

"Yes," said Erin, "but that won't be necessary." She walked across the floor and said to Hopper, who stood behind the bar, "I need a pan of clean water and a soft washcloth."

"No pan," said Hopper. "How about a bucket of water and a clean bar towel?"

"That will do nicely," said Erin.

A moment later, as she turned back toward the door, the bucket and towel in hand, Teto drew her to the side so he could speak low, just between the two of them.

"Make sure you understand," he said, "there's close to a hundred thousand dollars at stake here. If you get him to tell you where it's hidden, you bring the information straight to me, nobody else." He thumbed himself on the chest. "I'm the only one who handles the money. I'm the one who splits it up, *comprende*?"

Erin gave him a dismissing smile.

"It's not *if* I get him to tell me, Teto," she said close to his ear, "it's *when*."

Teto smiled. "I like your confidence. If you get him to talk, you will get a bigger cut, say . . . one thousand dollars?"

"*Sí, gracias*," Erin said with the same smile, turning and walking out the door.

Hector sat slumped, tied to the wooden chair in the middle of the floor of Three-Hand Defoe's living quarters. His head lolled to one side. Fresh blood

seeped from the corner of his swollen lips and trickled down his throat. Yet, in spite of his condition, he
had regained his senses enough to vaguely understand what was happening around him.

Having enough faculty to realize that being awake
right then was not in his best interest, he feigned
unconsciousness and observed his surroundings
through the purple swollen slits of eyelids. When he
saw Luis Torres step into the room through the side
door, he listened closely.

"The two of you can go," Hector heard Luis say to
the two gunmen who lounged against the wall. Truman Filo was tapping his knife blade against his
trouser leg.

"Go?" said Filo, straightening upright, appearing
disappointed at Luis' words. "What about carving
the squirrel?"

"Will you understand me better if my boot is in
your teeth?" Luis growled.

Filo shrank away. "We're gone, Luis," he said quickly,
the knife going out of sight. "Let's go, Lud," he said to
Blake.

The two gunmen turned without another word
and left the room. Seeing them leave helped Hector
feel a little better—not much, but a little. Behind his
back, his fingertips felt all around on the ropes tying
his wrists to the chair.

As his fingers searched for a way to free himself,
Hector watched the woman walk into the room and
stop and look at Luis, bucket of water and bar towel
in her hands.

"*Finally*, we can talk," Luis said to Erin, stepping

over close to her. He tried to embrace her, but she artfully maneuvered away from him and walked over toward Hector.

"Yes, we can talk," she said in a cautious, lowered voice, "but don't do something foolish. All it will take is someone walking in and seeing us in each other's arms."

"I—I almost wouldn't care if they did," Luis said, following behind her but stopping short of putting his hands on her shoulders.

"*I* care," Erin said over her shoulder, "and so should you, for all of our sakes."

"I have been going crazy out of my mind over you," Luis said. He hesitated, then asked, "Are you certain about the baby?"

"Oh yes," said Erin, setting the bucket down beside Hector's chair. She dipped the towel in the clean water and wrung it loosely. "I'm more certain every day."

"Then we must tell him," Luis said.

"Why, Luis?" Erin asked. "So the child will grow up with neither a mother nor a father? You know he will kill us both if he finds out. Isn't that what you were telling me all the while when we made love? That we must keep this a secret, that Teto will kill us both if he ever finds out?" She gave a faint smile, not facing him.

"It was different then," Luis said behind her, noting the vindictiveness in her voice. "I admit that I was only quenching my passion for you."

"Oh, your *lust*?" Erin said coolly over her shoulder. She laid the wet towel on Hector's battered forehead, gently letting it cover his purple eyes.

"All right, *yes*, my lust, if that is what you insist on

calling it," Luis said. "But now I am feeling much more than lust. You carry my child inside you."

He ventured his hands up onto her shoulders, but Erin shrugged them away and continued attending to Hector's battered face.

"It may interest you to know that your child was nearly torn from my belly and feasted upon by wolf cubs," she said with a sharpness in her voice, reminding him that whatever befell her befell the baby—*his* baby.

"Didn't you notice I'm limping a little?" she continued. "I have wolf bites on my ankle and my forearms. Shall I roll up my shirtsleeves, show them to you—?"

"Stop it, *por favor*!" said Luis. "You say these things only to make me crazy! All right, you have succeeded! I have lost my mind over you. What must I do? What must *we* do?"

"*We . . . ?*" Erin said quietly. "I'm glad to hear you're including me in *our* plans, whatever they may be."

"Of course I include you," Luis said, as if in submission.

She fell silent for a moment, attending to Hector, removing the towel, soaking and wringing it. She laid it across the bridge of Hector's nose and his cut and swollen cheeks.

Finally she said, "All right, we'll tell Teto everything." She paused, then said, "But I decide when and where we tell him . . . not a word from you before."

"Yes, *yes*, I understand," Luis said, eagerly agreeing with her. "Only when you are ready, not before." He again ventured his hands up onto her shoulders. This time she allowed it.

"I want this child of ours to have everything I have not had in my life," she said, her voice softer now as she dabbed a corner of the towel at dried blood on Hector's face. "Do you agree?"

"Yes, I agree," said Luis. "If it is a boy, I will see to it he grows up atop the finest horses and sits on the finest of saddles—"

"And if it is a girl child?" Erin asked him pointedly. "Will she still be welcome?"

"Oh . . . a girl child?" Luis said, seemingly taken aback by the possibility. "Well, even if it is a girl child," he said, "so what? She will still be welcome."

Erin smiled again to herself.

"Let me ask you one more thing, Luis," she said. "Does a thousand dollars really sound like a fair amount for my poor brother Bram's cut of the money?"

Hector relaxed a little in the chair, listening, hearing every word, feeling the coolness of the water on his throbbing, aching face.

PART 4

Chapter 24

At daylight, the Ranger had followed the hoofprints left by Erin's horse closely until they led into the narrow, walled canyon. There, he lifted the Winchester from across his lap and waited, listening warily, scanning rock and cliff for any glint of gunmetal, any sign of riflemen.

Nothing. . . .

He stepped the dun forward cautiously into the walled canyon until he realized that had anyone been lying in wait above him, they should have made their play by now.

So far so good. . . .

He stopped the dun again when he saw the tracks end around a turn in the trail in a cluster of boot prints. There, he noted that three other sets of horses' hooves joined with Erin's. He looked up along the ridge sixty feet above him for a moment, then back down and out past where the canyon walls stopped, as if sliced from the hillside by the sword of God.

Last chance for an ambush. . . .

His eyes followed the prints out of the canyon along the winding trail toward Rosas Salvajes.

Had some of the Gun Killers waited here to spring a trap on him? Yes, he was certain they had. They would have been fools not to, he told himself. Had Erin turned them away, led them away?

Charmed them away . . . He smiled to himself.

But if so, why? he wondered, nudging the dun forward. Was it because of the wolves? Did she figure she owed him something for saving her life—hers and her baby's? He liked to think that might be her reason. But he'd been around her enough to know that something as simple as genuine gratitude could have been the furthest thing from her mind. What he was certain he did not want to do was start thinking that he understood her.

Huh-uh, not this woman, he decided. Still, he felt like whispering a thanks to her for not setting him up here on this narrow canyon trail. He tapped his heels to the dun's sides and put the horse up into a quicker pace now that morning shone clearly on the rolling terrain.

He rode on.

At midmorning, he stepped down from his saddle beneath the edge of a low, rocky rise and let the dun's reins fall to the ground. The dun stayed in place, just as it had been trained to do. Sam walked up the rocky slope, going into a crouch the last few feet, until he gazed over the crest and looked down and out at the streets of Rosas Salvajes lying in the distance.

After a moment of studying the layout, the sun, the distance, he stepped back below the rise, picked up a handful of loose sand and stepped forward again until he could hold his closed hand above the edge of the rise. He watched the sand spill from his hand and bend sidelong on a hot passing breeze.

This would have to do.

He walked back to the dun, took down the big Swiss rifle case and opened it on the ground. Sunlight glinted on the smooth precision steel, the deep polished gun stock. He picked up the long scope from its seat, closed the box and carried it to the rise. With the rifle in the box beside him, ready to assemble, he lay down, stretched out in the dirt and raised the scope to his eye.

In the living quarters of the dead Henri Defoe, Erin Donovan dropped the bloody bar towel into the bucket of water, stepped over and peeped out the door, making certain Luis had really left. When she stepped back over to Hector, she shook him by his shoulder.

"Wake up! Wake up. I know you're not asleep. Open your eyes," she insisted.

Hector raised his slumped head and turned his purple swollen slits of eyes up to her.

"They are open," he whispered in a strained, slurred voice. "I have been . . . badly beaten," he rasped.

"I'm not here to listen to your sad story," Erin said. She stepped around behind him and looked down, seeing where he had nearly managed to get the rope loosened from his wrists. "My, but haven't you been a busy little squirrel?" she said.

"Do not . . . call me . . . squirrel," Hector managed to say.

"You're right. I'm sorry," Erin said, stooping and

untying his hands from the chair. "Anybody who took this kind of beating and has not given the money up is no squirrel. That's for certain."

"Why . . . are you here?" Hector asked, his voice recovering some. He brought his hands around and rubbed his raw wrists. He studied his fingers, as if to make sure none had been lopped off while he'd been unconscious.

"I told Teto I can get you to tell me where you hid the money," Erin said. "I told them beating you wouldn't do it, and killing you was even worse." She paused, looking down at him and added, "I took a chance on kindness working where all else has failed. Was I wrong?"

"You were . . . not only wrong, you were dead wrong," Hector said, struggling to rise from the chair. His words ended in a gasping, wheezing sound. Pain shot through his battered chest. Instead of making it to his feet, he crumpled toward the floor. Erin managed to catch him and steer him back onto the chair.

"Sit still for a minute," she said, fearing he might pass out on her. "You're going to have to keep your wits about you, if we're to get you out of here alive."

Hector coughed and wheezed and collected himself. "I told you . . . I will not reveal where I have hidden the money—"

"Yes, I know. I heard you," Erin said, cutting him short. "Now keep quiet until you regain some strength. I suspect you have broken ribs."

"I—I recognize you," Hector said. "You and your brother—"

Erin cut him off again, saying, "We'll make small

talk later, Hector. Right now you have to tell me where the money is hidden." She paused before asking, "Don't you have a house out of town along the land-wagon route? The doves all say you do."

"I used to," he said. "I used to have a wife there too. But not anymore. Go see if you don't believe me."

"Hector, I hope you wouldn't make me ride out there for nothing," said Erin.

"Call me Pancho," Hector said with a swollen, crooked trace of a smile. Fresh blood oozed from the cuts on his lips.

"Yes, Pancho," Erin said. "Now tell me where to find the money—"

He cut her off, saying, "Would I not . . . be a fool to tell you? You are one of them."

"No, I'm not," Erin said, speaking quickly, knowing Luis could return at any moment. "I'll get you out of here alive, but I want part of the money for doing it."

"No." Hector shook his head stubbornly. "I don't believe you . . . are not one of them."

"Geeze begorra!" Erin cursed in Celtic under her breath. "I come to save you! Don't be a fool! You can give me part of the hundred thousand, or you can die and never see a dollar of it!"

"A hundred thousand . . . ?" Hector managed to chuff. His voice seemed to gain strength. "It is three hundred thousand dollars—I counted it."

Erin clenched her teeth and stared away in anger.

"The bastards!" she hissed, realizing why Teto wanted no one else to see the money until it first went through his hands. She knew that Teto and Luis were both in on shorting everybody. *The dirty bastards!*

Upon hearing the sound of boots crossing the walk plank outside the door, she gave Hector a startled look. He threw his hands behind his back and let his head slump back to the side.

Erin backed away from him and stood next to a small table as Luis walked in, rifle in hand. He looked over at her.

"What's wrong?" he asked, seeing an expression on her face that she had not been able to shed quickly enough.

"Nothing," Erin said. She stood perfectly still as Luis stepped over closer to Hector.

Looking down first at Hector's battered face, then at the loose rope on the floor beside the chair, Luis stiffened. His thumb went over his rifle hammer, ready to cock it.

Seeing Luis through the swollen slits of eyelids, Hector tried to hurl himself forward and grab him. But Luis sidestepped him, threw his rifle up to take quick aim.

Hector hit the floor facedown and braced himself, knowing he'd hear the sound of the shot rip through him at any second. Yet, instead of a gunshot, he heard a deep grunt followed by a long gasp. Rolling onto his side, he looked up and saw the wooden handle of a large bread knife standing where Luis' ribs met in the center of his chest.

Luis staggered backward a step, his rifle slumping at his side, his eyes wide in disbelief. Staring down at the big knife that had been lying atop the wooden table where Erin had stood, he shook his head slowly.

"Why . . . ?" he asked Erin in a failing, muffled whisper.

"*One* hundred thousand dollars?" Erin said. "Does that tell you why?"

"I . . . didn't . . . *know*," Luis managed to say as Erin reached out and jerked the rifle from his hand. But she could tell he was lying.

Coldly she said, "Yes, well, *now* you do." She reached out with the rifle barrel and pushed him backward to the floor.

Hector stared up at her, stunned, as he struggled to rise onto his knees.

Erin pointed the rifle down at his forehead and cocked it.

"I don't know how you did it, *Pancho*," she said tightly. "But you got loose and got your hands on the knife. You killed poor Luis . . . then I shot you dead. It's that simple."

Hector hung as if frozen on his knees, staring up at her through his swollen eyes. His hands spread. A tense silence imposed itself on the room. There was no doubt she *would* kill him; there was no doubt she *could* let him live.

"What must I do?" he finally rasped.

"Take one guess, *partner*," Erin said drily.

"It's—it's out back," said Hector. He tried struggling to his feet but couldn't make it. "You'll have to help me." He reached a hand up to her.

"Don't worry, Pancho. I'll get you out of here," she said. "I'm going to take good care of you. You have my word." Leaning the rifle against the chair, she pulled

him to his feet, looped his arm across her shoulders
and led him out the back door.

From his spot on the low rise, the Ranger lay with the
big Swiss rifle assembled, the butt of it resting against
his right shoulder. With the scope mounted and
adjusted, he scanned back and forth once again along
the dusty street. He'd recognized Luis Torres as the
gunman walked around the side of the Perros Malos
and entered the side door of the attached living quarters behind the cantina.

All right, there was one of the brothers, he told himself, getting an idea of where to find everybody once
the shooting started. He scanned the rifle to his right,
taking in two gunmen who stood talking to one of the
cantina doves in the narrow shade of a tall flowering
cactus. Through the scope, he saw their lips move in
conversation. The young woman opened the loose
front of her blouse, jiggled her bare breasts, taunting
the two men, then jumped back in silent laughter as
one of them reached out and tried to grab her.

Sam moved the scope away from the gunmen and
the dove and scanned farther to his right, at the end
of town closest to him. Two riflemen were partially
hidden beneath a ragged canvas awning out in front
of a weathered shack, keeping watch along the trail.
Scanning back to his left, he counted a dozen horses
lined up along the hitch rails out front. At the edge of
the cantina, one man stood alone sipping on a bottle
of rye, rifle in hand. At the far end of town, two more
men stood guard. It was clear the Torres brothers had
the town covered from either end.

He did a quick head count. Two at either end of town, one at the edge of the cantina, two with the dove—Luis in the living quarters. Eight men accounted for, he told himself. That meant Teto and three others were either inside the cantina or off somewhere in town. There could even be others whose horses were inside the barn, he cautioned himself.

But his count was close enough. It was time to get to work, he told himself, ready to aim at one of the two guards nearest to him and make his first shot.

Wait. What's this?

Something had caught his eye. He moved back with the scope and homed in on Erin and the Mexican limping away from the back door of the adobe living quarters attached behind the cantina. His shot would have to wait, he told himself, watching the two hurry as best they could through a stretch of sand, dried brush, cactus and broken rock. He kept the circling scope on them, seeing them as if they were right in front of him until they both moved down out of sight. He relaxed his shoulder, but kept watch through the scope. He would wait.

In the brush fifty yards behind the cantina, Erin eased Hector down onto a rock and lifted his arm from across her shoulders.

"Wake up, Pancho!" she said, keeping her voice lowered but firm, seeing that Hector had begun to fade out on her. "Which one is it?" she asked as his swollen eyes tried to focus on her.

It took all of Hector's strength to raise his arm enough to point at a broken rock ten feet away. "It looks stuck . . . but it's not . . . ," he said, his words trailing.

"Goodness, I hope not," said Erin, appraising the heavy-looking rock, stepping over to it in a crouch.

She put her shoulder to the rock and shoved hard. Surprisingly, the rock rose off its flattened bottom, rolled a full turn and stopped. Erin's eyes widened in delight, gazing down at two burlap feed sacks lying crushed into the sandy ground. She sank to her knees, opened one of the sacks and looked inside.

"Oh yes . . . ," she purred, seeing the bundles of bills and loose gold coins.

She checked each bag in turn, dragged them up from the indentation of the rock and set them on the ground beside her. She sighed and looked at Hector.

Through swollen eyes, Hector saw her hand go to the big Starr shoved down in her waist.

"Now you . . . have the money," he said. "Do you . . . kill me?"

"*Kill* you?" she said incredulously. "A deal is a deal, Pancho. If it wouldn't hurt you so bad, I'd be kissing your swollen mug this very minute!" She adjusted the Starr in her waist and gathered the two sacks.

"*Gracias,*" Hector said weakly. "Take the money and go."

"No," said Erin, "we both go. I gave my word to get you out of here. That's what I'll do."

Hector only stared at her.

"We have to get the money closer to the barn," Erin said. "I'll get in and get us some horses. Then we'll cut out. How far is it to your house?"

"Two miles . . . straight out the land-wagon trail," Hector said.

"Are you up to it?" Erin asked.

"Get a horse between my legs . . . I can ride," Hector said. He struggled upward; Erin reached out and helped him. She steadied him onto his feet.

"But can you walk?" she asked, turning him loose, seeing that he didn't fall.

"I can walk. Let's go," he said.

Erin picked up a feed sack in either hand and swung them both back over her shoulders. She walked in the direction of the barn a hundred yards away, across broken rock and loose, sloping hillside. Hector struggled along behind her.

Sam watched the two from the low rise, through his scope, seeing the Mexican's battered condition as they struggled along toward the livery barn. He noted the two feed sacks hanging back over Erin's shoulders, knowing that money was the only thing that could be inside them. What else would be so important under these circumstances? he reasoned, watching Erin bound across the hillside toward the barn. *Watch out*, he cautioned her, knowing she couldn't see that one of the gunmen had spotted her from the street and started walking toward her, his rifle in one hand, a bottle of rye in the other.

Halfway to the livery barn, Erin heard Hector go down and begin sliding on the loose hillside. He didn't call out for help, but she dropped the sacks and ran to him as he stopped in a pile of brush. The money sacks slid along behind her, following her like slow-witted friends.

"I—I can walk," Hector insisted, grasping her forearm.

"No, you can't. This is no good, Pancho," Erin said, looking off toward the livery barn. "You stay right here with the money. I'll come back for you with horses."

The gunman, a young killer named Adle Price, stood at the corner of the livery barn and stepped out in front of her as Erin ran toward the big wooden doors.

"Well, well," he said, blocking her way. "What are you doing out here running around all by yourself?"

Erin saw the bottle of rye and smelled the whiskey on his breath. She thought of the Starr pistol stuck down in her waist, but if she were to reach for it, the gunman had only to grab her hand or smack her with his rifle butt, standing this close.

"I'm looking for you, Price!" Erin said, making up her story quickly. "Something terrible has happened! Teto said tell you—"

"Huh-uh," the gunman interrupted her, "I just saw Teto at the cantina. Nothing's happened." He gave her a suspicious look. "Maybe you best come with me." He reached out to grab her arm. "We'll see what Teto has to say—"

"Stay away . . . keep your hands off me!" Erin said, pulling against his grip. But just as she tried to yank free, she saw a large red hole blow out from the center of Price's chest. She gasped.

Price's head whiplashed back and forth from the

impact; a gout of blood, meat and bone matter splattered her face and shirt as it jettisoned past her. Then she heard the sound of the shot catch up to the bullet and resound across the rocky terrain.

Sam stared through the scope and watched Erin dive to the ground as if the next shot might be meant for her—but it wasn't.

"Get up and get out of there," Sam whispered under his breath. "It's commenced." He bolted the spent shell out of the big Swiss rifle and replaced it with a fresh one.

Chapter 25

Inside the cantina, Teto heard the rifle shot and immediately ran to the front door. He listened to the young dove scream and saw her run away from the gunmen she'd been talking to, her face covered with blood. Her open blouse billowed back behind her; her blood-streaked breasts bounced wildly. One of the gunmen stood clinging to the large cactus, its daggerlike spines pinning him as if he'd been crucified. A large hole poured blood from the center of his back.

"Stay back, Teto!" the other gunman shouted, having hit the dirt and crawled quickly around the cactus for cover.

Teto jumped back inside just as a large chunk of adobe and wood exploded from the spot where his head had been only a second before.

At a window, Filo and Blake peeped out, then looked over at Teto.

"Teto, are you all right?" Filo called out to him.

"Hell yes, I'm fine," said Teto, keeping the thick front

wall of the cantina between himself and the outside world. "Can you see where it's coming from?"

"I saw smoke up on the rise!" Blake called out, taking a quick look and ducking back away from the window. "But whoever it is, they're too far out of range for us to shoot back!"

"That damned *Ranger*!" Teto bellowed. "I knew I should have killed him myself and been done with it." He clenched his teeth. "Now he has us pinned down—like rats in a hole."

The rear door swung open; the three gunmen spun toward it, guns ready to fire.

"Don't shoot, it's me!" said Wade Carrico.

"Jesus, Wade!" said Teto, he and the others letting their guns slump a little.

Carrico stepped inside and shoved Erin in ahead of him. Her face and chest were covered with blood. She staggered and caught herself on a chair back without falling.

"Look who I found trying to steal a horse from the barn and get her knees in the wind," Carrico said.

"I wasn't trying to go anywhere," Erin said. "I was rattled! I was being shot at!"

Teto hurried over to her.

"Are you hit? Are you bleeding?" he asked, grabbing her, looking her up and down.

"No, I'm not hurt," said Erin, pulling herself away from him. "It's Price's blood, not mine. He's lying dead back there. His heart blew out all over me," she said, a terrible look coming to her blood-smeared face, recounting the scene in her mind. "It was awful!"

"Listen to me, Erin," Teto said calmly. "Does the lawman carry a long-shooter?"

"I—I believe he might," Erin said. "He has a wooden case that he carries beneath his bedroll—"

"It's him," Teto said, cutting her off. "Damn it to hell."

"Yeah, it's him sure enough," said Carrico, "and she's the one who said he wouldn't be coming along behind us."

"And I was *wrong*, Carrico," Erin said, convincingly. "How would I know he found himself a horse somewhere?" She stared at Teto for understanding.

"Wrong, *ha*!" said Carrico. "If you ask me, she's in with that lawman. She spent all that time on the trail with him. Who can say what they—"

He shut up when Teto swung his Colt toward him, cocked and pointed.

"Go gather the men, Carrico," said Teto. "It will keep *me* from killing you where you stand."

"What's the difference?" said Carrico. "If I go out there, the long-shooter is going to kill me."

"As you wish," Teto said, leveling the Colt toward Carrico's chest. Carrico's hand tightened around the butt of his holstered Remington.

"Stop it, both of you!" Erin shouted, coming very close to stepping between the two of them, but stopping short. "If we turn against one another we will all die! Is that what you want, either of you?" She looked back and forth. Her hand went to the big Starr revolver in her waist. "Fine, then. Let's all kill one another!"

Carrico was the first to flinch. He let his hand rest down away from his Remington.

"I'll go gather the men," he said quietly. "What's the plan?"

"We gather up and charge him," Teto said.

"Jesus!" said Blake, standing over by the window beside Truman Filo. "You mean we're going to charge a long-shooter like that? We'll be dead by the time we get into shooting range."

"He has to reload," Filo said, more optimistic. "He can't kill us all." A grin split his face. "We just can't slow down and enjoy the view along the way." He tipped a half bottle of rye toward the others as if in salute, then threw back a deep drink.

Wade Carrico stepped over, snatched the bottle from Filo's hand, threw back a long drink himself and handed the bottle on to Blake.

"Damned if we ain't all crazy," he cursed under his breath, turning, heading out the open back door.

"Watch for us!" Teto called out behind him. "When we run out, we'll send the horse down the street toward you."

Blake whispered sidelong to Filo, "We're going to die right there at the hitch rail." He raised the bottle and took a deep drink.

"Not all of us," Filo said, grinning like a madman. "I feel lucky as hell today."

Teto put his arm around Erin's waist.

"What did the squirrel tell you about the money?" he asked just between the two of them.

"That's what I was coming here to tell you," Erin said, "before Price got himself shot all over me." As she spoke, they began to hear and feel the swelling rumble of horses' hooves moving toward the far end of town.

Teto looked off toward the sound, then back at her, expectantly.

"The squirrel killed Luis and got away," she said quickly, both of them interested in the rumble of hooves growing stronger.

"Luis is *dead*?" Teto exclaimed, raising his voice above the sound of the approaching hooves.

"Yes," Erin said louder.

"She's . . . *lying*," Luis Torres growled, staggering in through the rear door, the knife handle standing in his chest. He wobbled in place, the front of him covered in blood, his Colt hanging in his bloody hand.

"Luis!" cried Erin, stunned at the sight of him.

"Jesus!" said Blake.

"Riders coming!" Filo shouted, staring at Luis.

"*She* . . . stabbed me," Luis said, using all his strength to raise the cocked Colt toward Erin. "She carries . . . my child."

"No, brother, no!" Teto shouted, seeing what Luis was attempting to do. He swung his Colt up and fired shot after shot into Luis' bloody chest, each bullet sending him farther out the open rear door.

The hooves rumbled louder. Teto grabbed Erin and ran to the front door to look out. Blake and Filo peeped out from the edge of the window toward the far end of town, mindful of the Ranger still atop the low rise with his big rifle.

"What was Luis saying?" Teto demanded. "Did you stab him? Are you carrying his baby?"

Erin looked into his smoldering eyes, feeling the tip of his gun barrel beneath her left breast.

"For God's sake, no!" said Erin. "The squirrel stabbed

him. Luis must have been out of his mind. You heard what he said, that I'm carrying his baby! You know better than that!"

Teto searched her eyes for any sign of deception as the rumble of hooves grew stronger.

"It's—it's true I'm carrying a child, Teto," Erin said, "but it's *your* child. It could belong to no one else. I told Luis about it." Her eyes welled with tears. "I thought you would both be happy about it." He voice trembled. "I had no idea Luis felt the way he did about me."

"*Por favor.* Don't cry, my Irish princess," Teto said. He lowered his Colt, uncocked it and drew her close to him. "You stay here and keep down out of sight. I don't know who is coming, but I am certain they are not our friends."

Lying on the ground beneath the crest of the rise, the Ranger had felt the rumble of hooves in the earth beneath him long before he'd caught sight of a rising dust drift upward west of the town. When he did see the dust streaming and swirling behind the riders, he turned the Swiss rifle toward them just to see them through the scope. At the head of the riders, he recognized the *rurale* posse leader.

Just now getting here . . . , the Ranger told himself, seeing the leader's face close up in the scope, through dust, sunlight and wavering heat. "You couldn't have arrived at a worse time," he murmured to himself.

The *rurale* leader's expression was set fiercely in both anger and determination. Sam studied his face through the scope for a moment longer, then lowered the rifle and let out a breath. Whatever plans he'd had would have to wait. It made him no difference if the Mexican posse wiped out the Gun Killers all by themselves. But that was highly unlikely, he reminded himself.

He had started to turn his scope back to the street in Rosas Salvajes when a bullet streaked in and thumped into the dirt near his right elbow. Turning quickly toward the sound of a rifle shot, he saw riders coming toward him fast—but he held his fire. These weren't Gun Killers. These were two of the *rurales* he'd seen dragging the dead horse down the street in San Pelipe.

"Drop the gun! *Drop the gun!*" one of them shouted as they raced in closer and slid their horses sideways to a halt thirty feet from him.

Sam laid the Swiss rifle carefully on the ground, took his hands away from it and raised them.

"On your feet!" the excited *rurale* ordered. "Do it now!"

Sam stood up slowly, his hands still in plain sight.

The two recognized him, he was certain. Turning to each other, they spoke in voices too low and fast for him to hear.

"You are the *Americano* lawman from Nogales— the one we met in San Felipe!" the excited one said, his rifle pointed at Sam.

"I knew that," Sam said calmly, staring at him.

"Lift your pistol and drop it," the other man demanded.

"No, *wait!*" said the excited one, not liking the idea of this lawman getting his hand on a gun. "Get on the ground," he ordered. Then quickly he corrected himself. "No, wait. Stay on your feet!"

"Make up your mind," Sam said. He paused, his hand halfway to the butt of his holstered Colt. "I don't have time for all this."

"You will make time, Señor Lawman," said the excited *rurale*. He turned to the other man and said, "Julio, get his gun and rifle. I have him covered."

"*Sí*, Eduardo," said Julio. He stepped down from his saddle and walked forward, a big French-made revolver in his hand.

Sam cut a glance toward the distant street as heavy gunfire erupted. The other *rurales* descended onto the town in a looming swirl of dust—dust that had already begun to obscure everything from sight. The *rurales* rode back and forth, shooting at the cantina and at anyone foolish enough to let themselves be seen.

"I hope you fellows brought shovels," Sam said quietly, lifting his Colt and handing it to Julio, who stood in front of him.

"Don't worry, lawman. We have plenty of shovels," Eduardo said with a smug grin, not catching the implication in Sam's words.

Sam let out a long breath as the shooting from the distant street intensified.

"Careful with the rifle, Julio," he said as the young man picked up the Swiss rifle and turned it back and forth in his hands.

"Don't worry, lawman," said the *rurale*. He lowered his rifle barrel a little now that he considered Sam unarmed. "Once Raul has taken down the Gun Killers, you will get these back. We do not want you getting in our way while we do what must be done."

"I understand," Sam said, keeping his hands chest

high, watching the young Mexican look the big Swiss
rifle over, deciding how to disassemble it. "Do you
mind if I break the rifle down?" he asked. "It might be
quicker."

"Julio, give him the rifle before you shoot your
foot off," said Eduardo. "But keep an eye on him." He
stared hard at the Ranger. "If he tries anything,
shoot him."

In Rosa Salvajes, the shooting continued to inten-
sify. The dust had grown to such a thick swell that all
Sam and the two *rurales* could see were the blossoms
of blue-orange gunfire streaking back and forth
between the mounted posse and the hard-fighting,
besieged Gun Killers. Behind the cantina, Sam watched
a string of riders race up out of the dust along a hillside and bound out of sight over a rise.

Sam shook his head as he quickly took the Swiss
rifle apart and placed it and the scope inside the
wooden box. He closed the box on the ground, stood
up and stepped back.

"There you are," he said as he raised his hands
chest high again. He gestured a nod toward the gun
battle. "The quicker we get down there, the quicker
your men can stop shooting one another."

"You make me laugh, you *gringo* lawman," the
mounted *rurale* said. "You always think you know
everything." To Julio he said, "Get on your horse and
keep this one between us."

"*Sí*, Eduardo," the young Mexican said. He started
toward his horse with the Swiss rifle case under his
arm. But Sam stopped him and took the case.

"If you don't mind, I'll carry the rifle case," he said.

The two looked at him. "No," Eduardo said. "You will get the rifle back *only* when Raul says you may have it. We are sick of you *Americanos* coming here thinking you can tell us to do whatever you want."

Sam clenched his jaw and kept his mouth shut as he swung up onto his saddle.

"Ready when you are," he said.

Chapter 26

———

When the Ranger and the *rurales* drew near Rosas Salvajes, the thick, blinding cloud of dust had begun to lift above the town and drift across the rocky land. The firing had stopped. Only a thin rise of dust stood above the path the Gun Killers had used as an escape route. Sam shook his head, realizing how many of the outlaws had gotten away. He hoped that among them Erin Donovan had managed to stay alive.

At the edge of town, the *rurale* leader's horse came pounding up to them. The big Mexican's hat was missing. He had tied a bandanna around his forehead to cover a bullet graze. He looked stunned by the fierceness with which the Gun Killers had faced his posse.

"They got away?" he said to Sam in the form of a question, a strange look on his face. "We could see nothing in the dust but *dust*. They got among us. We could not fight without shooting our own." He gave his strange look to Eduardo and Julio. "They have killed *my posse*!"

"I figured they would," the Ranger said. "These men are no easy kill."

"They killed all of our men?" Eduardo cut in.

"All but three," said Raul. "Those three are in pursuit of the killers right now."

"In *pursuit*?" Sam said, his very tone implying the foolishness of such an act.

"*Sí*, I sent them in pursuit," said the leader defensively. He looked Sam up and down. "Do you say sending them was a mistake?"

"A bad mistake," Sam responded, still gazing off along the high hillside trail. "You need to go stop them before it's too late."

As if on cue, a hard volley of rifle shots resounded in the distance, from the path the Gun Killers had taken.

Sam let out a low breath and shook his head again. "Never mind," he said quietly.

Raul appeared enraged, but he subdued his anger and said, "I will ride them down myself, as soon as we have buried our dead." He looked at Eduardo and Julio. "Eduardo, go bring the townspeople out of hiding. Tell them we need shovels to bury our dead."

"*Sí*, Raul," said Eduardo, avoiding Sam's knowing stare. "Come, Julio," he said. He started to turn his horse away.

"Wait a minute, Julio," said Sam. He reached over and jerked the Swiss rifle case from under the young Mexican's arm. "My Colt, too," he said, holding out a hand toward Julio.

Julio gave Raul a questioning look.

"Yes, damn it, give him his gun," said Raul, as if disgusted with Julio.

Sam took the Colt, checked and holstered it. He gave Julio a nod.

The two *rurales* turned their horses toward the dusty street as heads began to peep out from doorways and windows.

"Let me be honest with you, lawman," said Raul with a sigh. He touched his fingers to his bandaged head, examining his wound as he spoke. "I have much to do. I am going to need your help."

Sam looked him up and down.

"I don't dig graves," he said. He turned his dun and started to tap his heels to its sides.

"*Santa Madre*! Look at this!" Raul said in disbelief.

Sam turned in his saddle and saw a gunman staggering toward them from the alley beside the Perros Malos Cantina. The entire length of the gunman was soaked with blood. He left a trail of bloody footprints behind him. A knife handle stuck from the center of his chest; his gun hung from his right hand. His left hand held the strap to a canteen.

Raul jerked his pistol from across his chest, but Sam raised a hand toward him.

"No, wait," Sam said, stopping the *rurale* leader from shooting the wounded outlaw. "Let's see what this one has to say."

Luis Torres staggered in place and crumpled to the ground just as Sam swung down from his saddle, rifle case still in hand, and ran to him. Stooping down, Sam laid the rifle case in the dirt and raised the wounded man's head onto his knee. He looked at the bloody face closely.

"Luis Torres?" Sam said, recognizing him from a wanted poster in Nogales.

"Yes, yes, I am Luis," the outlaw groaned. "Get away from me. . . . I am cursed."

"You're dying, Torres," Sam said bluntly. "It wasn't one of this posse who stuck that knife in your chest. Who did it?"

"The . . . woman. The mother of my child . . . ," Luis said, his words ending in a deep, wet-sounding cough.

Sam knew there was only one woman he could be talking about.

"Erin did this to you?" he asked, not doubting it for a second.

Luis nodded and grasped Sam's shirtsleeve. "Am I cursed to hell . . . forever?"

"You'll have to take it up with God," Sam said. "Where are the Gun Killers headed? What are their plans from here."

"*Plans* . . . ?" said Luis. "No plans . . . not while you dog us so closely."

Good, Sam thought, his persistence had paid off. Had he not been on their trail, they might have gone off on another mission to rob and kill. He'd kept them too busy dodging him. He had forced them into this showdown—would have ended it here, had the *rurales* not ridden in unexpectedly and spoiled everything.

"Was it the posse who shot you?" he asked, recalling the gunshots from the cantina before the *rurales* rode in.

"No . . . my brother, Teto . . . shot me," Luis said. He managed a thin, weak smile. "Arrest him . . . eh?"

Sam only stared at him, knowing he wouldn't be breathing much longer.

"Over the woman," Sam said, not liking the picture that was coming to his mind. "Because she's carrying your baby."

"*Sí* . . . ," Luis said with a deep sigh. His eyes went to the knife handle standing on his chest. "She is . . . a bad woman," he said, shaking his head slowly.

"So it seems," Sam replied, not liking to have finally and so completely admitted it to himself.

"She caused me to . . . do my brother wrong," Luis said, fading fast. His eyes began to glaze over and look away aimlessly.

No, that was your fault, the Ranger said silently, realizing it did no good to tell Luis while he drew his last breath. *He must have known it anyway*, Sam thought as he reached a hand down and closed the outlaw's eyes.

"What did he tell you?" Raul asked, stepping over from his horse with his pistol drawn and cocked.

"Nothing helpful," Sam said. He stood, picked up his rifle case and walked back to the dun.

Raul uncocked his pistol and shoved it back into his holster.

"You tell me!" he demanded. "I will decide if it is helpful or not."

"Go home, Raul," Sam said as he tied his rifle case under his bedroll.

"*Go home*, you tell me! How dare you say such a thing," Raul shouted. He pounded himself on the chest. "Mexico is *my* home—what's left of it after you gringos cut it, divide it and steal it *one piece at a time*!"

"Right," Sam said flatly, turning to him with a cold stare, "I almost forgot."

He swung up into his saddle and adjusted his dusty sombrero.

"Where are you going?" Raul demanded. "I am not through talking!"

"Yes, you are," Sam said, turning his horse away from the hillside and the trail the Gun Killers had taken.

Seeing his direction, Raul called out, "You are running away from them?"

"They're stirred up like hornets. I'm riding *around* them until they settle," Sam said. "You three would be wise to do the same."

"No," said Raul, "the three of us will not run *around* them. We will ride them down and kill them as soon as we bury our dead."

The Ranger looked down the dusty street at the dead men and horses strewn about. Julio, Eduardo and some townspeople walked among the dead, shovels in hand. One of the doves from the cantina stood watching, wrapped in a bedsheet, smoking a thin cigar.

"*Vaya con Dios*," Sam said to Raul. "Take a shovel with you."

In the rocks behind the livery barn, Hector had lain on the hillside, hugging the ground as bullets flew in

the street below. He had kept an arm over the sacks of
money beside him as if they were living things. He'd
even watched through swollen eyes as Erin, Teto Torres and five of the remaining Gun Killers ran from
the rear of the cantina into the barn and raced out
moments later atop any horses they could get their
hands on—most of their own horses lay dead in the
street, shot down at the hitch rails by the *rurales*.

When the woman had ridden out of the barn, she'd
led two horses behind her. Hector saw her look in his
direction as she turned loose of the two spare horses'
reins. He'd watched the horses race away, but veer off
from the rest of the riders and slow to halt farther up
the hillside.

What was her intention? he asked himself. Had she
left the horses for him? He believed so. Yet, did he
not think he would take the money and ride away,
never to be seen again? She could have told Teto and
the Gun Killers he was there hiding with the money,
he reminded himself. He would be dead, and they
would have split the money and ridden on. At least
she would have had a share. As it turned out, she
would have nothing now, unless he—the squirrel—
could be trusted to keep her share safe for her.

With great pain in his chest, his cracked ribs and
his badly beaten head, Hector gathered the tops of
the sacks of money in his right hand. He crawled on
his belly, pulling himself up the hillside with his free
hand toward the two loose horses. He would show
her what a squirrel would do.

When he had gotten to the spare horses, one

turned and trotted away. But the other horse stayed put, staring at his battered face curiously until he reached out and took a hold of its dangling reins.

"Ah, I can see you are a good *caballo*," he whispered in a strained voice.

Pulling himself up the horse's sides, the two sacks in hand, he loosened both strings on the sack tops, tied them together and draped them over the horse's back behind the saddle. It would have to do for now, he told himself. Looking back down the hillside, he saw two of the *rurales* and some townspeople walk out the rear door of *his* cantina and head for the livery barn.

"I will be back . . . to claim what is mine," he whispered to himself in a ragged voice. He hefted himself up onto the saddle with much effort, pain throbbing throughout his body. Lying forward on the horse's neck, reins in hand, he whispered, "Take me away from here, *caballo*. I have seen far too much."

Five miles along the hill trail, Teto, Paco Sterns and Truman Filo had climbed down from the rocks and stood over the bodies of the three *rurales* who had followed them from Rosas Salvajes.

"Gather their horses," Teto said, his gun belt hanging over his shoulder. As he spoke, he reloaded his smoking pistol. "We'll be needing them before long."

Climbing down from the rocks behind them, Wade Carrico, Ludlow Blake and Jete Longley stepped out on the trail—all that remained of the Gun Killers that had been in Rosas Salvajes when the shooting started.

"We lost two spare horses when your lady-friend let them get away," Carrico said, gesturing toward Erin, who stood off to the side, her forearms wrapped around her midsection.

"Are you going to start arguing again?" Teto asked in a warning tone, clicking his reloaded revolver shut and staring hard at Carrico.

"No," said Carrico, unafraid. "If you don't give a damn, neither do I. I was just curious why she let them go, is all."

Teto considered the matter. Then he turned to Erin and said, "Why *did* you let the spare horses go?"

"For God's sake, Teto," Erin said in a shaky voice. "I was scared, and sick . . . and being shot at."

Teto turned to Carrico, with his loaded pistol pointed loosely toward him.

"Wade, she was scared and sick and being shot at," he said. "Does that do it for you?"

Carrico only shook his head and looked away.

"Were the lawman and the *rurales* working together?" he asked, changing the subject.

Teto gave a little laugh and said, "I'd have to say so, Wade, whether they meant to be or not."

Carrico let out a breath, chuckled a little to himself and said, "If they weren't, I expect they damn sure should have been. That turned into a real tight spot there for a minute or two."

Paco Sterns looked back warily along the hill trail.

"We have the horses. Let's *vamos*," he said.

"What about the squirrel and our money?" Erin asked just to get a feel on where things stood with Teto.

"As soon as it's safe, we find the squirrel and skin his back with a bullwhip," Teto replied. "But for now, our situation has changed. We do not risk getting ourselves killed over money." He grinned. "Not when there is a whole country full of it waiting across the border."

Chapter 27

The Ranger had spotted the lone rider moving along the high trail in the afternoon sunlight. As soon as he saw the bulging feed sacks hanging over the horse's rump, he realized it was the Mexican, not one of the Gun Killers, riding the high trail away from town. He lagged back a safe distance and kept out of sight. He wasn't after the money. Yet, he would bet that wherever the money went, Erin Donovan would follow. And wherever Erin Donovan went . . .

He let his thoughts fade as he watched the Mexican guide the horse down the rocky, sloping hillside to the lower trail, leading out of town across the rolling desert floor. From the looks of the battered Mexican, and the way he sat slumped loose in his saddle, Sam doubted he could make it very far without pitching sidelong into the dirt.

Never underestimate the healing power of money, Sam reminded himself, letting the Mexican get to the bottom of the treacherous hillside and on to the lower trail before nudging his dun down behind him. Sam stayed back out of sight and followed the hoofprints of Hector's horse until they turned off the lower trail back toward a bleak, little adobe hovel.

The house stood at the end of a worn path, beneath a hillside covered with cactus, creosote and mesquite brush. Sam had a hunch that this was the Mexican's home, or at least a place where he felt safe enough to lie low and rest himself overnight—let himself heal a little.

Or meet someone? Sam asked himself, looking all around, studying the lay of the land. *We'll see. . . .*

He rode the dun away from the trail, found a rise strewn with brush and cactus and stepped the horse down out of sight. He climbed down from his saddle, took the Swiss rifle case from beneath this bedroll and opened it on the ground. Instead of taking out the rifle, he only took out the scope. Lying down at the edge of the rise, he made himself comfortable and looked across the purple evening toward the open front window of the adobe.

It's going to be a long night, he told himself, the brass-trimmed scope to his eye.

At a camp, lit only by the pale light of a half-moon, Wade Carrico stooped down and shook Teto Torres by the shoulder.

"Teto, wake up," he said. "She's gone."

The Mexican outlaw leader sat up, rubbing his face, and looked at Carrico with a questioning expression.

"The hell are you talking about, Wade?" he asked angrily.

"I'm talking about your woman," said Carrico, his

voice turning equally angry. "I watched her go get her horse and lead it away from here."

"You didn't try to stop her?" Teto asked.

"I figured it being your woman, you wouldn't want me laying hands on her," Carrico said. "There's been bad blood between us over her as it is."

In truth, Carrico was glad to see her go. Had he stopped her and brought her to Teto, she would've lied and put him in a tight spot. This way, Teto had no one to blame but Erin herself.

Teto just stared at him for a moment, realizing he was right.

"How long ago?" he asked.

"No more than five minutes," Carrico said.

"Damn it," Teto said, "she's always been bad about slipping off in the night." He stood and looked down where Erin had slept on a blanket beside him. When he'd gone to sleep, she'd been lying against him, her arm over his chest.

"Want me to start grabbing everybody's horses?" Carrico asked.

"No," said Teto, "just mine. I'll get her. I'll see what this is all about."

As he spoke to Carrico, Teto thought about the missing money, the missing Mexican. He thought about his brother, Luis, standing with the knife in his chest, declaring that Erin carried his child in her womb.

"Alone? Shouldn't I go with you, at least?" Carrico suggested. He stared at Teto in the thin light of the moon, but the leader's face revealed nothing.

"No," Teto said, "you should do like I said and get

my horse for me. I'll find her and bring her back. We'll catch up to you and the others on the trail."

As Teto pulled on his boots and gathered his hat and gun belt, Carrico hurried to where the men had lined their horses along a rope stretched between the two scrub piñons. When Carrico returned to Teto, the outlaw leader climbed up into his saddle and looked down.

"Keep the men on this trail. Keep moving north," he said to Carrico. "I'm putting you in charge until I get back and catch up to you."

"You got it," Carrico said. "But are you sure this is the right thing—"

"Not now, Wade," said Teto. "I've got no time to argue with you." He gave a wry smile that went unseen in the pale moonlight. "She's my Irish princess."

Without seeing Teto's smile, Carrico thought his words sounded weak for the leader of a gang like the Gun Killers. His were more the words of a small child still yearning for his mother's milk.

"Go, then," Carrico said, raising a hand, not knowing how else he should respond to such a frivolous statement.

As Teto left, his horse's hooves clacking away across the wide rock shelf lying beneath them, heads rose from saddles and blankets. The remaining Gun Killers frantically gathered around Carrico in the darkness.

"Easy, fellows," Carrico said. "It's only Teto going after his woman."

"What the hell?" Ludlow Blake asked, his Colt hanging in his right hand, his hair disheveled.

"You've got to be kidding," said Truman Filo, his rifle in hand.

"There's no *kidding* here, Filo," Carrico replied quietly. "He left me in charge. Anybody don't like it, make yourself heard."

"It's all right with us, you being in charge, Wade," said Paco Sterns.

The gunmen stared after the sound of the horse's hooves until the animal crossed the rock shelf and stepped off onto softer ground.

"There he goes," said Filo as the hooves fell silent. "Jesus, after all that went on between them back in Wild Roses? Now she up and runs off?"

"Nothing new for her," said Paco Sterns. "She's always running off . . . always in the night too."

"Yeah, but why is Teto always following her?" said Filo. "Hell, let her go, is what I would do."

"Really?" said Carrico, contemplating the situation as he spoke.

"Hell yes, *really*," said Filo. "Damned if I'd go running after her, in the middle of the night—make a fool of myself in front of my men."

"Not even for a hundred thousand dollars?" Carrico asked in a quiet tone.

"*Oh*," said Filo.

The gunmen stood in dead silence while Carrico's words sank in.

"Damn it!" Jete Longley said at length.

"Let's get our horses!" said Ludlow Blake.

"Easy, fellows," Carrico repeated, holding up a hand in the darkness to stop them.

"You mean we're not going after them?" asked Jete Longley. "You're the one mentioned the money!"

"That I am," said Carrico. "There might be money

behind this, and there might not. So let's keep our
heads in case we're wrong."

"What do you say, then?" Filo asked.

"We're going after them, sure enough," said Carrico. "But we're going to shy back and see what it
looks like before we go accusing anybody."

When Hector had arrived at the abandoned adobe
that once was his home, the first thing he'd done was
water the horse and himself. Then he'd forced himself
forward, led the tired animal inside the hovel and
into the back room that served as a stall. He'd lifted
the money sacks from the horse's back and dragged
them to what used to be his and his wife's bedroom.

There he'd laid the sacks of money on the dirt floor
and gathered loose straw and a ragged blanket that
had been thrashed about and shredded by playing
coyote pups. When he'd finished making a pallet of
money, straw and blanket, he'd crawled atop it and
lain on his back, hoping his pain would subside with
sleep. But it did not.

It was dark when the pain forced him awake. As
he sat up stiffly on the pallet, he saw red eyes flash in
the darkness across the dark empty room.

"Get out you . . . son of *a bitch*," he growled in pain,
grabbing a handful of straw—the nearest thing he
could find to throw at the prowler. He heard paws
race away through the empty house and out the
rear door.

Hector dragged himself up to the open window,
where he stood in the pale moonlight for a moment,
as if to deliver himself from the greater darkness and

remind himself he was still alive. Noting a lump in his trouser pocket, he reached in and found the folded-over, nearly empty leather bag of cocaine powder that Sidel Tereze—or one of the other doves, he thought hazily—had left on the small table in Three-Hand Defoe's living quarters.

No, *his* living quarters, he corrected himself. Or, it had been his living quarters, before the Gun Killers arrived, wanting what he had so foolishly thought belonged to him.

He turned the leather bag in his hand and shook his head slowly. Would things have been different had he kept his head clear and his wits about him? He had to think about that for a moment. He could not blame the tequila and ground cocaine powder for the loss of his wife and son. He had lost them well before he'd started drinking and using the powder.

He unwrapped the leather bag as he thought about it. He shook out a small mound of the powder onto his palm and looked at it, seeing it silvery blue in the slanted moonlight. Pain throbbed behind his swollen eyes, inside his raw, puffy lips.

After a moment, he let out a breath, closed the leather bag one-handed, folded it over and shoved it back down into his trouser pocket.

Here goes, he told himself. Lifting his palm to his mouth, he took the mound of powder onto his tongue and swallowed it. He licked his bruised and battered lips, and in seconds noted the pain had left them.

Outside, across the roll of the desert floor, Sam had been lying at rest, his head on his forearm. But he perked up when he saw the faint glow of a candle move through the hovel and stop inside the window.

Didn't the Mexican realize that a light, even one this faint, could be seen a long way across these rolling flatlands?

Yes, Sam decided, *of course he realized it. That's why he lit it.*

Raising the scope back to his eye, Sam studied the window, seeing the shadowy silhouette of the Mexican move about inside.

Getting around pretty good, Sam noted, *for a man as battered as he'd appeared to be earlier.*

In the distance, along the rolling trail, Erin saw the dim candlelight as soon as it reached out from the window into the dark night.

Was it Hector? she wondered, riding with the big Starr out across her lap in quick reach. The wolves had taught her a terrible lesson about traveling in the dark in this wild, brutal land.

Yes, it must be, she thought. It was about where he'd said his house would be, two miles west of Rosas Salvajes. Anyway, that's where she was headed, she told herself. She looked back along the trail behind her. Then, in spite of the darkness, she booted the horse forward, up into a gallop on the sandy trail.

Nearly an hour had passed by the time she reached the house. She had already slowed the horse back to a walk as she turned onto the narrow path leading to the front door. But before she made it all the way to the house, Hector called out to her from within the darkness.

"Is that you, Irish *señorita*?" he asked, his voice sounding stronger.

"Yes, Hect—Pancho," she said, catching herself. "It's me, Erin Donovan. I'm alone. Don't shoot."

After a second, Hector stepped out of the darkness, holding a broken ax handle in his hand.

"Don't worry. I have no gun," he said. He eyed a rifle butt sticking up from a saddle boot. It was a rifle Paco Stern had given her in case they ran into more *rurales* on the trail.

Erin stopped her horse and slipped down its side. She made no offer of the rifle to him.

"You sound a lot better than you did earlier," she said, leading the horse toward the house twenty yards away. "Where's the money?"

"It is safe inside," Hector said, walking along beside her. He seemed tense but well, walking straight, with almost a little bounce in his step.

"What has gotten into you, Pancho?" she asked.

"*Cocaína!*" Hector replied readily, his swollen lips even allowing him to speak better in spite of their rawness.

"Careful with that stuff," Erin warned him.

"*Sí*, I will be careful," Hector said.

Erin followed him into the house, leading her horse to the room where Hector had stalled his.

"I knew you would come here for the money," Hector said as she closed the door and turned to face him.

"And you were right." Erin smiled. "Now may I see it?"

"*Sí*, this way," Hector said. He walked into the bedroom and gestured toward the pallet on the floor.

"Oh, so this is how it is," Erin said knowingly, eyeing the makeshift bed in the light of a short candle.

"No, no," Hector said quickly. "I am showing you the money. It is there, in the pallet."

"Oh, I see," Erin said, relieved. She shook her head, embarrassed. "You must excuse me, Pancho. I'm not used to men being such gentlemen as you."

Hector understood, but he only nodded, walked over to the window and picked up the short candle from the sill. "Now that you are here, if you will permit me, I will put out the light, lest we draw trouble for ourselves."

From his spot in the dirt, Sam watched Hector appear in the window and blow out the candle. But before the young Mexican extinguished the flame, Sam caught sight of the woman's shadowy silhouette in the room behind him. She held a big revolver out at arm's length, aimed toward the back of Hector's head.

Chapter 28

———

Staring out the window, Hector had been speaking and did not hear the sound of the big Starr revolver cock six feet from his head. Or, if he had heard it, he simply had not recognized the sound, Erin told herself, the gun leveled and ready to fire.

"You trusted me to bring your part of the money to you," Hector said to her as he stared out into the purple, Mexican night. "It was a trust I could not betray, short of death."

"Yes, and you trusted me to get you out of Rosas Salvajes alive," Erin said, sighting down the long gun barrel. "So our trust of each other was well founded. Now we are evened up."

"*Sí*, now we are even," said Hector, feeling the cocaine boiling in his system, making him feel strong, bold, invincible, his pain gone for the time being. "Now you can take your part and go," he said. "I will hide my part until I have ridden back to town to claim what is mine."

"You're going back to Rosa Salvajes?" questioned Erin. "To run the cantina?"

"Yes, until I find someone else to take it over," said Hector. "It belongs to me now. I will not give it up."

Gripping the gun tightly, Erin shook her head.

"You are a bold, brave and honorable man, Pancho," she said with regret in her voice. A tear formed in her eye. She sighed. "If only you weren't so crazy, you wonderful squirrel."

She clenched her teeth and pulled the trigger.

"*Crazy?* Am I so crazy," he said, staring straight ahead into the night with no idea what had just happened behind him, "to want what every man wants for himself, a place on this earth that he can call his own? A home, a good woman, a family? A way to work and feed and shelter his family, to be able to hold his head up as a man and stand before the world unashamed?"

Erin stared at the big revolver wide-eyed, stunned that it had misfired. She shook it and looked at it again, as if shaking it might be all it needed. She started to cock the gun, raise it and try again, but Hector turned around facing her in the darkness before she could do so. He continued talking with no letup, feeling the affects of the cocaine forcing him to say things he might otherwise never say.

"No," she said, "that's not *crazy* at all."

"When I have taken back what is mine," Hector continued as if she weren't even there, "I will find myself a woman, and I will treat her like a queen. We will have a son. He will not replace the son Ana took from me, but that is all right—"

"You had a son, Pancho?" Erin asked. She held the gun back behind her, trying to get her thumb over the big hammer to recock it. But she couldn't.

"*Sí*, I had a son," said Hector. He shrugged. "He was not the blood of my blood, but that did not matter. Even though he was the son of another man, I loved him as my own, and I treated him no different than I would have had he been—"

"Oh?" She cut him off again. "You mean your wife had been widowed?"

"No," said Hector. "She had a child out of the church. He was born shortly after we were married. The *Padre* at San Carlos blessed us on our wedding day and said that in God's eyes, it was meant for us to marry, and to give the boy a name. I would be his father. Everything should have been fine. But I am a poor man, and I could not meet even our most basic needs. That is why she left me. That is why she took my son, and went to join the boy's real father." His voice cracked with emotion.

"I'm—I'm sorry, Pancho," Erin said in earnest. She quit trying to cock the Starr. Instead, she stepped over and sat down on the edge of the bed made of money. She laid the Starr beside her and flipped back the ragged blanket.

"Come sit down, rest a minute," she said. She patted the money sacks beneath the straw. She felt an urge to reach inside the sacks and make sure all the money was there. But she didn't. She knew she could trust the squirr—*Pancho,* she corrected herself.

Hector seated himself beside her on the edge of the pallet.

"I'll tell you a secret, Pancho," she said. "I am carrying a child."

Hector just looked at her.

"It's true," she said. "And I have no father for my child, no home here, no name, nothing. . . ."

Across from the adobe hovel, the Ranger had jumped up from the ground at the sight the silhouette of the woman holding a gun in the window. But as one tense second overlapped onto the next and no sound of gunshot resounded, and no blast of fire exploded inside the room, he eased back down and waited. He didn't want to barge into the adobe. He didn't want to do anything that might alert Teto and the remaining Gun Killers when they rode back looking for the money. And he was certain they *would* be coming back for the money. He gazed off to the east, where the first silver light of morning wreathed the jagged horizon.

He hoped it wouldn't be much longer.

Teto knew he was being followed. Wade Carrico was a smart Texas outlaw—too smart to let him or anyone else ride away in the night when a large cache of money was at stake. *Not without following them*, Teto told himself. Carrico was only doing what he himself would do under these same circumstances. But still, the fact remained, Teto had put him in charge and told him to keep the men moving north until he caught up with them. Carrico had disobeyed him. He couldn't let that go unmentioned.

Teto had followed the woman close enough that, at

times, he feared she would hear his horse's hooves. But when she had turned onto a winding trail where a light shone in the distance, he'd let his horse fall back a little, knowing there was no way he would lose her now. The light was a signal from someone, he was sure of it. Who? He wasn't certain. A beautiful woman like Erin, it could be anyone.

I have questions for you, my Irish princess, he thought, speaking to her in his mind. He might have let things go, had she not run away. But now that she had left him in the middle of the night, he wanted to know why Luis would have thought such a thing—that the baby she carried belonged to him. How could Luis have thought such a thing had he not been sleeping with her?

His own brother . . . , Teto thought. He shook his head and rode on.

When the small, shining light in the distance went out, Teto made a mental note of its position and rode on in the pale moonlight until he found a dark dry wash running alongside the trail. He turned the horse down into the wash and sat quietly in his saddle, rifle in hand, until he heard the sound of quiet hooves walking along the trail behind him.

"There went the light," Jete Longley said under his breath, riding amid the five Gun Killers. "Suppose that means he's there already?"

"No," Wade Carrico replied in a lowered voice of his own, "he couldn't have gotten that far ahead without running his horse to death."

"We don't even know that light has anything to do

with Teto and the woman," Blake said. "It might not have been her signaling him at all. It might've been just what they call a *coincidence*."

"Look around you, Lud," said Carrico. "This god-forsaken desert, nothing or nobody around for miles. It would be a coincidence if the light *wasn't* somebody signaling."

"I'm speaking for nobody but myself," said Paco Sterns, "but Teto and Luis have both always shot straight with me. I feel like a skunk thinking Teto is up to something, trying to beat us out of our money."

"Nobody is blaming anybody of anything," said Carrico, at the head of the riders. "But it hurts nothing to check and see what's going on. I couldn't believe we were just going to ride away from all that money to begin with."

"Yeah, you heard Teto," Truman Filo said mockingly, " 'There's a whole country full of money waiting across the border.' "

The men chuckled.

"I never saw Teto Torres get so loose when it comes to money," said Carrico. "That in itself put me on guard—"

He stopped abruptly, pulling his horse to halt, seeing the dark figure, horse and rider, jump up onto the trail facing them.

"On guard against *me*, Carrico?" Teto said, his rifle leveled at Carrico's chest.

"*Whoa!*" Carrico said to his spooked horse, getting it under control. "Damn it, Teto! We were talking, that's all!"

His horse settled, his right hand slipped to his holstered Colt. But he didn't draw it.

"Talk now," said Teto, his rifle still leveled on Carrico.

"Jesus, Teto," Paco Sterns cut in, "he was just saying how it didn't add up, you acting like the money was no big deal, talking about how we could get more anytime we wanted it."

"Yeah," said Filo, "tell us you wouldn't be thinking the same way if it was the other way around."

Teto didn't answer. Instead, he stared at Carrico in the darkness above his cocked and leveled rifle.

"I told you to take the men and ride on, Wade," he said. "You didn't follow my orders."

"I did what I thought was best for all of us," Carrico said, not backing an inch. His hand was firm around the butt on his Colt; his thumb was over the hammer. "If that doesn't sit well with you, we can settle it up right here and now—"

Almost before he got the words out of his mouth, a rifle shot exploded to their left, twenty yards off in a shadowy stand of rock and brush—the bullet whistled through the air between him and Teto.

Even as Teto and Carrico drew away from each other, another shot exploded, then another.

"Cover up!" Carrico shouted to the men.

"Get off the trail!" Teto ordered at the same second, he and Carrico both turning their horses as more gunfire streaked and exploded from the brush.

"Follow me!" Teto shouted, his horse rearing a little before he booted it off the trail, back down into the dark dry wash, Carrico right behind him.

"Who the hell is out there?" Carrico asked Teto, the two of them dropping from their saddles, hugging the cutbank of the dry wash for cover. Along the wash, the rest of the men did the same.

"I don't know," said Teto with a dark grin. He fired, levered a fresh round and fired again. "Now that you are the big *jefe in charge*, you tell me." He turned and fired again as shots resounded from the brush.

"Damn it, Teto, I wasn't trying to take over, I was looking out for everybody's interests," said Carrico.

"Forget it," said Teto. "My guess is, this is what's left of the *rurales* back in Rosas Salvajes." He fired again and levered another round.

"Makes sense to me," said Carrico. "I would have thought they'd had enough of us." He rose and fired six quick shots with his Colt.

"They're hardheaded," said Teto. "I hate a hardheaded *pinchazo* worse than anything."

"What do we do now?" Carrico asked. He reloaded his smoking Colt as he spoke.

"If it's the *rurales*, I make it there's no more than three or four guns left at most," said Teto.

"I wish we knew for sure. We could sit them out until daylight, then shoot them all the way back to Wild Roses if we feel like it," said Carrico.

"Huh-uh. We're going to have to hit hard and fast and keep moving," said Teto. He gestured away from the gunfire toward the direction where the candlelight had been. "Whoever was signaling has heard all this. They'll be hightailing on us."

"You're right," Carrico said. "Still, I wish we knew

for sure it's the *rurales*." He clicked his reloaded Colt shut.

The rifles in the brush stopped firing. After a second of silence, a strong voice called from the rocks and brush.

"This is Raul Sanchez, the leader of the posse you men killed in Rosas Salvajes," said the voice. "We have you pinned and outgunned. You must give yourselves up, if you wish to live."

Teto grinned in the moonlight and said to Wade Carrico, who was crouched down beside him, "See? All you had to do is ask."

"Did you hear me there, *banditos*?" the *rurale* leader called out. "Those of you who give yourselves up will not be killed—except for the *bastardo* who stole my horse and left his dead horse in its place! Him I will hang by the neck until he is dead."

"What's that about?" Carrico asked.

"Damned if I know," Teto replied. "But he sure sounds upset over it."

"Think we ought to give up, so we can get going?" Carrico asked.

Teto thought about it for a second.

"Why not?" he said. He checked his rifle and said along the cutbank to the others, "Everybody get ready. Paco, gather our horses and get them away from here. Hurry back."

"*Sí*, I will hurry back," Paco said, crawling away a few feet, then rising into a crouch and running along the wash.

Teto called out to the *rurale* leader, "We want to

give ourselves up, but we know nothing about your horse, Señor Sanchez."

A silence; then the *rurale* leader called out grudgingly, "All right, then. Give yourselves up. We will discuss my stolen horse later."

"That sounds like a hell of a deal," Carrico said wryly to Teto.

Teto called out to the *rurale* leader, "We are coming out with our hands raised. Please do not shoot us."

Raul turned to Eduardo and Julio lying spread out alongside him, their rifles pointed toward the Gun Killers.

"They are not so bold when they are faced by real men, eh, amigos?" he whispered.

Eduardo and Julio stared grimly ahead.

Paco Sterns slid back in among the men, having tied the horses to a bush farther down the wash.

"Ready!" he said in a whisper, even though no one asked.

As the *rurales* watched, four of the six Gun Killers stepped up in the purple darkness, their arms clearly raised in the air. Their rifles lay in the dry wash behind them. Their holsters were empty on their hips.

As the four stepped forward, Teto and Wade Carrico hurried along the wash in opposite directions until they were positioned five yards on either end of the surrendering gunmen.

"Come," Raul said quietly to his two men, "let's take them as prisoners. Once they are in my charge, I will beat out of them which one stole my horse."

The two men stood up and flanked Raul as he moved forward, a big French pistol in his hand.

When the Gun Killers were as close as twenty feet, Filo glanced back and forth in the darkness.

"Now!" he shouted as his hand reached back around his empty holster and snatched the gun from behind his back.

On either end of the gunmen, Teto and Carrico opened up with rifle fire. The other three men followed suit with Filo, their hands jerking pistols from behind their backs and firing rapidly into the *rurales*.

The three *rurales* crumpled to rocky ground. Only one of them, the young Julio, even got off a shot. But as his shot exploded wildly, three bullets pounded him backward and to the ground.

Almost before the ringing after-silence set in, Paco Sterns raced away, got the horses and ran back, leading the animals up from the dry wash and across the rocky ground.

As he hurried up behind Teto, he saw him looking down at the bloody face of the *rurale* leader.

"You—you lied," the *rurale* gasped, clutching both hands to his bullet-riddled chest.

"I know," said Teto, almost apologetically. He held his smoking rifle pointed down, less than a foot from Raul's forehead. "It is getting to where you can't trust anyone, eh?"

The horses jerked as Teto pulled the trigger, but Paco held them firmly as the men stepped in and took their reins from him.

Turning to Carrico, Teto, with his smoking rifle

still in hand, asked, "Are we square, you and me? Or do we still need to get that way?"

"We're square, damn it," Carrico said. "Don't be pointing that rifle at me." He swung up into his saddle and turned his horse beside Teto's. "Are you coming or what?"

Chapter 29

The Ranger heard the gun battle spring up suddenly farther out along the land-wagon trail. When he saw the flash of muzzles explode like flat sheets of lightning across the harsh Mexican terrain, he stood up and stared toward the battle, judging its distance. Was it the Gun Killers? He had little doubt. Against the *rurales* he'd left behind in Rosas Salvajes?

Yes, that would be his first guess, he told himself.

No sooner had the gunshots risen in the near distance than the candlelight came back on in the window of the adobe hovel—but it only burned for a moment. He turned and studied the two silhouettes as they busied themselves inside.

"I knew I might be followed, but I didn't think they could be this close," Erin said as she raked away loose straw and the ragged blanket. She pulled up the two sacks of money and rolled them over onto the dirt floor. "Choose which one you want," she said, "in case we get split up again."

"No, you choose," Hector said, the cocaine still keeping him up above the pain coursing throughout his battered body. "I will go get the horses."

When he left the room, Erin hefted one sack, then the other, finding them to be about equal in size and weight. When he walked back in, leading the two horses, she looked up and saw him staring at her with the rifle from the saddle boot in his hand. She noted the strange look on his face.

"These feed sacks are a dead giveaway," she said, noting the coins and stacks of paper money showing through the burlap. "We've both got saddlebags, so let's use them." She paused, then said, "I see no reason why we can't ride together . . . for a while anyway. That is, if it's all right with you."

Hector didn't answer. Instead, he levered a round into the rifle chamber and eased the tip of the barrel toward her.

Erin reread the look on his face. It wasn't so strange now that she understood its implication. It was more a look of resolve. She shot a glance toward the big Starr revolver lying on what was left of the straw pallet.

"Do not reach for the gun," Hector cautioned her. "It does not fire anyway, remember?"

He knew? she thought. He'd heard the gun cock? But he'd said nothing? He'd kept it to himself until he got his hands on the rifle?

"Yes," he said, as if answering her inner questions. "I know what you want to do. I know what you *would have* done."

She looked at the rifle barrel; she thought about her unborn baby.

"Hector, listen to me," she said, struggling to keep her voice cool and steady, even as she realized death stared her in the face. "Yes, it's true, I was going to kill you and take all the money. If the gun hadn't misfired, I would have done so, I can't deny it."

"No, you cannot," Hector said quietly.

"But I'm glad it misfired, Hector," she said. "Do you hear me, I'm *glad*!"

"*Sí*, so am I," Hector said flatly.

"I want you to understand something," she said. "My life has been much the same as yours. I have done nothing but struggle to keep myself alive since the day I was born. It's hard living like that every day. It makes one do things they would never dream of doing otherwise."

Hector only stared at her, the rifle tight in his hands.

Erin reached a toe out and nudged one of the sacks of money.

"But with this money, things can be different for me now," she said. "I know they can be different. I don't have to kill someone else in order for me and my baby to live. With this money, I can live and let live. I can raise my baby in peace, and not have to worry how I will feed and clothe it."

Hector found himself staring at the sacks of money, realizing how different things would have been for him if he'd had the money sooner, before his wife, Ana, and his son left him.

"It is true what you say," he whispered almost to himself. "There are those who would have us believe that money is not everything, and I envy those people. My life would not have been so bad if only I had money to make it better." He shook his head slightly in regret.

"But not now, Hector," she said, stepping forward toward him, the sacks of money lying at their feet.

Hector's wary look caused her to stop.

"You wanted to kill me," he said, letting her know to keep her distance.

"Yes, and I am sorry for that," she said, "deeply sorry. But that was before I knew how you felt—what you've been through. I don't want to kill you, Hector. I want to be your friend, your *compañero*." She paused and gave him an intimate look. "I'll even be your *íntimo compañero*, if you will have me."

His *intimate companion . . . ?* Hector swallowed the tightness in his throat and looked her up and down. *My God, she is beautiful*, he told himself.

This was not the time or the place to judge people hastily or harshly, he thought. Like most creatures here in the brutal desert lands, people did what they had to do for the very moment in which they lived. This was no time to discern what life demanded next from them. There was only this hot, insistent moment that demanded attention in order to stay alive.

"I—I want to believe you," Hector said. "I would give anything to believe you. . . ."

"Then *do* believe me, Hector," she said. "All you have to do is let yourself believe me." She ventured a step closer to him, farther away from the big Starr revolver.

Hector let the rifle slump in his right hand, but he raised a finger for emphasis.

"You must give me your word not to try to kill me again," he said with a half smile, the soothing feel of the cocaine surrounding him.

"You have my word, Pancho," Erin said, stepping and putting her arms around him. "I will never try to kill you again."

From the other room, the Ranger stepped out of the darkness and into the moonlit bedroom, his Winchester rifle in hand.

"Easy, *Pancho*," he said quietly, having heard the woman use the name while he'd stood listening from the other room. "I'm not after either one of you." He glanced at Erin as he spoke.

Hector's rifle lowered and hung in his hand.

"How long have you been there, Ranger Burrack?" Erin asked, taking a step back from Hector.

No longer "Sam." Ranger Burrack now, Sam noted.

"Not long," he said. He stepped around to where the Starr lay on the remaining loose straw.

"This money is ours, Ranger," Hector said firmly with a warning tone to his voice. He turned with the Ranger, keeping squarely faced toward him.

"If this was U.S. territory, I'd take the money and turn it in," Sam said. "Down here, I have no claim on it. I don't even know which side of the border it came from."

Hector gave Erin a look. "Do you believe him?" he asked.

"I believe him," she said. "He's here for the Gun Killers, nothing more. Right, Sam?"

"Right," Sam replied. He looked closely at Erin.

Erin thought she saw disappointment in his eyes. "Sam, I didn't mean to—"

"Take the money and get going," Sam said, cutting her off. "There's nothing to explain."

Erin hesitated, then said, "Sam . . . there's enough money here for us to share it. If it hadn't been for you dogging the gang so hard . . ."

The look Sam gave her caused her words to trail to a halt.

Hector looked at the two of them with curiosity. Was something playing out here, or was it just the cocaine toying with his mind?

Sam grabbed the big Starr revolver, walked over to the open window and laid it on the sill. He picked up the candle, lit it and placed it in the window beside the gun.

"The gun battle is over. They're on their way," he said.

"You will not fight them alone," Hector said, stepping forward. "I will stay and fight beside you."

"No," Sam said, "I fight alone. This has nothing to do with you."

"Nothing to do with *me*?" said Hector. "Look at what they did to me."

Sam gestured a nod toward the sacks of money on the floor.

"The money is what did that to you," he said. "It'd be a shame to get yourself killed before you enjoy what it brings you."

Hector looked at the sacks of money, then up at the woman. He tipped his swollen, battered head a bit.

"You are right, Ranger," he said. He stepped out

and stood between the sacks on the floor. "But before I go, I tell you this. If you think you have seen the last of me, you are wrong. I will soon return to Rosas Salvajes and take my cantina from whoever is running it."

"Good luck, Pancho," Sam said, trying to dismiss the matter. He picked up the big Starr and turned it back and forth in his hand.

But Hector wasn't finished. He thumbed himself on the chest, the cocaine still hard at work, doing its job, starting to bring things to the surface that usually only boiled and simmered deep inside him.

"I will tell you something else," he said. "You and your country have not heard the last of Pancho Pasada. I will use this money and whatever resources I have to bring other men like myself together. Bold men! Men who will not be denied what is ours just because you have made a mark in the dirt between our country and yours. We will be coming, Lawman from Nogales," he said in a scornful warning.

"I'll be waiting," Sam replied quietly but firmly. He held the big Starr up, his thumb over its hammer, knowing that the longer they talked the farther apart they would find themselves.

"Now get going." He reached out arm's length through the open window, pointed the revolver straight up and fired it once.

Hector and Erin stared at each other in amazement, hearing the blast, seeing the streak of blue-orange muzzle fire.

Sam fired it again, this time two shots.

"Oh my . . . ," said Erin. Why had it not fired for her?

He fired again, three shots. Then he laid the empty smoking gun on the windowsill.

"Are we through talking, Pancho?" he asked.

Hector started to say something more, but the woman took his arm and pulled him away.

"Help me with the money," she said to Hector. Having taken a set of saddlebags from behind her saddle, she tossed them on the floor beside the money sacks. To Sam she said, "He has taken cocaine powder for his pain."

"I figured as much," Sam replied, watching Hector stoop down, open the sack and start stuffing the money down into the saddlebags.

Erin took a pair of saddlebags from behind Hector's saddle and put them on the floor to be filled.

She stepped in closer to the Ranger. "Sam, I feel like there is something I should say or do."

"There's not," Sam replied.

"You *did* save my life," she said softly.

"And *you* saved mine," Sam replied. "Now get moving before you end up in the middle of things here. You've got your baby to think of, and a life waiting for you in Ireland."

"Sam," she said, "I must confess to you. I've never been to Ireland in my life."

He just stared at her.

"It's true," she said. "My father came from Ireland before Bram and I were born. He was a Texan who came to Mexico in forty-six to fight in the Mexican army in the Batallón de San Patricio. I am named after Ireland, but I was born here in Mexico. My mother was Mexican. *This* is my native land." She gestured a hand toward the darkness, taking in all of the wild, rugged terrain.

"So, the story about you and your brother, Bram, being orphans—?"

"Lies," she said bluntly, "along with everything else I told you. I lied to you. I lied to Teto and Luis. I have lied to everyone throughout my life because I was born on the wrong side of the border."

The wrong side of the border . . .

Sam shook his head and gazed out across the dark purple night. In the east, silver sunlight began to swell above the jagged, black horizon.

"There's no right or wrong side of the border," he said. "We're all the same."

"That's easier to believe when you come here from Nogales," she said. "It's harder to believe when you go to Nogales from here."

Sam stared out in silence for a moment.

"Why are you telling me the truth now?" he asked quietly.

"I don't know," she said. "I suppose I just needed to tell someone the truth—just once in my life." She paused and added, "You were honest, and fair with me."

"How do you know?" Sam said quietly. He turned and looked at her. "How do you know I was being fair and honest? I could have been lying—playing along with you just to get you to lead me to the Gun Killers."

Sam glanced at Hector, who was still busy stuffing the money into the saddlebags. *Reward money for the Gun Killers?* he thought, but he didn't say anything.

"You could have been, but you weren't," Erin replied. "I would have known if you were."

"So you think," Sam said. He looked at her for a moment longer. "Get out of here, Erin. There'll be things happening here you won't want to see." He turned and handed her the big Starr revolver. She shoved it back down into her waist.

Chapter 30

———◆———

Teto and the five other Gun Killers put their horses into an easy gallop when the candlelight reappeared in the purple darkness. Riding up alongside Teto, Wade Carrico called out to him above the squeak of tack and the rumble of hooves.

"We need to slow down, Teto," he said, "in case this turns out to be some kind of trap."

"Keep your mouth shut, Wade; I'm warning you!" Teto called back to him.

"Listen to me, Teto, damn it," said Carrico. "Whoever lit the candle did it to guide Erin to them, not us."

Teto started to slow down, considering Carrico's words. But as he did, the signal shots rang out in the night from the same direction as the candlelight.

"Aw, hell," said Carrico, seeing Teto boot his horse up into a faster gallop.

Teto laughed as all six of them raced along the dark trail.

"Don't you ever get tired of being wrong, Wade?" he called out.

Carrico cursed to himself as he booted his horse right alongside Teto's.

"This little Irish trollop is going to get us all killed one day," he swore under his breath.

They rode on.

Four miles ahead of them, in the open rear door of the Pasadas' abandoned adobe hovel, Sam stood and watched Erin and Hector swing up into their saddles and turn their horses east into the first rays of rising sun. Sam raised a hand to Erin as she looked back at him from her saddle.

"Keep moving until you put a few river crossings between here and yourselves," he said. But then he caught himself and stopped—he didn't need to tell Erin Donovan anything when it came to leaving no trail.

But she looked back and raised her hand. Then she turned and put her horse forward, her pair of bulging saddlebags tied down firmly behind her saddle.

Hector sidled his horse over closer to her as they rode along, his own money-filled saddlebags riding behind his saddle.

Sam watched them become smaller and more grainy as they rode on, until the purple darkness seemed to reach in and swallow them.

Walking back inside the adobe, to the window where the candle sat burning on the sill, he stood and listened closely until he heard the sound of hooves moving across the desert floor.

"Time to go to work," he murmured to himself, stepping away from the open window.

When Teto and his men were close enough that they could see the window framing the glowing candle-light, they slowed to a stop and sat staring for a moment at the abandoned adobe, checking their rifles and the pistols on their hips.

"Everybody spread out," Teto said in a lowered voice. He nudged his horse forward at a walk. "Nobody shoots until we find out what this is." He looked over at Carrico. "Wade, flank us like earlier. Get behind the house, but don't get an itchy trigger finger."

"I never do," Carrico said, pulling his horse away from the others.

With their mounts spread a few feet apart, Carrico off covering their left flank, the five horsemen advanced their horses forward slowly and stopped again twenty yards from the glowing candlelight.

"Wait here," Teto said to the other four horsemen. He gigged his horse forward and rode on to the front of the adobe.

"*Hola* the house," he called out to the open front door, seeing the flickering candlelight dimly through-out the abandoned hovel.

He waited for a tense, silent moment. The men sat their horses, staring at the candlelight, guns in hand, ready to fire.

"Erin, my Irish princess!" Teto called out, mocking her pet name. "I know you are in there. I followed you as soon as you left. Come out!"

Another silence. Then Teto said to the adobe, "I will come and drag you out if I have to. Or you can come out on your own. You can tell me everything and I will forgive you."

Another silence.

"Damn it, what's he waiting for?" Paco Sterns said sidelong under his breath.

"He's *loco* for the woman," Jete Longley whispered back from a few feet away. "Him and Luis both were always crazy over her."

"You need to keep that kind of talk to yourself, Jete," said Blake.

"I've been thinking," Teto called out to the shadowy hovel, "the squirrel didn't get himself loose. You cut him loose. You and him partnered up on the money—don't try denying it!"

"Jesus," Sterns whispered, "has he lost his mind?"

No one replied. The men only stared and listened.

"My brother was not lying," Teto called out. "You stabbed him! Were you sleeping with my brother—my brother who I killed for you?"

"Je-*sus*!" Sterns whispered again, this time with more emphasis. "We trusted these two holding our money?" He shook his head in disbelief.

Behind the house, Carrico had climbed down from his horse and looked all around on the ground.

"Teto, I've got two sets of hooves leading away from here," he called out. He hoped his information would shut Teto up. Nobody wanted to hear this kind of raving from their leader.

"Damn it to hell!" Teto shouted. He hammered his bootheels against his horse, sending it recklessly bolting in the open front door of the abandoned hovel.

The men looked at each other in the silvery darkness of dawn.

"She's gone!" Teto called out, appearing at the window in the candlelight, down from his saddle, his rifle in hand. His horse milled a few feet behind him. "But she was here! So was our money!" He held up the empty feed sacks. "I found these . . . and I found three gold coins lying on the floor!"

"All right, Teto!" Carrico called out from behind the house. "I've got their tracks! What the hell are we waiting for?"

"You heard him, damn it!" Teto shouted, still standing in the light of the candle. "Don't just sit there. Let's get after the—"

The men heard a rifle shot reach in out of the darkness and cut Teto Torres' words short. They saw the impact of the bullet pick their leader up and hurl him backward like a limber scarecrow. Teto hit the wall on the other side of the room and slid down, trailing blood.

The men took control of their spooked horses before the animals could rear and bolt away. Turning his horse quickly, Paco Sterns pointed at the gray sliver of smoke thirty yards away.

"There's the shooter!" he cried out, pointing with his big Remington revolver.

The three other men turned their horses in time to see a streak of blue flame explode from Sterns' gun barrel. But as Paco Sterns' shot blasted out, so did a second shot from the Ranger's Winchester rifle. This time, his shot came from a different spot, twenty feet to the left of the first looming curl of smoke.

The Ranger's second shot flung Sterns backward out of his saddle and sent him rolling limp on the ground.

Truman Filo saw the flash from the Ranger's shot.

"It has to be that damned lawman!" he shouted to Jete Longley and Ludlow Blake. "Ride him down!"

The three horsemen bolted out across the sandy ground toward the second curl of rifle smoke standing in the grainy darkness. But as their horses pounded forward, Filo drew his horse back from between them, circled wide of the adobe hovel toward Wade Carrico, who had remounted his horse and was pointing it in the direction of Hector's and Erin's hoofprints.

"*Wade*! Wait for *me*!" he cried out.

Carrico turned in his saddle just in time to see a streak of fire reach out ten yards to the left of the Ranger's second curl of smoke. The shot hit Filo in his back and sent him tumbling forward, horse and all, end over end in a cloud of dust.

"Damn *this*!" cried Wade Carrico. He sent his horse pounding out along the set of hoofprints.

Longley and Blake spotted the Ranger's muzzle flash in time to start firing before he could take a new position on them.

"There he is!" shouted Longley. "Kill him!"

The two rode hard, firing repeatedly. Their pistol shots whistled past Sam's head as he dropped onto one knee and took aim in the gray-silver dawn.

Two shots exploded from the Winchester and the two riders went down, leaving their saddles as if they'd been snatched up from behind by some large, vengeful hand.

Sam straightened up from his position on his knee and looked all around. Hearing something close behind him, he swung around, the rifle ready and cocked. Then he let out a tight breath, almost in silent prayer.

"You were supposed to *stay*," he said to the coppery, black-point dun.

The horse sawed its head, chuffed and pawed a hoof at the ground.

Sam looked at the big Swiss rifle he'd assembled and left tied down atop his bedroll just in case he needed it.

"Oh, I see," he said, stepping over the dun. He uncocked the smoking Winchester and shoved it down into the saddle boot. He slid the Swiss rifle from under its tie-downs and swung up into the saddle.

Riding toward the hovel, he circled the dun to the left, getting the house out from between himself and his fleeing target. Seeing a brownish gray rise of dust climbing upward toward the horizon, he stopped the dun and reached his hand far down its left rein. As he gripped the rein short and drew it back tight, he raised his left knee and pressed it down firmly on the horse's withers.

The dun obeyed his command, sank onto its front knees and rolled easily down onto its side. As the horse lay down, Sam stepped out of his saddle, Swiss rifle in hand, and also lay down. He stretched himself out on the ground, holding the rifle out across the dun's side.

He put the rifle's scope to his eye and studied the rising dust in the distance until he saw the outline of the rider move up into the early sunlight. At this distance, even through the scope, the rider looked small—the shot hard to make.

Sam settled himself in. He reached his left hand out, rubbed the dun's neck and patted it, telling it to keep still. Then he put his hand back to the front of the rifle stock and eased his breathing into the same rhythm as that of the horse.

He pinned the scope to the center of Wade Carrico's back and let his rifle barrel drift up and down with the steady rise and fall of the dun's sides.

In the soft, silver glow of dawn, he squeezed the trigger on the barrel's rise, seeing the circle of the scope climb from the small of Carrico's back to a point between his shoulder blades just as the rifle bucked against his shoulder.

The dun did not stir. But Sam laid his left hand back over its neck as if to calm all the same.

"Easy, boy," he whispered.

He studied the target and watched Carrico stiffen for a second before he slumped to one side, spilled from his saddle and rolled away in the dirt.

Sam let out a breath and stood up, the big Swiss rifle smoking in his hand. He gazed out as the horse continued to climb without its rider into early sunlight. After a moment, he picked up the dun's reins and tapped his boot to its rump. As the horse rose to its hooves, Sam swung a leg over its back and slipped easily into his saddle.

The dun shook out its mane as Sam laid the Swiss

rifle across his lap. Sam turned the horse toward the hovel and patted its withers with his left hand.

"You're as good as I've ever seen," he said quietly to the dun.

Inside the hovel, Teto Torres had crawled to the rear door and sat gazing off into the swell of sunrise. He clasped an empty feed sack to his bloody chest. In one blood-streaked hand, he squeezed the loose gold coins he'd found on the floor. When he heard the Ranger lead the dun through the house up behind him, he didn't try to turn around.

"So, lawman," he said, "did you finally kill everybody?"

Sam didn't answer. He noted how strong Teto's voice sounded for a man who'd taken a bullet dead center.

"How bad are you hit?" he asked, stopping two feet behind the wounded outlaw leader, his Colt hanging in his hand, the big rifle back beneath its tie-downs.

"Oh, I am what . . . they call . . . a goner," Teto said, pain in his halting voice in spite of its strength.

Sam stepped forward into the doorway and looked down over Teto's shoulder, making sure there was no gun in his hands.

Seeing the Ranger standing over him, Teto opened his bloody hands and exposed the large bullet hole in his chest.

"See . . . I'm dead," he said quietly. He clamped his right hand back over the wound to steady a flow of blood, but he opened his left hand and showed Sam the blood-smeared coins. "She . . . left me these." He gave a chuckle that turned into a deep cough. "Just something . . . to remember her by, eh?"

Sam only stared down at the coins. He couldn't say if Erin had left them for Teto, or if maybe Hector had simply dropped them while stuffing the saddlebags. But the man was dying—let him believe what he needed to believe.

"Lawman," Teto asked after a moment of silence, "have you ever loved a woman?"

Sam looked up, off in the direction of the hoofprints.

"Yes, I have," he said.

Teto heard something in the Ranger's voice that caused him to raise his face and look up at him. Blood trickled down the corner of his lips, but he managed a weak smile.

"Ah, she . . . got to you too, eh?" he said.

Sam didn't answer.

"You can tell me. After all," Teto said, managing to shrug, "what can I do?"

"How well did you know her?" Sam asked.

"Well enough," Teto said. "She is *Mejicana*. Did you know that?"

Sam didn't answer; instead he said, "She told you?"

"She did not have . . . to tell me," said Teto. "I am *Mejicano* . . . so I know." He smiled. "But I never . . . let on to know. She likes . . . to think she is *all* Irish. And she wants to be *Americana* . . ." He shook his head. "I don't . . . know why. You *Americanos* . . . are nothing but trouble. Still, everyone wants to be *you*."

Sam only stared down at him and let him talk. He'd stop talking soon.

A silence set in while Teto shook his head and regained his thoughts. "You slept with her, *sí*?" he said.

"No," Sam said. "It wasn't that way."

"My brother slept with her," Teto said. "But it is my baby . . . she will bring into the world."

Sam only listened.

"And it is I who she loves . . . not my brother, not you, no one but me," he said. He held up the coins. "This is why she left *me* these, to tell me . . ."

Sam only nodded and said noting.

"You do not believe me, do you?" Teto said. "I can tell you do not."

"It doesn't matter what I believe, Teto," Sam said quietly. "I came here to do a job. Our paths crossed, hers and mine—"

"*Shhh*. Listen, lawman," Teto said, cutting him off as a single gunshot resounded in the far distance. Teto smiled. "It's her signal."

A second passed, then two shots, then a pause followed by three shots. Teto was right—it was the big Starr, Sam thought. There was no mistaking its sound.

Teto coughed and wheezed.

He said, "She does this to tell me where she is . . . that she has made it away from here . . . that everything is well. Ah, but that is good to hear. . . ." His voice trailed away to a whisper, then fell silent.

Sam gazed off in the direction of the distant gunshots. He liked to think that for some reason, she was signaling *him*.

Having heard Teto Torres' last breath, he stooped down beside him, looked at the thin smile on his bloody lips and closed the outlaw leader's eyes.

When he stood up, he caught a glimpse of a figure in the doorway and swung his cocked Colt toward it instinctively.

"Don't shoot, *señor! Por favor!*" said the little well tender, his arms stretched toward the low ceiling.

"Mister, what are you doing here?" Sam asked, relieved, his Colt slumping toward the dirt floor. The dun grumbled under its breath toward the well tender, its rear hoof half-cocked, as if ready to launch the little man back through the doorway.

"I—I am only passing by, on my way back to the ghost town. Rosas Salvajes is too dangerous!"

"I understand," Sam said.

"I like *living* with the dead better than I like *dying* with the living." The well tender grinned at his cleverness and lowered his hands a little. "I hear all the shooting, and when it stopped I come running pronto!" He looked at Teto's bloody body sitting slumped in the rear doorway.

"Why?" Sam asked, looking past him and out the front door, seeing who might be behind him.

"After so much shooting," the well tender said, wide-eyed, "I thought someone might need a bath?"

Sam looked at him curiously.

"You brought your tub with you?" he asked.

"I bring the tub everywhere I go," the well tender said. "It is outside in the yard. Is the *señorita* here? She likes to take the bath."

"She does," Sam said, remembering she took one after the wolves had attacked her, "but she's gone. I don't think you'll be seeing her."

"And you?" the well tender asked. "Do you need a bath?"

Sam looked at Teto's body, and out in the direction of the dead lying strewn about in the silver-gray sunlight.

"Yes, I need one," he said quietly. "But it'll have to wait. Besides, is there water here?"

"Agua . . . ?" The well tender scratched his head and looked all around; he hadn't thought of that.

Sam took the dun's reins and led it through the abandoned hovel and out the front door.

"You can bury these bodies, if you can find a shovel somewhere," he said as the little man followed him outside.

"For free?" the little man asked, sounding disappointed at the prospect of digging in the hard ground on what would soon become a scorching hot day.

"Teto will pay you. He has the burial money in his hand," Sam said, nodding toward the adobe where Teto Torres sat in the rear door facing the morning sun.

Maybe she did leave the coins for you, Teto, Sam said to himself.

But he put the thought out of his mind, swung up into his saddle and turned the dun toward the trail leading north. He was headed home. He could ride northeast and be in Laredo in three days, four at the most. But for some reason, he didn't want to run into her, not now, not this soon. He would ride back straight up-country. It was harder, hotter and would take three times as long. But after all, he told himself, he'd come here from Nogales. He would go back the same way.

He put the dun into an easy pace, the Mexican sunlight rising across him and the horse from the east. Alone now, he thought, but soon the horse's shadow and his own would appear alongside them and ride there most of the day. Times like these, wasn't that all the company he needed?

Yes, he believed it was, he told himself with some small degree of satisfaction. He adjusted his sombrero down on his forehead—and he rode on.

Don't miss a page of
action from America's most
exciting Western author,
Ralph Cotton, in

INCIDENT AT GUNN POINT

Coming from Signet in February 2012.

Will Summers heard the sudden blasts of rifle and pistol fire echo out to him along the rocky hills far to his left. He stopped his dapple gray and pulled his four-horse string up alongside him. He listened intently as the gunfire raged for only a matter of seconds before falling away as quickly as it had started.

What was that about . . . ?

Summers scanned the black roofline of Gunn Point, beyond the fresh layer of snow lying between him and the small town. His first thought was that the shooting could've been a couple of range hands who'd awakened surly and hungover in the rooms above Caster Stems's Maplethorpe Saloon and crossed each other's paths on the way to their horses. He'd known it to happen just that way.

But no, that wasn't it. Not cowhands . . . too many guns involved.

He watched wood smoke curl upward from tin stovepipes and stone chimneys, drifting away on the crisp morning air. Beside him, steam billowed and swirled on the breath of the four-horse string. Their backs glistened, half-frosted, half-wet—more steam wafting from the heat of their bodies.

His dapple gray chuffed and snorted beneath him, and now that they had come to a halt, the big barb scraped a forehoof on the snow-covered ground, revealing a patch of dried wild grass.

"Pay attention, here," Summers said quietly to the dapple gray. "You'll get your breakfast . . ."

He touched up the reins to keep the barb from dipping his head. The dapple shook out his mane and blew out a hot breath.

As Summers continued scanning the distant rooflines, shooting broke out again, this time on the trail leading out of Gunn Point in his direction. *All right, whatever it is,* he told himself, *don't get caught midtrail on open flatlands when it arrives.*

Summers levered a round into the Winchester's chamber and kept the rifle in his gloved right hand, the same hand holding the lead rope to his horse string. Like the dapple gray, the four horses had begun scraping their forehoofs and dipping their heads. He gave a tug on the lead rope as he tapped his heels to the dapple's side.

"Sorry, fellows. Not yet," he murmured to the string. "Let's clear out of here."

As he led the horses away from the trail and across the snow-streaked ground, Summers began to suspect the shooting must have been a robbery—a raid of some sort. That would have been plausible, had he been able to think of any business in Gunn Point worth robbing. But it had been more than a year since he'd last been in town. Change came quickly in this rocky hill country, especially if there were any traces of ore in the ground.

But that was neither here nor there, he reminded himself, looking all around the barren flatlands. What mattered now was cover—a safe spot for him and his horses. Whatever was coming would be here soon enough and he would be prepared to deal with it. But given the choice, he'd rather deal with it with his shoulder against a rock and his horses out of sight.

No cover, he thought to himself as he slowed the dapple and the string almost to a halt. "Now what?" he heard himself say aloud. His breath steamed off on a cold breeze. He looked toward Gunn Point as he heard heavy firing coming from town, followed by a few shots farther along on the trail.

"Yep, a robbery of some sort," he concluded. He could picture it now: a band of thieves leaving town in a hurry, a sheriff and a group of hastily gathered townsmen in hot pursuit. *That was it,* he told himself, looking toward the sound of the gunfire as two black dots rode into sight at the head of a white trail of swirling snow.

Two more black dots came into sight, riding hard to catch up to their partners. *There are the thieves . . .*

Summers turned his gray and jerked the string along beside him. Farther back on the trail, he saw another rise of swirling snow. *And there's the sheriff and his posse . . .*

He felt a little better knowing what to expect. But knowing didn't provide much comfort, not when he and his animals were still out in the open, standing amidst their own steam, about to be caught up in the fighting.

"What a spot to be in . . ." he said, still searching back and forth for any cover large enough to stop a bullet. There were times to pitch in and help the law, and there were times it was better to drop back out of the way and let the law do its job.

He considered quickly how this could all look to an angry posse—him out here on the flats with four horses, which just happened to be the right number of mounts to have waiting. He heard the shots firing back and forth along the trail, drawing closer every second.

This was not the time or place to get in the law's way. In the swirl of snow, their bullets had no way of knowing which side he was on. This was the time to lie back, let the thieves get past him—offering them no resistance—and wait for the posse. With any luck, the sheriff and his posse would believe he had nothing to do with whatever the four riders were running away from.

All right, it wasn't the best idea he'd ever had, he told himself, turning the dapple gray, but it would have to do. He loped farther away from the trail at an easy pace, leading his string, careful not to raise more powdery snow than he had to. He wondered if Turner Goss was still the sheriff in Gunn Point. *I hope so*, he thought, looking back over his shoulder at the second cloud of snow rising along the trail.

Three miles back along the trail, riding sightless in the billowing snow, Deputy Parley Stiles stopped firing and raised a gloved hand.

"Stop shooting!" he called out over his shoulder. He carefully slowed his horse down until he realized the men following him had done as they were told. As he came to a halt, the deputy could see the wake of powdery snow raised by the gunmen's horses already beginning to clear a little.

"Why are we stopping, Parley?" a townsman called out a few feet behind him. "We can't stop now! Not while we've got them in our gun sights. Let's ride them down!"

"Settle down, Dewitt," said the young deputy. "We're not stopping any longer than it takes to clear the air some."

"But damn it, Deputy—!" a mining engineer named Horace Dewitt cursed before the deputy cut him off.

"Strike that language from your mouth, Dewitt," the young deputy demanded, "else you won't ride another step with this posse."

"I meant nothing by it, Parley," Dewitt said, fuming but keeping his temper in check. "I'm speaking for all of us! We need to stay right down their shirts until we—"

"Don't call me Parley again," the young deputy snapped, once more cutting the miner short.

"It is your name!" the engineer countered. "What the hell—I mean *heck*—are we being so formal about?"

"I'm Deputy Stiles to every one of you," the deputy said, loud enough for all to hear. "Especially while I'm leading this posse." He looked around in turn from one face to the next through the steaming breath of men and animals.

"We understand, Deputy," said a meek voice among

the townsmen. "But why are we stopping? Shouldn't we—?"

"To keep from breaking our necks and ruining some good horses," the deputy said with authority, before the timid apothecary clerk could finish his words.

"Our deputy is right," said a gambler named Herbert Long. "As long as they've got a clear trail and we're stuck riding in their wake, they've got the odds working in their favor."

Dewitt grumbled something cross under his breath, spat and looked away. "This ain't no poker game, Herbert," he said sorely, settling a little but still clearly not happy about following the young deputy's orders.

"Oh, but I beg to differ with you, my *ore-craving* friend," Long replied, a hint of disdain lying beneath his rich Southern accent. "It's *all* poker." He passed a small, knowing smile around to the others. "We've only just been dealt this hand. Now we need to study our cards closely before we commit to any—"

"Anybody needs to step down and relieve themselves, this might be the best chance for a while," said Deputy Stiles, cutting the gambler off as readily as he had the others.

The gambler gave a toss of his gloved hand as if in submission. He swung down from his saddle and stepped away a reins' length from his horse. Four more of the seven riders followed suit. Deputy Stiles stayed in his saddle, staring straight ahead into the settling crystalline veil. As did Horace Dewitt and Martin Heintz, the town druggist.

As the splatter of the four dismounted men's urine

set new rises of steam curling up from the cold ground, Dewitt shook his head in disgust and turned away.

Noting Dewitt's gesture, the gambler grinned, shook himself off and said, "I don't suppose any of you gentlemen had the foresight to bring along a bottle of whiskey, perchance."

"There will be no drinking, and no *talk of drinking* in this posse," Stiles called out before anyone could respond in any manner.

"There you have it," Long murmured to himself, buttoning the fly on his frayed and faded pinstripe trousers. He put on his right glove and closed the front of his wool overcoat. "The voice of the law has spoken . . ."

Leading the thieves, Jackie Warren spotted Summers and his four-horse string sitting a hundred yards off the trail. With no warning to the three other speeding horsemen behind him, the young outlaw jerked his horse to a reckless halt.

"What the hell!" shouted Henry Grayson, almost thrown from his saddle as his horse veered to keep from slamming into Warren's animal and tumbling end over end. The other two also veered and reined down. When all three horses had stumbled and slid to a stop, their riders glared at Jackie Warren.

"What's wrong with you, Little Jackie?" Grayson shouted from behind his bandana mask. He circled in close.

"Not a damn thing, Henry!" the young outlaw shouted in reply. He jerked his bandana down from across the bridge of his nose and nodded toward the lone rider and the four horses sitting staring at them across the snowy flatlands. "Take a look at this." He gave a grin. "Are those *our* horses?"

The other three masked riders looked out at Summers, who sat with his Winchester propped up on his thigh—his warning for the four of them to ride on.

"Hell no," Henry Grayson said. He stared for a second, then said to Warren and the others, "All right, let's get going. We still got the law on our rumps." But before he could slap his reins to his horse and bat his boots to its sides, young Jackie reached out and grabbed his horse by its bridle.

"What's your hurry, Henry?" he said. "That posse has quit us. This is all going our way."

"Like hell, they've quit us," said Lewis Fallon, a young Texas outlaw out of Waco. He looked back warily toward the swirl of white still adrift on their back trail.

"You don't hear any shooting, do you?" Jackie said.

"That doesn't mean they've turned back," said Avrial Rochenbach, known to the others as a former Pinkerton detective turned bandit.

"What about this one?" Jackie said, nodding at the single figure looking back at them from a hundred yards out.

"What about him?" said Grayson.

"He's got horses," Jackie Warren said, a Spencer rifle in his gloved hand. "We ought to take them just in case ours wear out. Especially mine." His saddlebags bulged with stolen money.

"We've got horses waiting. We don't need his," Grayson said. "We don't need nothing he's got."

"But he might have seen our faces," Jackie said, searching for any reason to create mayhem.

"Not ours, he hasn't," said Grayson. "We kept our masks on like we *all* agreed to do." He jerked his horse away from Jackie's hand and slapped his reins to its withers. "This thing is set up perfect. Stick to our plan. Let's ride!" he shouted.

The other two outlaws booted their horses along behind him. But before turning his horse, Jackie threw his rifle against his shoulder and shouted, *"Yi-hiiii!"* out across the flatlands. He fired wildly.

Summers saw the bullet strike the ground ten feet in front of him. Instinctively, he raised his rifle, yet he held his fire, hoping the outlaw was only giving him a warning.

"That's it—ride on," Summers murmured. "We've both got better things to do than shoot one another . . ."

He saw the first three horses already pulling away; the fourth rider was ready to bat his horse's sides to catch up with them. But before the last outlaw left, he pulled off one more wild shot.

From the string beside him, Summers heard one of his horses whinny in pain. He caught a sidelong glance as the horse half rose on its hind legs and toppled to the ground in a spray of blood and snow.

As soon as the bullet hit one of his string horses, Summers had leaped out of his saddle and slapped his dapple gray's rump. He hurriedly cut the rope holding the three live string horses to the dead one and sent them racing out behind his gray. He hadn't wanted a fight; he hadn't wanted to lose a horse. But now that he had a horse down, he threw himself behind the body and laid his Winchester out across its side.

Kill my horse . . . ! He jerked a fresh round up into the rifle chamber. Steam curled from the gaping bullet hole in the dead horse's neck. He was in the fight now, whether he wanted it or not.